"It is done."

Hearing the words, young Loren Soth breathed a deep sigh of relief. "Well done, Caradoc. You have served me well."

Soth's seneschal stepped into the cottage and began disrobing. He tossed his clothes upon the hearth, watching the blood of his victims burn in shades of orange and blue.

Aynkell Soth looked up at his son for the first time in hours. "Now when you take over rule of Nightlund, no other heir can come forward to lay claim to it." He turned to Caradoc. "Thank you for the removal of the black marks upon my soul."

"The black marks may have been removed from your soul," said Knight Soth, "but they are not gone. They have merely been transferred. The weight of my father's sins is now mine alone to bear. What a lovely gift to receive so soon before my wedding day."

"Don't be so quick to blame and condemn me, my son," Aynkell said. "You are of my flesh and of my blood. You always will be. There's too much of me in you for you to be so critical of my life."

The knight's face darkened into a scowl. His father began to laugh. Loren stormed out of the cottage.

As he joined Caradoc and began his homeward ride, the young knight could still hear his father's mocking laughter ringing in his ears . . .

Haunting him for many, many miles.

From the Creators of the
DRAGONLANCE® Saga
WARRIORS

Knights of the Crown
Roland Green

Maquesta Kar-Thon
Tina Daniell

Knights of the Sword
Roland Green

Theros Ironfeld
Don Perrin

Knights of the Rose
Roland Green

Lord Soth
Edo van Belkom

Saga

WARRIORS
Volume Six

Lord Soth

Edo van Belkom

DRAGONLANCE®
Warriors Series
Volume Six

LORD SOTH

©1996 TSR, Inc.

All Rights Reserved.

Distributed to the book trade in the United States by Random House, Inc. and in Canada by Random House of Canada Ltd.

Distributed in the United Kingdom by TSR Ltd.

Distributed to the toy and hobby trade by regional distributors.

Cover art by Jeff Easley. Interior art by Valerie A. Valusek.

First Printing: December, 1996
Printed in the United States of America.
Library of Congress Catalog Card Number: 95-62260

9 8 7 6 5 4 3 2 1

8377XXX1501

ISBN: 0-7869-0519-0

TSR, Inc.
201 Sheridan Springs Rd.
Lake Geneva, WI 53147
U.S.A.

TSR Ltd.
120 Church End, Cherry Hinton
Cambridge CB1 3LB
United Kingdom

DEDICATION

For my brother, Lou van Belkom
who thought I was pursuing a fool's dream
but thankfully kept his opinion to himself.

ACKNOWLEDGEMENTS

A lot of people played a part in bringing this novel into being. I'd like to thank Executive Editor Brian Thomsen for having confidence in my ability; Margaret Weis and Tracy Hickman for creating such an interesting character to write about; editor Barbara G. Young for helping me smooth out some of the rough spots; fellow TSR author Ed Greenwood for advice and encouragement early on; and beta-testers Don Bassingthwaite, David Livingstone Clink and David Nickle for helping me make sure *Lord Soth* remained true to form.

Dear Astinus,

I know it has been your intention for many years to pen a volume chronicling the spectacular rise and fall of Lord Loren Soth of Dargaard Keep. Understandably, work on the literally thousands upon thousands of other volumes in your wondrous library has always kept you from this important task.

That is why I accepted this assignment with both eagerness and trepidation. While I was anxious to show you that your confidence in my abilities was well-founded, I was also unsure about those same abilities and concerned that they might not be up to the challenge of recording a life story so tangled and mysterious as that of Lord Soth's.

The history of the Lord of Dargaard Keep is a fascinating one, full of as much honor, devotion to duty, love, knightly law and discipline, as cruelty, jealousy, greed, falsehood, unbridled lust, infidelity and murder.

Putting it to paper was not an easy task.

For despite how well his exploits are known to the people of Krynn, the details of each are as varied as the number of people who are familiar enough to speak of them.

Before this volume was completed, the life story of Lord Soth—also known to many by such names as Knight of the Black Rose, the Death Knight, or the Death Lord—had been a mixture of legend, fable, myth, spoken histories and long-lost tales.

For example, there are many variations of the story concerning the death of Soth's first wife, Lady Korinne Gladria of Palanthas. (Even in this, something as simple as a name, there have been errors as the woman has sometimes been incorrectly referred to as Lady Gladria of Korinne.) Lady Korinne wed Soth in a magnificent ceremony on the grounds outside Dargaard Keep. But while some histories have reported that she died during childbirth, or merely under "mysterious circumstances," they are all only partly true.

But you, Astinus of Palanthas, Master Historian of Krynn, did not become a master historian by chronicling half-truths and lies, and neither shall I. The reputation and respect you have earned in every corner of Krynn has been won by your tireless pursuit of truth in all matters pertaining to its history. It has been my goal to produce a history worthy of that same respect.

Whether I have achieved that goal or not, only you are qualified to judge. On my own behalf, I will say only this. While this is as well a researched history of Lord Soth's life as I could pen, I cannot say in all honesty that it is the one true version. For while I worked diligently to confirm each fact found in the various written records scattered throughout Solamnia and across the four corners of Krynn, far too many aspects of the story could only be verified verbally, and even then by—how shall I say?—less than reputable sources.

Speaking in more general terms, I found Soth's tale to be an utterly shocking one. Yet, as startling as it is, I suspect that there were even more disturbing elements that, even with the utmost diligence, I was unable to unearth. With much regret, I fear that those parts of Soth's history might be lost to us forever.

Nevertheless, I have combined all of the reliable facts concerning Lord Soth's sordid life and gathered them together in a single volume for the very first time. The result is as true a history of the knight's life as is within my ability to produce.

I submit it for your approval.

Verril Esteros, Second Aesthetic
Great Library of Astinus of Palanthas
401 A.C.

Prologue

Three moons might well have been in the sky, but only two dared show their faces. Lunitari glowed a dark shade of red while Solinari shone a bright white, leaving the dark moon Nuitari to be hidden by the night.

Lunitari and Solinari hung over the dark rippling waters of the northern sea like a pair of watchful eyes, shining crimson and white light down onto the sleeping port city of Kalaman, and casting spiderlike shadows across its dim, quiet streets.

A dark figure moved swiftly through the shadows. His movements were strong and sure, like those of a nobleman, but his dress was an ill-fitting patchwork of worn and tattered garments, suggesting the man was no more noble than a petty thief or common rogue.

Whatever the man's class, he moved quietly from shadow to shadow, avoiding the light as much as he shunned the open spaces between the scattered homes and shops.

When he reached the open mouth of a darkened alley, he stepped into its blackness and paused for a moment to catch his breath. As he stood there, he felt for the weapons hidden beneath his cloak, making sure everything was in place. He'd have only one chance to complete his task and he knew failure would not be tolerated.

After he had rested and his breathing had slowed, he ventured deeper into the alley's uncertain darkness.

After a short walk, he came upon the open back door of a popular tavern—The Rose and Thistle. From inside, the faint sound of laughter and song echoed into the alley while flickering firelight blazed through the half-open doorway like rays from the midday sun.

The dark figure stopped and strained to hear the people singing merrily inside, all the while making sure to keep his distance from the warm light emanating from within.

Next to the door, on the side closest to him, one of the tavern's more inebriated patrons—a dwarf—was propped up against the back wall of the establishment, no doubt sleeping off the effects of an over-indulgence of its finest ale. The dwarf was sleeping so peacefully it seemed a shame to wake him, but there was no time for such polite considerations.

Not tonight.

So without further hesitation the shadowy figure reared back and gave the dwarf a hard kick in the upper thigh.

"Ow!" exclaimed the dwarf, then muttered sleepily, "I assure you sir, I had no idea she was the daughter of a—"

So the dwarf was a scoundrel as well as a drunkard! He gave the dwarf another hard kick, this time causing the dwarf's ale-soaked eyes to flutter open. After taking a moment to wipe the last remnants of sleep from his eyes, the dwarf looked up at the dark, hooded figure standing over him. . . . And gasped in fear. "What do you want?" he asked.

"I'm looking for a young man, a *bard*"—he said the word as if it were a bad thing—"by the name of Argol Birdsong. Is it true that he performs in this tavern on occasion?"

"Now," the dwarf said casually, foolishly thinking he held a position of power over the dark figure standing before him. "Who wants to know?"

The hooded man stepped on the dwarf's foot then, pressing down hard with the heel of his boot. "I'm not interested in, nor do I have the time for dwarven games. Is he here or not?" He turned his boot to emphasize the point.

"Ow!" the dwarf cried, then quickly nodded. "Y-yes, he's here, he's here," he said. "In fact, that's him singing now."

The dark man held his breath for a moment and listened. He could just make out the sound of some ballad coming from inside the tavern. Satisfied, he lifted his boot from the dwarf's foot and fished inside his pouch for some coins.

"Go inside and tell Argol Birdsong there's an old friend waiting for him out in the alley." He dropped a few coins onto the dwarf's lap. "Then remain inside until you've drunk your fill . . . and then some."

The dwarf immediately stopped rubbing his aching foot and picked up the scattered coins. "Yes sir!" he said, jumping to his feet and limping back inside the tavern.

When the dwarf was gone, the dark figure looked up and down the alley then retreated into the safety of the shadows. There, he waited for the singing inside to come to an end. When the tavern was filled with the soft mumble of drunken voices carrying on in contented conversation, he tensed his body and listened for the sound of approaching footsteps.

When the sound came moments later, he drew back his cloak and took hold of the heavy dwarven warhammer that had been hanging from a loop on his belt.

"Hello?" called Argol Birdsong in a melodic voice. "Is someone here?" The bard paused a moment, then smiled broadly. "Aristal, my love? Are you here waiting for me?"

The man in the shadows took a moment to examine the features of the bard. Yes, the singer certainly bore the family resemblance that he had been told to look for. He stepped forward, partway into the light, but his face remained obscured by the folds of his hood.

"Who are you?" asked the bard, his voice no longer so birdlike and perhaps just a little bit frightened.

The stranger ignored the question and asked one of his

own. "Are you Argol Birdsong?"

"Yes, but—"

The man's next word died in his throat as the warhammer suddenly appeared, glinting at the top of its arc for a brief moment before slamming down onto the bard's head.

Once . . .

Twice . . .

Three times . . .

The bard's body slumped forward, then crumpled lifelessly, thudding heavily onto the alley floor.

And then all that could be heard was the rustle of a cloak and the fading click of boots as they hurried out of the alley.

Into the night.

* * * * *

The assassin ran quickly through the streets of Kalaman, staying away from the main roads and always remaining close to the protective cover of shadows. After running for several blocks, he slowed his pace and added a slight stumble to his gait to suggest that he'd spent most of the night sampling ale and wine of dubious merit.

When he reached the livery stable housing his horse, he tipped the stableman handsomely and was quickly on his way, riding fast enough to appear as if he were headed somewhere, but not so fast as to appear as if he were running away from something.

Outside of the city's limits, he hastened his horse's pace to a trot and then to a full gallop. He continued riding hard and fast for several minutes until he came upon a sharp bend in the Vingaard River.

The water was as black as the darkest night, even in the middle of the day. It was also deep as a well, as much as a hundred feet or more at its center.

It was the perfect place to make something vanish.

Remaining on his horse, the assassin moved to the edges of the southern river bank and opened his cloak. He unfastened the blood-stained warhammer from his belt and swung it wildly over his head by the leather thong tied to the end of its handle. After several quick rotations, he let go of the thong, flinging the hammer out over the water. The weapon whistled slightly as it twirled and sliced through the air, then made a faint splash as it broke the water's surface midway between the two banks.

The hammer remained on top of the water for a moment, reflecting a sliver of moonlight as the hammerhead turned for the bottom, and then it was gone.

Without a second glance, he turned from the river, kicked at his horse's ribs and was soon riding hard once more, heading west.

One more stop. One more task, and this night would be over.

As the moons slowly arced overhead, he came upon a small hamlet on the western outskirts of Kalaman called Villand. When he began to recognize the outlines of individual homes and cottages, he dismounted from his now heaving horse and gave it a hard slap on its haunches. The startled horse reared back and leaped forward. After two frantic strides it slowed to a more comfortable pace that would see it return to its home in a day or two.

Now alone in the village, the assassin again moved stealthily through winding streets, clinging to the cover afforded by the rough-hewn buildings and scattered trees. When he was near what felt like the center of the village he took a map from his inside cloak pocket and unfurled it beneath Solinari's generous moonlight.

Several of the bigger homes and shops were detailed on the map and after recognizing two of them, he was better able to orient himself and learn of his position within the village. If he wasn't mistaken, his destination was just four houses down the street on the left.

He clenched the map in his left hand and quietly counted off the houses as he passed.

When he arrived at the small unassuming cottage, he

checked the front door for a sign. It was there. A double loop connected at its center.

He checked the sign with the one scribbled next to the note on the map. It was the same double loop. The sign of Mishakal—a benevolent goddess known as the Healing Hand—had brought him here to this home. Except, unlike Mishakal, the assassin wasn't here to heal.

With the careful and deft hand of a thief, the assassin picked the lock on the door and eased it open, praying that the owner of the house had been particular about keeping his hinges well oiled. Fortunately he had been, and the door swung quietly open and closed. In seconds he was inside, moving about the house in utter silence.

The first room he checked was just off the kitchen. As promised by the notes written on the map in his hand, it was empty. He moved through the larger room in the center of the house and came upon another smaller room. This had to be the bedroom he was looking for.

It was separated from the adjoining room by a simple white sheet hung in the doorway. With a gentle hand, the assassin pulled the sheet aside and stepped into the room.

The window set in the outside wall was bare and moonlight bathed the room with a soft, incandescent glow, as if the light of Mishakal herself were shining down on the room's sole occupant.

He moved closer to the bed for a better look.

There was a half-elven female lying there. She was attractive for a half-elf. In fact, she was attractive by any standard of measure.

As with the bard, there could be no mistaking this woman's identity. She was indeed the one he sought. Her name was Alsin Felgaard, and she was a milkmaid working on one of the many farms that surrounded Villand.

He moved still closer, then recoiled slightly. Even though he knew what to expect, the features of the half-elf's face were strikingly similar to those of Argol Birdsong. In fact, if the creature lying on the bed hadn't been half-elven, he would have sworn that they were full brother and sister.

The assassin pondered that thought for a moment, then did his best to dismiss it from his mind. His task was not to think, only to do as he'd been told. If he thought about it for too long, his loyalty might waver, and he couldn't afford to have that happen.

If it ever did, he'd be a dead man.

After taking a deep breath to calm himself, he drew back his cloak once more. This time he removed the battle-axe from where it hung on his belt and gripped it firmly in both of his gloved hands.

Slowly, he raised the axe over his head. . . .

And hesitated.

The half-elf was far too young and beautiful a flower to be cut down so early in what would be a long, long life.

He inhaled a ragged breath, his shaking hands causing the battle-axe to tremble. He let a shiver run its course, then closed his eyes and let out a sigh. As he slowly reopened them, he shook his head.

He'd foolishly allowed himself to think again.

He took another breath, this time making sure his mind and body were hardened by resolve to complete his mission, a resolve stronger and colder than any steel could ever be.

This wouldn't be the first time he'd killed, he told himself. Nor would it be the last.

He raised the battle-axe over his head again, and quickly brought it down with a mighty stroke, cutting through the body of the sleeping maiden and splintering the hard wooden boards of the bed she lay upon.

Her eyes opened in horror, but no sound escaped her lips.

If she'd been lucky, she hadn't suffered.

The assassin turned from the ruined and bloodied corpse, and left the house as quietly as he'd entered.

When he stepped outside, the sweat soaking his body cooled like ice upon his skin.

It chilled him.

To the bone.

He silently slipped from shadow to shadow to a spot just outside the village where there was a fresh horse tethered to a tree waiting for him. He mounted it easily and in seconds both horse and rider were off, riding west across the plain toward Dargaard Keep.

He stopped only once during his ride.

When he came upon a small creek, one of the dozens of tributaries feeding the Vingaard River, he brought his horse to a stop at the water's edge. Unlike the waters of the Vingaard River itself, the water here was shallow and slow moving. However, the creek's bottom was quite muddy and the water murky, making it another desirable spot in which to rid himself of the murder weapon.

As he did earlier that night with the warhammer, he tossed the battle-axe into the creek. After it smacked the surface it was almost immediately gone from view.

And now, for the first time that night, he let out a long, deep sigh of something resembling relief.

The deeds had been done.

He remounted and allowed his horse to walk slowly for several minutes as both horse and rider tried to catch their breath. Then, at the call of its rider, the horse suddenly charged forward in a gallop.

After several hours, as the first rays of dawning sunlight just began to creep over the horizon, he came upon a small and simple cottage at the northernmost foot of the Dargaard Mountains. There was light inside the cottage and, judging from the smoke rising out of the chimney, a roaring fire in its hearth.

He pulled back on the reins and the horse gratefully slowed to a walk. He guided the horse into the stable, covered it with a blanket, provided it with small amounts of food and water, and then headed for the cottage.

He knocked three times and waited for someone to answer the door.

* * * * *

Two men sat by the fire in the small wooden cottage, one rocking in his chair, the other still and silent, as if in deep meditation. The cottage was small, perhaps even cramped, but because they were using it for just this one clandestine meeting, it was more than adequate for their purpose.

Although the flickering light of the fire was dim, the physical similarities between the two were obvious. Both were big men, tall and heavy-boned, suggesting they were formidable fighters. Their facial features were almost identical, and judging from the square jaw, the prominent brow and high cheekbones, the only real distinction between the two was the passage of time.

The older man had salt and pepper hair—somewhat thinned up top and around the edges—and a full beard which had been blanched white by years of worry. By contrast the younger man's hair was a thick dark shock hanging down over his shoulders in curls, and his pitch black mustache was stylishly long and tapered. He appeared as yet untouched by life's more weighty burdens.

Beside their ages, the only other difference between the two men could be found in their eyes. The elder's eyes seemed old and tired, the color of dead embers the morning after a fire. In comparison, the younger man's steel-gray eyes were sharp and piercing despite their being set deeply into the dark sockets under his brow. And even though his eyes were slightly obscured in shadow, they still had the appearance of being mysteriously alight from within—some might even say, blazing.

Suddenly the younger of the two sat upright in his chair. As he listened carefully to the sounds of the night outside, he could just make out the hoofbeats of an approaching horse.

Slowly the elder rose from his rocker, moving to the hearth to stoke the fire.

In minutes there came three sharp knocks on the door.

The younger man hurried to the door and opened it. A

man dressed in the guise of a thief stood in the doorway, his body leaning against the jamb for support.

"Well?"

"It is done."

Hearing the words, the younger of the two men, a Knight of the Sword named Loren Soth, breathed a deep sigh of relief. "Well done, Caradoc. You have served me well. Please, come inside now and rest for a while."

The older man, Knight Soth's father, Aynkell Soth, busied himself with the fire to make it appear as if he were unconcerned about the other's arrival.

Caradoc stepped into the cottage and began disrobing, tossing his cloak upon the hearth. It hissed and sizzled as his sweat evaporated from the cloth, then all at once it burst into flames. His shirt and britches followed, the blood of his victims burning in colorful shades of orange and blue.

Without another word, Caradoc began dressing himself in his more comfortable—and familiar—knightly garb. In addition to being a Knight of the Crown, Caradoc was also the younger Soth's steward, or seneschal, serving his master with unwavering loyalty.

Knight Soth returned to his seat and watched his most loyal steward finish getting dressed.

"Any problems?" he asked. "Did anyone see you?"

"There was a drunkard behind the Rose and Thistle, but I never revealed my face to him."

Soth nodded. "And the weapons?"

"A warhammer and a battle-axe, making the deeds appear to be the work of renegade dwarves." A pause. "Both weapons are currently resting beneath some very cold and very dark waters."

"Excellent," Knight Soth said. "You've done well."

Aynkell Soth returned to his rocker and looked up at his son for the first time in hours. "Yes," he said in a voice that was surprisingly devoid of emotion. "Now when you take over rule of Knightlund, you can be certain that no other heir will come forward to lay claim to it."

Knight Soth looked at his father for several seconds before speaking to him in a voice that was dripping with contempt. "It seems to me that as a bard and a milkmaid, neither of the two products of your affairs would have been of the type inclined to claim it."

"Perhaps not," said Aynkell Soth. "But if they had known of their lineage, known of their birthright, then perhaps . . ."

"It's of little consequence now," Caradoc said flatly. "They are both dead."

"Yes," said Aynkell, nodding. "Thank you."

"For what?" asked Caradoc, doing nothing to stop his voice from rising in anger. He was loyal to Knight Soth, not to the knight's father, who was nothing more than a second-rate clerk and first-rate philanderer. "For the murder of your own flesh and blood, the half-kin of my master?"

If the elder Soth was surprised by the young man's impertinence, he did not show it. "Why? For the removal of the black marks upon my soul," Aynkell answered, his voice still strong, still confident.

"The black marks might have been removed from your soul," said Knight Soth, "but they are not gone. They have merely been transferred. The black marks that were once upon your soul, are now upon mine. The full weight of my father's sins are now mine alone to bear. What a lovely gift to receive scant months before my wedding day."

Soth knew that the evil deeds were necessary to assure his ascension to the lordship of Dargaard Keep—and he would let nothing interfere with that—but he resented the fact that his father had made such murders necessary.

The sarcasm in young Soth's words was too much for the elder Soth to bear. He turned away from his son in order to avoid having to look him in the face.

"You might not have been a Knight of Solamnia," said Knight Soth. "But you were familiar enough with the Oath and the Measure to have at least tried to live by its code."

"I was never suited to become a knight, nor to live like one," Aynkell said, his voice sad and apologetic. His face appeared to have aged over the last few minutes with the realization that his son would likely never forgive him his past indiscretions.

"A poor excuse."

"Perhaps, but it is the only one I have."

Soth shook his head and sighed. "You may attend the wedding and take your place of honor upon the high table. But it is only at Korinne's request that you will be there."

Aynkell nodded.

"I want as little to do with you as possible."

Aynkell stood motionless and impassive.

"Come, Caradoc," said Knight Soth. "Light is dawning and we must return to the keep before we become conspicuous by our absence."

"I'll ready the horses," said Caradoc, now fully dressed and looking every inch a Knight of the Crown. He left the cottage, giving Soth the chance to spend a final few minutes alone with his father.

Knight Soth turned to face the older man.

"Good-bye, father," he said, knowing that the words were much more than just a casual farewell.

The elder Soth looked at his son for a long time and the disgrace he felt slowly disappeared. A cynical, almost mocking, smile appeared on his face.

"Don't be so quick to condemn me, my son," Aynkell said. "You are of my flesh and of my blood. You always will be. There's too much of me in you for you to be so critical of my life."

For a moment Knight Soth was speechless.

In the intervening silence, Aynkell began to laugh.

The knight's face darkened in a scowl as he turned abruptly away from his father and stormed out of the cottage.

As he joined Caradoc and began his homeward ride, the young knight could still hear his father's mocking laughter ringing in his ears . . .

Haunting him for many, many miles.

BOOK ONE

SON'S RISE

Chapter 1

Dargaard Keep was an impressive sight, even to those who had watched it slowly being constructed and had been familiar with its commanding presence for years. It was a keep unlike any other on the face of Krynn, looking for all the world as if it had grown up out of the ground, rather than been painstakingly built stone by stone.

It was an appearance that had not happened by chance. With its unique shape, labyrinthine hallways, spires and towers, and deep multiple levels of caverns and dungeons, it had taken over a hundred of the best stone cutters, masons and smiths from the four corners of Krynn more than five years to complete. But all who set their eyes upon it agreed that the years of hard labor had been more than worth it, for now that it was finished it stood triumphantly at the northern end of the Dargaard Mountains as one of the true architectural wonders of Solamnia, perhaps even of all of Krynn.

The keep had been designed by Knight Soth himself, who'd wanted to create a fitting tribute not only to those

Solamnic Knights who had so bravely fallen in battle over the ages, but to his numerous uncles and cousins, all of them knights, who had died when the great plagues swept across Solamnia in the latter years of the Age of Might. Therefore the keep had been constructed in the shape of a rose, its towers, battlements and ramparts curling out from its center like the petals of a flower under the warm light of the mid-morning sun. Closer to the ground, a long column twisted up from the earth with portholes and windows dotting the structure at various points, their intricate and decorative brickwork giving the column the appearance of having thorns. Protecting the keep was a high and thick stone wall which, ringing the structure with a solid line of defense against even the most persistent attacker, at the same time created a spacious courtyard on the grounds for the training of knights and for the conducting of ceremonies and other festivities.

And finally, surrounding the keep was a deep and dark chasm, said to be bottomless but in reality no more than a hundred or so feet deep. The only entrance to the keep was across a sturdy drawbridge which spanned the chasm and led visitors through a well guarded gatehouse. The gatehouse featured a heavy steel portcullis fashioned in the shape of interlocking swords and adorned with small crowns and large roses. The overall design of the keep made it both a wonder to behold and an impregnable fortress. As a result, plans had been made to designate the keep as the strategic headquarters of the Knights of the Rose, the highest order of the Solamnic Knights.

But despite its many wonders, the most unique of all of the keep's features was its color. At Knight Soth's insistence, the keep had been built from a rose-colored granite popularly referred to as "bloodstone" which had been quarried from a very rich vein in the heart of the Dargaard Mountains. When he had first hinted that the keep should be made of the crimson stone, the cutters and masons rebelled knowing all too well that bloodstone was the hardest of all building materials to work with. But now, mere months after its completion, all agreed that the additional effort and hard work had been more than worthwhile.

The keep was a thing of beauty and a source of pride to all the people of Knightlund. It was also a structure worthy of its most noble inhabitant, Knight Loren Soth, currently a Knight of the Sword and a great and noble soldier for the cause of Good.

The mood around the estate on this morning was a spirited one as a carnival-like atmosphere had pervaded all of the proceedings in and around Dargaard Keep for the past few weeks. What else could be expected as one of Solamnia's greatest knights prepared to be wed?

And, with a higher concentration of knights and noblemen than could be found even on the greatest of battlefields, the merchants and tradesmen of Solamnia had all flocked to Dargaard Keep, setting up shop weeks in advance, trying to secure the best spots in which to sell their wares to the wedding guests they hoped would all be in a spending mood.

On the grounds just west of the keep, blacksmiths and other skilled tradesmen were selling newly forged armor and swords, all of which glinted with gold, silver and brass accents and shone blindingly bright beneath the hot morning sun. Many of them had already done great business, selling all that they had brought and taking orders for more custom-made articles. Around the back of the keep, tailors and seamstresses sold resplendent garments suitable for wearing to the wedding ceremony of a knight, while still others were busy making new clothes specifically ordered for the occasion.

The rest of the crowd was filled out by jugglers, conjurers, minstrels and bards, and an assortment of other fortune tellers, con artists and prestidigitators. Busiest of these were the herbalists who purported to be selling all varieties of love potions, the potency of which were verified nightly by some of the more amorous of the wedding's guests.

But while the mood outside was festive, within the walls of the keep's courtyard there was an event underway, the tone of which was somewhat more subdued.

"Knight Soth, please come forward," said Lord Olthar Uth Wistan, High Warrior, and one of the presiding knights on the assembled Rose Knights Council. Olthar sat at one end of a group of five knights seated at the high table which was elevated atop a wooden platform positioned against one of the courtyard's inside walls. At Olthar's immediate left were two elderly Knights of the Rose, both of whom had long since retired from their active knightly duties. Oren Brightblade and Dag Kurrold had both been asked to sit on the Rose Knights Council out of respect for their long years of distinguished service to the knighthood. Both had accepted the honorary appointment with pleasure.

Sadly, Solamnic Grand Master Leopold Gwyn Davis had fallen ill the previous week and was bedridden and unable to attend. A seat was left empty upon the platform in his honor.

Soth stepped forward dressed in a combination of gleaming plate armor and chain mail, a scarlet cloak trailing behind him. His breastplate bore the symbol of the Order of the Sword and in contrast to the rest of his armor, it was worn and dented, evidence of just some of the heroic battles he had fought and won against the forces of Evil. He knelt in front of the high table and kept his head bowed, waiting to be spoken to.

Lord Olthar nodded to the fourth council member, signaling to the member that he was no longer presiding over the council.

The fourth member nodded, accepting control of the ceremony.

"Are you the supplicant wishing to apply to the Order of the Rose?" asked High Justice Lord Adam Caladen, who along with High Clerist Lord Cyril Mordren occupied the remaining two spots on the five-member Rose Knights Council.

Soth looked up at the high justice and nodded.

"You may begin with your family's lineage," said High Justice Caladen.

"I am Loren Soth, Knight of the Sword," he said proudly. "My family has been one of the ruling houses of Solamnia for many, many years. For generations, the Soth name has carried on the proud tradition of the Solamnic Knights, pursuing the virtues of loyalty, obedience, heroism, courage, justice and wisdom. So well have my ancestors served the knights, and so stringent is their adherence to the ways of the Oath and the Measure, that they were deeded the province of Knightlund in recognition of their years of loyal service and undying devotion to the cause of Good." Soth paused in honor of his ancestors. "It is my intention to make sure that the same level of commitment continues under the Soth family name for many generations to come."

A slight good-natured laugh rippled through the crowd of knights, family and guests that had gathered within the courtyard to witness the ceremony.

"While my father, Aynkell Soth, was not a knight, he has done his best to serve the Knights of Solamnia well. In addition, many of my father's brothers—my uncles— were some of the bravest and most noble knights Solamnia has ever seen."

"Yes," someone called from the rear of the crowd.

"And although my father was just a humble clerk, he was never without honor, pledging loyalty to the knighthood and living his life as if he himself were bound by the code prescribed by the Oath and the Measure." Soth raised the volume of his voice slightly as he said these words in order to prevent it from wavering. "For many years, he has acted as a most capable steward of Knightlund, ensuring that the realm would be strong and prosperous for the day that I, his only son and the one true heir to Knightlund"—these words were also spoken loudly, almost as if they were a challenge—"became of age and the province could rightly be passed from his capable hands to mine."

The crowd behind Soth broke into a small cheer that grew in strength until the high justice was forced to raise a hand and restore order. "And what of your deeds of honor?"

Another laugh rippled through the crowd, only now it was a little livelier. Asking Soth about his deeds of honor was like asking the great and legendary Knight Huma Dragonbane, "And what of the dragons?"

"I have led a successful expedition to Southern Ergoth to rescue two knights who had been captured and unjustly held as hostages by a band of ogres while on a peaceful journey to Qualinesti."

Members of the Knights Council nodded, none more emphatically than Dag Kurrold, whose son Degan was one of the two knights rescued in that very raid.

"While escorting a religious pilgrimage of women to Istar to visit the Temple of the Kingpriest, my party was crossed by a band of marauding thieves in one of the passes leading through the mountains of Thoradin. During the subsequent battle, I single-handedly slew four ogres and a minotaur." Some in the crowd gasped at the mention of a minotaur, but Soth continued. "But most important of all was that none of the women on the pilgrimage, nor any of the knights under my command, were killed or injured in the fight, while each and every one of our attackers was dispatched and the pilgrimage continued on without further incident."

"Paladine be praised," came a cry from somewhere in the courtyard, no doubt from one of the women who had been on the pilgrimage.

"Last spring," continued Soth, "while traveling through Kelwick Pass on my way to Throtyl, I rescued a child from inside a burning cottage, then brought that child back to

Dargaard Keep where the healer was able to save its young life."

"Hurrah!" came the faint voice of a boy, the same boy Soth had saved from the fire.

"I successfully defended the honor of Lady Wandra after accusations had been made against her chastity by a scorned suitor."

"Enough! Enough!" cried Lord Caladen sternly, raising his hands as if Soth's deeds were a rising tide which needed to be stanched. "You know as well as anyone here that a supplicant need only offer three honorable deeds. If we were to listen to all of the deeds on your list, Knight Soth, we might all be late for the wedding." The high justice smiled and the tension was broken by the sound of laughter.

The tone of such council meetings was usually quite solemn, but that was usually the result of an uncertainty about a knight's suitability for acceptance into the Order of the Rose. For Soth, however, his ascension into the highest order of the Knights of Solamnia was little more than a formality. The Knights of the Rose had been eager to bring Soth into their order for years and in fact had waived the stipulation which would have required Soth to venture on a quest to prove his loyalty to the order and its cause. Sending him on a thirty-day quest to restore something which was lost, to defeat an evil and more powerful opponent and to conduct one test of wisdom and three of generosity seemed unnecessary in Soth's case. He had been undergoing such tests, and passing them with flying colors for years.

"Now," said Lord Caladen. "If anyone present has any knowledge as to why this noble knight should not ascend to the Order of the Rose, or rule over Knightlund as its lord, now is your chance to be heard."

Although Lord Caladen said the words jovially and as if they were little more than a mere formality, Soth's heart leapt up into his throat as he waited for a faint voice to break the quiet stillness of the moment.

No one said a word.

Or perhaps dared to.

"Very well, then, Knight Soth," Lord Caladen said rising to his feet. "Your lineage is impeccable, your deeds most honorable, and your supplication unchallenged. However, it is the custom of the Rose Knights Council to adjourn in private to determine whether a petition should be accepted or rejected, and we shall do so now."

Lord Caladen moved away from the high table, stepped off the platform and was followed into a room just off the courtyard by Lord Cyril and Lord Olthar. Oren Brightblade and Dag Kurrold also followed the others off the platform, but they were helped down the steps by several eager Knights of the Crown who were more than willing to lend a hand to the gallant knights who had fought beside their fathers and grandfathers so many years ago.

When the Knights Council had left, Soth turned around to take a look at the gathering. To his right, seated in the small gallery reserved for honored guests, was Caradoc, who as Soth's seneschal, would also be ascending an order of the knighthood soon, becoming a Knight of the Sword. To Caradoc's left was Korinne Gladria, waving to her shining knight with a look that was proud, loving and somehow seductive. Soth waved back at her, then stopped as he caught sight of his father. Aynkell Soth had raised his clenched fist as a sign of congratulations, but Soth quickly looked away before it became obvious that he had seen the man and was forced to acknowledge the gesture.

Soth turned his head the other way and saw scores of his fellow knights from all three of the orders offering their congratulations and best wishes. Soth nodded to each in turn as he continued to scan the gathering. Then when he looked directly behind him, he saw a wall of bodies crammed into every available corner of the courtyard, some even sitting atop the shoulders of the more sturdy in the crowd. Even the balconies and battlements were full of onlookers and well-wishers. This was a momentous occasion in Soth's life and he was glad there were record numbers of people who wanted to be a witness to it.

The low murmur of voices was silenced by the opening of the door to the Rose Knights Council's room. Oren Brightblade and Dag Kurrold were first to exit and were quickly escorted back onto the platform by the young knights who, like everyone else, were eager to hear the Rose Knights Council's decision.

A moment later High Warrior Lord Olthar Uth Wistan, High Clerist Lord Cyril Mordren, and High Justice Lord Adam Caladen took their places at the high table.

They were all silent and their faces were strangely solemn.

Watching them take their seats, Soth was suddenly worried that things were about to go terribly wrong. Had the Knights Council been made aware of his father's indiscretions? Had they somehow learned about the measures he had taken six months previous? If they had, it would mean his ascension to the Order of the Rose would be rejected; indeed, even his life as a Knight of Solamnia might well be over.

The sweat began to bubble up on his brow.

Lord Adam Caladen looked down at Soth. "Knight Soth," he said. Lord Caladen raised his head to address the gathering. "The Knights Council has considered your application carefully and it is our opinion that—"

Soth drew a breath and held it.

"—you immediately be admitted into the Order of the Rose."

Soth exhaled.

The courtyard erupted in applause. Hats, helms and gloves flew into the air in celebration.

Soth remained kneeling, knowing the ceremony was still not completed.

Lord Caladen stepped down off the platform and walked out into the courtyard until he stood in front of the young Knight of the Sword. After a few seconds, the cheering died down, allowing Lord Caladen the chance to be heard. "Arise, Knight Soth."

Soth got to his feet.

"And from this day forward be known to all as *Lord* Loren Soth of Dargaard Keep, Knight of the Rose."

Four knights stepped into the courtyard carrying a shining new breastplate bearing the symbol of the rose in its center. After placing the breastplate at Soth's feet, they helped him remove his scarred and dented one bearing the symbol of the sword, then placed the new breastplate into position.

With his armor now complete, Lord Soth absolutely gleamed.

He bowed to Lord Caladen and the rest of the Rose Knights Council, then turned to face the bulk of the crowd. He drew his sword, raised it high over his head, and said, "Est Sularus oth Mithas."

Then he repeated the words in Common.

"My Honor is My Life!"

The crowd erupted in thunderous applause, this time accompanied by a shower of yellow, white and red roses.

* * * * *

"He is so very handsome," said one of the many maids and ladies who had gathered in Korinne's bedchamber to help her pass the hours before her greatly anticipated wedding to Lord Soth in the morning.

"Not to mention big and strong," said another.

"That he is," agreed several others.

"If you are lucky," said Lady Gelbmartin, a large, robust woman who was a cousin of Korinne, and whose husband, Lord Gelbmartin, was the steward of Vingaard Keep, "he'll put both those qualities to good use on that bed over there." She pointed to the huge canopied four-poster bed on the other side of the room.

All of the women laughed.

"If he's anything like his father," said Lady Gelbmartin, "you two should be busy just about every night, Palast morn to Linaras eve."

Again, laughter coursed through the room.

Korinne smiled. Although she'd never said so in as many words, she was looking forward to her wedding night with great anticipation. And she knew Soth was, too.

When the laughter died down, Lady Gelbmartin chattered on. "Aynkell Soth is getting on in years, but that hasn't stopped him from flirting with every pretty woman he sees. Why, just today I was—"

Lady Gelbmartin stopped talking when she saw three maids approaching the gathering carrying a gift-wrapped box and a bundle of six red roses.

"Milady Korinne," said one of the maids, a woman by the name of Mirrel who'd lived and worked in Dargaard Keep as a laundress even before it had been completed. "Allow us to welcome you to the keep. It will be our pleasure to serve you as loyally and faithfully as we have served our Lord Soth."

One of the maids gave Korinne the roses and box. She sniffed at the roses, then pulled the ribbons off the box and opened it. Inside was a white gown made of the softest and sheerest of fabric, which when worn would do nothing for the sake of modesty.

"Thank you," said Korinne, standing up and holding the gown against her body at the shoulders. "Do you think he'll like it?"

"If he has a heartbeat!" said Lady Gelbmartin.

Korinne blushed.

The rest of the women laughed.

* * * * *

Elsewhere, Lord Loren Soth sat comfortably in one of the keep's smaller dining halls in the company of his fellow knights, including the thirteen loyal knights under his command. He finished his tankard of ale in a gulp and before he could place it back on the table, a footman made sure another frosty tankard was there waiting for him to sample.

"Thank you my good man," he said, blowing the white head of foam from the top of the tankard. Then he picked the tankard up from the table and raised it high in the air. "To wedded bliss!" he shouted.

"To wedded bliss!" came the cry of dozens of voices, a few of which were slow to answer the call causing a strange echo to reverberate through the room.

"Bliss! Wedded bliss! Bliss! Bliss!"

And finally one last cry from a knight rudely awakened by all the noise. "To bedded wiss!" he stammered, grabbing his tankard and raising it up, only to realize it was empty.

The knights laughed raucously and easily. After what seemed to be endless quests and journeys across the continent of Ansalon, battling evil forces in the never ending fight for the cause of Good, this gathering, filled with such camaraderie and good cheer, was a more than welcome relief. In fact, so happy were the men to see old friends and fellow knights that (although no one would be foolish or brave enough to suggest it) the atmosphere pervading the room would have likely been as warm even without the lubricating effects of the ale.

"With a woman as beautiful as Korinne Gladria," said Wersten Kern, one of the most loyal of Soth's own knights, "I should think wedded bliss would be a certainty."

"Truth be told."

"Hear, hear."

"Paladine speaks!" came the call of the knights, followed by the sounds of clinking tankards and the slosh of ale.

"Yes," continued Wersten Kern. "And if Lady Gladria doesn't give our good Lord Soth the desire to produce many, many heirs, then he has no business being such a famed Knight of Solamnia."

At another time Kern's comment might have been construed as being covetous of Lady Gladria, but in the company of his fellow knights, the sentiment was understood.

The room erupted again in laughter and the sound of more clinking tankards, even a shattered one, which brought on still more laughter.

Meyer Seril, a Crown knight originally from Caergoth, the capital city of Southlund, was next to speak. "Certainly Dargaard Keep shall soon be filling up with young knights eager to follow in their father's footsteps."

"It's my solemn promise," Lord Soth said, "that the Soth name will live in glory throughout Solamnia, by the deeds of its namesakes, my sons, grandsons and great-great grandsons, for many, many years to come."

Dag Kurrold, the semiretired knight who had been sitting off by himself, half-asleep in a corner, suddenly perked up at hearing the new direction of the conversation. "If the younger Soth is anything like his father," he said in a hoarse, yet powerful voice, "there won't be a lack of children for want of trying." He laughed then, a wheezing cackle that caused everyone to stop and look in the direction of the old knight.

Everyone, including Soth.

The mention of his father hit Soth like a cold slap in the face. He stood up, his wide piercing eyes and dark scowl causing everyone in the room to fall silent.

"Leave the room!" Soth said harshly.

Dag Kurrold looked at Soth, a stunned and apologetic look on his bearded face. "I'm sorry," he said. "I meant no—"

"No, it's not you," Soth said, his voice much softer, as if he'd reconsidered the harsh tone of his earlier words. In fact he was now almost as apologetic as the elder knight had been. "It's just that I've suddenly been overcome by the whole day. I'm afraid I'm going to need my rest if I'm going to be a presentable bridegroom at tomorrow's ceremony. Please, if everyone could leave now . . ."

"The lord of the keep needs his rest," declared Wersten Kern. "There are many other rooms in the keep we can move the festivities to."

The knights slowly began to rise, many of them taking their tankards with them, some even carrying barrels. Indeed, the party would be continuing in scattered parts of the keep well into the night.

"Good night, my lord."

"Good night, sir."

"Night, *Lord* Soth."

Each of the knights said farewell, then quickly left the dining hall. Dag Kurrold was one of the last to leave, his face long and troubled.

"I'm sorry for ruining the merriment," said the elder knight.

"Not to worry," said Soth, slapping a hand on the older man's back. "You can rest easy tonight. It was not your words which troubled me."

Dag smiled. "All right, then. Good night."

The hall was soon empty.

Except for Soth.

Except for Caradoc.

Together, knight and steward filled their tankards then sat down at the table, facing each other.

"To the glory of the noble Soth clan," Caradoc said, raising his tankard.

Letting out a sigh, Soth raised his tankard as well. "Yes," he said. "To an unblemished future, for generations to come."

They clanked tankards, the sound of which echoed hollowly off the cold stone walls.

Chapter 2

The sun had risen several hours ago but was still barely visible over the eastern horizon as the sky over Dargaard Keep was gray and full of thick, dark clouds. Obviously these were not the best weather conditions under which to celebrate a wedding. But as the dark clouds continued to gather and roll across the sky, threatening a downpour at any moment, a kind of reverse optimism began to infect the wedding's guests until they were all of the opinion that a stormy wedding day could only bode well for the bright future of the marriage.

So, content in the knowledge that the wedding ceremony would go on, rain or shine, the squires and footmen worked quickly to assemble the benches which would seat the more than one hundred invited guests on the grounds just outside Dargaard Keep. The decision to move the day's festivities outside had been made not only to accommodate the large number of guests, but also to allow everyone who wanted to witness the spectacle a chance to do so.

Those without official invitations would find a spot for themselves on the hills and knolls surrounding the makeshift chapel that had been built on the grounds. In fact, some had already secured a place for themselves on the grassy slopes near the altar even though the wedding itself wouldn't begin for several hours yet. All this, simply for the sake of catching a close-up glimpse of the regal Lord Soth and his resplendent bride-to-be, Korinne Gladria.

Conducting such an early vigil for something as simple as a good vantage point might have seemed a bit excessive for some, but certainly not to those native to Solamnia who looked upon a marriage between the houses of Soth and Gladria as nothing less than a royal wedding.

Which in many ways it was.

Korinne Gladria was the daughter of Lord Reynard Gladria, one of the most highly regarded and respected noblemen of Palanthas, not to mention a distant cousin to the High Clerist himself. And Soth, although the son of a humble clerk, was also a distinguished Knight of Solamnia and member of the Order of the Rose. And, while all the Knights of Solamnia could lay claim to royal blood, the Order of the Rose was open to only those of the "purest" blood, making it the order of royalty within the Knights of Solamnia.

And so, as the last few benches were set into place, the grassy lands surrounding the altar slowly began to fill up with footmen, maids and commoners from Dargaard Keep, as well as the many farmers who tended the fertile farmlands of Knightlund.

Overhead, there was a slight shift in the clouds, allowing the sun to peek through the curtain of gray for the first time that morning.

* * * * *

"Please don't worry, Mother. He's a wonderful man," said Korinne Gladria, as her bridesmaids attended to her long, flowing white gown.

Lady Leyla Gladria looked into her daughter's eyes and smiled. "I have no doubt that he is, dear Korinne."

"Then why do I have the feeling that you are still uneasy on a day which is supposed to be one of the happiest of my life?"

Leyla took a breath and exhaled slowly. "I just wish you were marrying someone more like—"

"More like Father," Korinne said. "Oh, Mother."

"Your father might not have been heralded as a valiant and courageous hero, but he was still a very distinguished politician and diplomat, not to mention a good husband and father. There was nothing he liked more than to be at home with his family. Nothing in the world made him more happy." She shook her head. "Soth is a warrior, perhaps even a great warrior. But that is his life. He craves adventure, lives for the battle. When I think of the violence he's been a party to . . ."

"All in the name of justice and freedom."

Leyla paused. "My dear, sweet, innocent girl. Men never do evil so completely and cheerfully as when they do it under the guise of doing good."

Korinne looked at her mother curiously. "Whose fine words are those?"

"It's a preface to one of the volumes by Vinas Solamnus, volume seven I believe. It is a warning to those who foolishly believe that all warriors who fight on the side of good can do no wrong."

"Soth is a good man. And he will be a good father, too."

Leyla sighed. Obviously this was a topic that had been discussed many times before, each time ending with the same result. "I just want you to be happy," she said, giving her daughter a hug.

"I will be, Mother," said Korinne, returning the hug warmly. "I will be."

* * * * *

"Do you, Lord Loren Soth, take Korinne Gladria, to be your wife, to love her with a pure heart, and honor her as you would the Oath and the Measure?" asked Lord Cyril Mordren. The elderly knight was flanked by two silver-and-white robed Priests of Paladine who had conducted the more mundane aspects of the ceremony before relinquishing duties to Lord Mordren, the High Clerist of the Knights of Solamnia.

Soth turned to his bride and held his breath lest her beauty take it away. She was absolutely stunning in her long white gown, which was highlighted by swirling sky-blue accents that followed the contours of her shapely form like a second skin. Under her veil, her red hair hung down past her waist in thick, full curls. Her green eyes looked up at him, large and alluring, possessing both an innocence and an eagerness, neither of which ever seemed to wane. She smiled at him, and for a moment Soth felt himself grow weak.

He turned back to face Lord Mordren. "With all my heart."

Lord Mordren smiled and nodded approvingly.

"Do you, Korinne Gladria, take Lord Loren Soth, to be your wedded husband, to love him with a pure and loyal heart, and to honor him and the Oath and the Measure, the knightly code by which he has vowed to live his life?"

Korinne turned from Lord Mordren and gazed upon her husband to be. Her eyes were alight with something akin to pure joy, and her smile was broad, as much from relief as from happiness.

The moment had finally come.

Soth felt his heart skip a beat. Here was possibly the greatest moment of the young Soth's life. In the span of days he'd been inducted into the highest order within the Knights of Solamnia, had been instituted as the new Lord of Knightlund, and now, he was to be wedded to one of the most beautiful and loving women in all of Solamnia, no, the entire continent of Ansalon if not Krynn itself.

Forgotten were the indiscretions of his father, the murders committed by Caradoc on his behalf.

The past was behind him now and he was anxious to begin life anew as a Knight of the Rose. To start fresh with new resolve to live his life according to the Oath and the Measure. And he was eager to start living his other new life, that of a husband, the head of a family, and a father to the heir of the Soth legacy.

If only she would say the words.

"With all my heart," she said.

Lord Mordren nodded, then turned to Soth. "You may kiss her, if you wish."

Soth turned to face his new bride, Lady Korinne Soth, and gently lifted the veil over her head. Her pale skin was soft, smooth and flawless, radiating a vibrant glow full of love, life and happiness. Her copper-colored hair curled and shimmered like flames in the light of the midday sun which had just started to break through the clouds in earnest. He hesitated for a moment, admiring her beauty, then leaned forward, bending at the waist so their lips could meet.

A rousing cheer rose up around them as the guests, some of whom had been waiting for this one moment for months, shouted their enthusiastic approval of the marriage.

The kiss lasted a long, long time, with neither Soth nor Gladria wishing for it to end.

But when the cheering lessened somewhat, Lord Mordren cleared his throat, interrupting the newlyweds' kiss, and allowing the ceremony to be completed.

"You are now husband and wife. Go forth and live with love, honor, wisdom, and above all loyalty to one another, now and forever."

Another cheer from the crowd.

Minstrels began to play.

The couple turned to face the assembly, then slowly began walking down the center aisle left open between the benches filled to capacity with family, friends and fellow knights. Their path, which led around toward the other side of the keep, was carpeted with multi-colored rose petals.

After they'd passed through the crowd of guests, the rest of their way was lined with Knights of the Sword who'd drawn their weapons and crossed them over the aisle to form a canopy under which the couple could walk.

The gesture was an unexpected tribute, and Soth was both surprised and honored by it. As he walked under the arc of gleaming swords held aloft by his fellow knights, he began to think about how everything to do with the wedding had been so right, so wonderful. It was as if the wedding had been blessed by Paladine himself, perhaps even Mishakal as well.

Soth looked up to offer thanks, and noticed that the sun was finally shining brightly for the first time that day.

* * * * *

As the day wore on, the clouds continued to dissipate, leaving the hot summer sun of Fierswelt to blaze down upon the festivities, making it warmer than was welcome. But, considering the questionable weather conditions that had started the day, no one was complaining, especially the women, whose new gowns and dresses would have been all but ruined by any sudden downpour.

That the Vingaard River valley enjoyed some of the most advantageous weather on the continent of Ansalon was never more evident than on this day. After a three month winter in which the fields had lain fallow, there had come the two short months of spring used for planting. Indeed much of the planting this season had been done in specific preparation for today's wedding feast. And now the people of Knightlund were finally able to reap and enjoy the fruits of their labor.

Strewn across the long tables set out in rows were barrels and bowls full of fresh fruits and vegetables, including four different kinds of apples, three different kinds of squash, two kinds of tomatoes and as many different other "greens" as had ever been grown in the fertile valley to the north and west of Dargaard Keep.

There were even other delicacies from such places as Istar, Silvanesti and Ergoth, all of which had been brought by guests or sent as gifts to the bride and groom by friends who were unable to attend.

At one end of the food tables, several fires were being stoked as many different types of game were being roasted, a process that filled the air with an enticing aroma which promised that today's meal would be the best many had ever tasted.

At the other end of the food tables were barrels of ale, casks of wine and pitchers of sweetwater, all properly chilled with ice and snow brought down from the white-capped peaks of the Dargaard Mountains especially for the occasion.

And above the tables filled with food and the others lined with guests, Lord Soth and his Lady Korinne sat at the high table set upon a slight rise in the ground, a setup which gave the couple a place of honor and allowed their guests to offer congratulations while the festivities were underway.

"Lord Soth," said Colm Farold, a young Knight of the Sword who had stepped up to the high table to make his offering of a wedding gift. "While I have not brought a gift I can hold in my hand, I nevertheless offer you something more valuable than any gift of material wealth." Farold paused. "I offer you my undying loyalty as a Knight of the Sword." He dropped down on one knee before Soth's table and bowed his head deeply.

For a moment Soth was made speechless by the gesture. He knew he had the loyalty of many of the knights in attendance such as Caradoc, and Wersten Kern, and could count on several others when their services were required, but to have a knight as distinguished as Farold publicly declare his loyalty was a rare thing indeed.

Soth got up from the high table. "Thank you Knight Farold. I'm deeply touched by your pledge—one that I assure you is priceless in value. My only hope is that I can prove myself worthy of your loyalty." A pause. "Arise, and welcome to Dargaard Keep."

A cheer erupted from the guests as Farold rose to his feet. After a nod to Soth and Lady Korinne he returned to his seat, receiving applause and congratulations every step of the way.

The presentation of wedding gifts carried on for quite some time, and after a while it became apparent that many of the wedding guests were of a similar mind. No less than five cradles were set up in front of the high table, ranging in style from simple wooden bassinets made by Knightlund farmers to gilded wood and metal cradles fixed upon wheels to allow them to be easily moved from one part of the keep to another.

But despite the number of duplicates, Soth and Korinne had accepted each gift with the same courteous and gracious "thank you," and even laughed heartily (if not politely) each and every time the inevitable jokes were made about the number of children the couple would be expected to have considering the number of cradles they now had to fill.

But at last the presentation of gifts came to an end.

Guests finished their meals and suddenly became eager to walk the grounds surrounding the keep, or else loosen the waistbands of their britches so that they might more easily partake in the rest of the day's planned activities.

But before the feast could be officially concluded, Lord Reynard Gladria and his wife Leyla had to make the presentation of Lady Korinne's dowry. Rumors had been circulating for weeks about the size and contents of the dowry, but specific details had yet to be divulged.

At last, all would know.

Leyla Gladria stepped up before the table, holding her

aged husband by the left arm, while Eiwon van Sickle, a Knight of the Sword from Palanthas who had escorted the Gladrias to Dargaard Keep, held firmly onto the man's left.

When they were in place, a chair was brought for Reynard Gladria while Lady Gladria made the presentation standing up.

"Dearest daughter," she said, then turning to Lord Soth. "And my new *son* . . ."

Soth wasn't sure the woman was saying the word affectionately or sarcastically, but he nevertheless nodded graciously.

"My husband and I have awaited this day for many, many years. And I know I speak for my husband when I say that we couldn't have wished for a more suitable man for our precious daughter than the heralded Lord Loren Soth, Knight of the Rose."

Lady Gladria reached over and took Soth's hand in hers, squeezing it tight.

"And with our daughter married, we find that we are no longer in need of much of our holdings. Therefore, it is with great pleasure that we present to you the deeds to the lands surrounding Maelgoth as well as those spanning the northern edge of the Plains of Solamnia. This will extend Knightlund's western border across the Vingaard River, bridging much of the gap between Palanthas and Knightlund, and making the distance between our homeland and the new home of our daughter a much shorter one to traverse."

For the second time in a very short while, Soth was at a loss for words. So too was Lady Korinne, for all she was able to offer in response to her parent's gift were tears of joy.

At last Soth got up from the high table and walked down the slight slope to thank his new in-laws for their extremely generous gift.

He approached Reynard Gladria first, kneeling by the seated man and bowing his head deeply. "Thank you *milord*," he said, using the word somewhat improperly in order to show the extent of his gratitude.

The elderly man smiled, exposing a gap-toothed row of teeth. He placed a frail and bony hand on Soth's shoulder and said, "Quite all right, my boy." His voice wheezed out the words like a steelsmith's bellows clogged with coal dust. "There's no one I'd rather see have it than a Knight of the Rose."

Soth nodded again, then stood up. He waited for Lady Korinne to finish thanking her mother, then he moved over and knelt before the woman. "Thank you, *milady*."

The elder Gladria remained stern faced. "Treating my daughter well will be thanks enough, young man."

Soth looked at her, realized that she was now his mother-in-law, and simply said, "Yes, milady."

Leyla Gladria nodded her approval.

* * * * *

A breeze blew down off the Dargaard Mountains, cooling the early evening air and making it more comfortable for the assembled knights to continue their games and amusements.

At the foot of the mountains, on the south side of the keep, several knights were busy testing their skills against one another by fighting mock battles commonly referred to as "friendlies."

"Knights prepare!" cried Oren Brightblade, the honorary referee for the evening's contests.

The two opponents stood up and entered the large circle drawn upon the ground. Wearing a red sash on his right arm was Meyer Seril, a Knight of the Crown. Wearing the blue sash was Caradoc, also a Knight of the Crown.

Although the winner and loser of each friendly neither gained nor lost any standing in the order, the Knights of Solamnia were a proud group and none took losing such contests lightly. As a result, many of the friendlies between knights were as fiercely contested as many of the battles they fought against their usual foes such as the ogres or minotaurs.

"May the best knight win," said Seril, smiling at his opponent.

Caradoc nodded and smiled politely. "May the winner be the best knight."

The combatants touched swords and stepped back so that their footmen could give the lightweight ringmail and leather armor covering the upper parts of their bodies a final check.

A moment later, the two men stood at the ready.

"Hup!" cried Oren Brightblade.

Suddenly the air rang with the clink and clang of steel against steel as each of the knight's thin, lightweight practice swords slashed through the air in search of a weakness in their opponent's defenses.

Whether Caradoc was tired from the long day of ceremony and festivities, or Meyer Seril was a more nimble fighter, was unclear. What was clear however, was that Seril was by far the better swordsman. He was able to block most of Caradoc's attempted blows and easily knocked Caradoc off-balance by slapping him gently on his arms and legs with the flat side of his broadsword, which was the primary object of the whole contest.

As the two knights continued to battle, other knights, those slightly older and perhaps more battle-weary, looked on, cheering on the combatants between gulps of frosty ale.

The time limit on the bout was close to running out and it was obvious to everyone present that Knight Seril would be declared the winner as he had easily outscored Caradoc by a margin of four-to-one.

But suddenly Caradoc faltered, as if he had been hurt by Seril's most recent blow to his armorless thigh.

"Caradoc, are you all right?" asked Seril, dropping his guard for a moment and leaving the right side of his body open to attack.

Caradoc rose up, swung his sword in a short and powerful arc and caught Seril on the shoulder with the sharp leading edge of his blade. The ringmail connecting the patches of leather armor covering Seril's arm broke away allowing Caradoc's sword to cut a long, gash across Seril's upper arm.

"Stop the friendly!" called Oren Brightblade. "Put down your swords!"

Seril grabbed his bleeding arm and fell to one knee. "If I didn't know you better, Knight Caradoc," he said. "I would have thought you did that on purpose."

"Who's to say he didn't?" called Arnol Kraas, Seril's squire and a recent supplicant to the Order of the Crown. Although it was not his place to pose such a question, none of the assembled knights objected to it. Perhaps many of them had been thinking the very same thing.

"On my honor as a Knight of Solamnia, I would never consciously hurt one of my fellows."

"You feigned being hurt—" continued Kraas.

"Enough! Enough!" interjected Brightblade. "Caradoc says the blow was accidental, and since he is bound to the Oath and the Measure, we must take him at his word."

Kraas said no more, but was obviously dissatisfied.

The other knights also said nothing, but were seemingly more content to abide by Brightblade's decision.

"Now, bring this man to see Istvan, the healer," said Brightblade. "It's only a flesh wound, but I've seen many a man die from less."

Two knights quickly dropped to the ground, took hold of Knight Seril and gently lifted him up, carrying him gingerly back to the keep.

After Seril was gone, and the footman had begun preparing the two knights competing in the evening's final friendly, Caradoc approached Brightblade and asked, "Do you declare a winner?"

Brightblade looked at Caradoc strangely. "A knight has been injured. Does it really matter who won?"

"According to the writings of Vinas Solamnus, as every battle must have a winner, so too must every friendly."

This was true, but the knights had long ago learned that open interpretation of the writings of Vinas Solamnus was far more practical than any literal adherence to their words. They were guidelines rather than laws carved in stone. For true honor lies in the heart of each knight, not in a set of old and dusty tomes. However, if the laws were cited verbatim in situations such as this, their authority could not be questioned.

"Very well," said Brightblade, no doubt as familiar with the thirty-seven volumes as Caradoc was. He cleared his throat and announced the winner. "Since Meyer Seril was unable to complete the friendly, Caradoc is declared winner by forfeit."

Caradoc raised his sword to acknowledge his victory.

Few cheered.

In fact, following Seril's wounding, many of the knights had gone inside the keep to partake of some of the evening's more sedate celebrations or to the north end where another group of knights had gathered beneath the cool shade of a vallenwood tree. On the side of the broad trunk that faced west, a large circular patch of wood had been cut flat with an axe and its pale-colored surface had been painted with three dark red rings, each larger than the one inside it.

"Who's next?" barked Olthar Uth Wistan, High Warrior presiding over the contest.

"I believe I shall give it a try," said High Justice Lord Adam Caladen. "It's been years since I've thrown a sword, but perhaps I'll get lucky, eh?"

"Hear that, men?" said Lord Wistan jovially. "Stand back, give him lots of room, and remember to keep your eyes on the sword."

A good-natured laugh coursed through the assembled knights, footmen and onlookers as Lord Caladen selected a sword from those standing upright in the rack to his left.

After finding one with a length and weight to his liking, he hefted it in his hand and practiced the movement that would soon send it hurtling through the air toward its target.

Like friendlies, swordthrowing was an amiable sort of sporting event contested by the Knights of Solamnia whenever they were gathered in sufficient numbers and had the free time to spend in good-natured competition. But unlike the friendly, which pitted knight against knight, swordthrowing tested individual knights against the strength, skill and marksmanship of the legendary Huma Dragonbane, Hero of the Lance and the greatest knight the Knights of Solamnia had ever known.

The origin of the contest came from a little known story about the fabled knight's battle with a particularly ferocious red dragon. According to the tale, Huma's initial attack against the dragon had knocked his dragonlance from its mount and completely out of his hands. Despite being weaponless, he brought his beloved silver dragon around for another pass. But before the dragons came into range of each other's breath weapons, Huma drew his broadsword and flung it through the air in the direction of the red. Although not designed to be used as a throwing weapon, the sword flew true, slicing the air like an arrow and piercing the vulnerable soft spot of the red dragon's underbelly. The wound so startled the red that it was sent into a long downward spiral from which it never recovered.

And today, the Knights of Solamnia celebrated the near-miraculous feat by throwing swords, not at a dragon, but at the symbolic red rings painted into the trunk of a sturdy vallenwood tree.

Satisfied with his weapon, Lord Caladen walked off the twenty paces from the tree then turned back around to face it. "Ready!" he said, lifting the sword to his shoulder.

The assembled knights and others in the crowd fell silent.

Lord Caladen took three steps forward and let go of the sword. Its flight was straight and unwavering, but it was slightly off the mark, clipping the right edge of the tree trunk and sending a sliver of bark spinning through the air before landing heavily on the grass behind the tree.

Even though he'd missed, the throw had been a respectable one for such a senior knight.

"Well done, Caladen!"

"A good effort."

The knights applauded, forcing Lord Caladen to accept their cheers with a broad smile and prideful wave, gestures that would have been more than enough acknowledgement even if he had hit the target dead center. "You're too kind," he said. "A lucky throw, no more."

Just then, Lord Soth came upon the pitch. He'd been circling the keep, greeting his guests one last time before retiring for the night—his wedding night.

Seeing Soth approach, Lord Wistan put his hands to his mouth and shouted, "Perhaps the bridegroom would care to test his mettle?"

The knights turned around and, seeing Soth, beckoned him to try a throw.

"Yes, give a try."

"Come on, Soth!"

Soth hesitated, then said, "All right, perhaps just a single throw."

The words were followed by a rousing cheer.

A footman quickly helped Soth with his cloak, then stood back as the knight selected a sword. To no one's surprise he lifted one of the heavier weapons into the air. Then, after finding its center of balance, he hefted it in his hand to check its weight.

"Make room!" cried Lord Wistan.

The knights surrounding Lord Soth fanned out, clearing a path toward the tree. Soth then walked over to the tree, marched off twenty paces, and turned on his heel.

"Ready," he said.

Lord Wistan nodded.

The crowd of knights and numerous other onlookers

that had suddenly gathered around the tree were never more silent.

Soth took three long strides, then threw the sword.

The blade whistled as it sliced through the air . . .

And an instant later it struck the tree with a hard *thwok!*

Soth looked up, and saw that the sword had hit the exact middle of the center ring, its haft wavering like the stiffened tail of a hungry cat.

For a moment, all were silent as they looked with awe upon the sword as it jutted out from the tree like a new branch.

"Huma could have done no better!" someone shouted.

"A sword never flew more true!" yelled another.

The cheers continued to ring out until they combined together in a single loud wash of exultant voices.

Soth acknowledged the cheers with a slight nod of his head, then raised his hands to restore quiet once more. "If you'll excuse me, I hate to keep a lady waiting, especially when that lady is my wife."

The words were followed by good-natured and knowing laughter.

Soth turned and headed for the keep.

At the vallenwood tree, several footmen tried to pull the sword from the trunk, but with half the length of the blade embedded in the wood, it would not budge.

Finally, three of them combined their efforts and the heavy broadsword slowly came free.

* * * * *

Soth came around to the entrance of the keep.

Standing on the drawbridge was Lady Korinne talking to a young knight draped in a blue cloak. They stood close together, barely inches apart—a distance which could be considered almost intimate.

Soth moved into the shadows cast by a large oak, and watched.

They talked for a minute, maybe longer, then kissed.

Moments later they parted, Korinne entering the keep, the young knight mounting his horse and riding away.

Soth waited until the knight was gone, then followed Korinne.

Once inside, he paused to stand at the open window of the master bedchamber overlooking the grounds outside the entrance to the keep. The fires that had been lit as the sun began its descent were themselves dying out, spotting the land with points of flickering orange-yellow light.

It had been a long day, thought Soth. A good day. The happiest, the proudest, the best yet in his relatively short life. And now the best day's night, his wedding night, was about to begin. Would it prove to be as special as the day had been?

He hoped so.

But before he could enjoy his special night, he had to deal with something that was troubling him.

Just then, the door to the chamber's dressing room opened. Soth turned in time to see Lady Korinne step into the room.

Even in the dim light of the candles set about the room, the woman's beauty was obvious and enchanting. She was dressed in a white nightgown made of a thin, almost sheer, material which clung to her every curve and left little to Soth's imagination.

Soth felt desire for his new bride, a desire he'd been suppressing throughout the day, suddenly erupt within him like sparked tinder. But despite his wish to rush across the room, he stood stock-still, watching patiently.

She moved to the middle of the bedchamber, stopped and looked up at him. "Does what you see please you?"

Soth knew it wasn't the time for such questions, but he couldn't help himself—he had to know.

"Who was that knight you were speaking to on the drawbridge?"

"A knight?" asked Korinne. "I'm afraid I don't recall."

"A young man dressed in a blue cloak. You kissed him."

"Oh, you mean Trebor Reywas. He's a friend of the family, a Crown knight from Palanthas. He was departing early and came looking for me in order to say goodbye."

"A friend of the family?" asked Soth.

"Why, Loren Soth," said Lady Korinne, her hands placed firmly on her hips. "If I didn't know any better, I'd say that you're jealous."

Soth sighed. Perhaps he *was* jealous, but even if he was it was a weakness he'd never admit to. He answered Korinne by shaking his head. "No, not jealous. Only envious of the kiss you gave him."

She smiled at him. "That's so sweet," she said, moving to the foot of the bed. There, she reached up for the string about her neck which held the gown in place. She untied the knot, moved the gown over her shoulders and let it fall to the floor. "I'm sorry you've had to wait. But, am I not worth waiting for?" she asked.

Soth merely nodded.

"Then, please," she said, "love me!"

Soth went to her, took her in his arms . . .

And loved her.

Chapter 3

"What constitutes an evil deed?" the Kingpriest said, standing in front a large group of his followers in the largest assembly hall within the Temple of the Kingpriest in Istar. The group was made up of mages, priests, acolytes and other loyal supporters of the cause, which was the purging of Evil from the face of Krynn.

Several hands shot up in response to the question.

The Kingpriest nodded in the direction of a young man dressed in slightly faded green and brown robes. Judging by his clothing, he was one of the Kingpriest's lesser priests, but nevertheless a devout follower and crusader for the worldwide promotion of Good over Evil.

"An act which is morally wrong, or bad," said the young priest.

The Kingpriest paced in front of his followers, his hands clasped together before him as if in prayer, or perhaps just deep in thought.

"Yes, yes, that is part of it. But what else? What constitutes an evil deed?"

Again, hands rose up before him.

He pointed to a woman dressed in pale yellow and white robes which had the insignia of the Kingpriest sewn over the left breast. She was a mage, a renegade mage who used her considerable power to help strengthen the Kingpriest's domination of Istar and to promote the Kingpriest's edicts and ideology across the entire continent of Ansalon.

"Anything causing injury or harm. A harmful effect or consequence," she said with strength of conviction.

"It is that too," said the Kingpriest. "But what is the basis for evil deeds, the thing that lurks behind them, pushing them forward, turning them into deeds?"

This time the Kingpriest indicated an older yellow-and-white-robed mage sitting toward the back of the assembly.

"Depravity, viciousness, corruption, wickedness . . ."

The Kingpriest began nodding his head with delight, "Yes, yes, yes . . ." Obviously, he was finally hearing just what he wanted to hear. "Evil deeds have all of those things at their core." He paused a moment to reflect. "But what must occur before an evil deed is enacted?"

The followers were unsure about the wording of the question and looked at each other in confusion.

"Before there can be an evil deed," said the Kingpriest, "there must be . . ." He paused to allow his followers the chance to complete the sentence.

He pointed at various people in the group.

"Evil purpose?"

The Kingpriest shook his head. "Not exactly."

"An evil concept?"

"Yes, but more precisely . . ."

"Evil intent?"

"Yes, but . . ."

"Evil thoughts?"

The Kingpriest stopped in his tracks, silent. "Yes," he said at last, seemingly relieved. "Evil thoughts. Before an evil act can even be committed, it must be preceded by an evil thought."

The followers continued to listen intently, realizing that the Kingpriest was getting closer to the reason he'd brought them all together.

"The Proclamation of Manifest Virtue was a great step toward the total defeat of Evil because it declared absolutely that Evil in the world was an utter affront to both gods and mortals alike. But the creation of the List of Evil Acts, acts for which the perpetrators faced execution, or death in the gladiatorial arena, was only a beginning. In the years since, the Istarian clergy has grown even stronger. Istar has become not only the center of religion, but also a leading center for art, culture and commerce. Today, the clergy oversees almost every aspect of daily Istarian life." The Kingpriest paused a moment, obviously satisfied by how powerful the priesthood had become under his rule.

"And then came the Siege on Sorcery, in which the people of Krynn laid siege to the Towers of High Sorcery, which effectively banished the evil magic wielders from Istar and allowed the benevolent powers of Good to flourish in a region of Krynn that was free of the stiflingly wicked forces of Evil."

The Kingpriest paced back and forth in front of his followers, knowing that his next words would be absolutely crucial.

"But despite Istar's spectacular rise to power, both at home and across the face of Krynn, and despite the banishment of Evil and the continuous fight for the cause of Good that is waged by the people of Istar and the good Knights of Solamnia, Evil still exists. Anywhere you look you can find it rearing its hideous head."

The Kingpriest's followers nodded in agreement.

"The time has come for new and drastic measures which will help us in the noble fight against Evil. That is why I propose to enact the following Edict of Thought Control."

A low buzz of voices circulated the room.

"Evil thoughts equal evil deeds," said the Kingpriest. "Anger is a capital offense equal to murder; lust is a capital offense equal to adultery."

The Kingpriest paused to allow the concept to sink in.

"Under this new Edict of Thought Control, you, my good friends and followers will be empowered to identify evil thoughts and prevent them from becoming evil deeds, thereby ensuring that Good will once again reign supreme in a land where virtuous, righteous and, above all, moral people wish to live without fear of the forces of Evil and its denizens.

There was silence in the room for a long time.

Finally, a single hand rose up from the crowd. It was a hand belonging to the elderly mage. "But how will we be able to detect evil thoughts, let alone control them?"

The Kingpriest smiled. "Ah, a very good question, but one that is simply answered. You forget that we stand for the cause of Good and with it on our side, anything is possible."

"Are you saying we shall use magic and spells to carry out this edict, to read the minds of the citizens of Istar?"

"Some would call it magic. Some others would call it spell-casting," answered the Kingpriest. "But those terms are used by wizards and sorcerers. You, loyal clerics and faithful followers, will be able to look into the minds of the people of Istar and read their thoughts through the power of a divine invocation. As a result, you will be able to go about your task safe and secure in the knowledge that you have been empowered to do so by the highest possible authority."

The followers looked uneasy, most likely unsure what had been meant by the "highest possible authority" given that the Kingpriest himself was the head of the clergy.

"Such magnificent power can not be handed down by those who simply perform magic. Such strength of conviction does not come from those who merely practice the incantation of spells."

A pause.

"It comes from, and is, quite simply, the will of the gods."

Chapter 4

"It was my tree and he had no right to cut it down!" said Vin Dowell, a tall wiry farmer from Tyrell, a small village to the west of Dargaard Keep located on the eastern bank of the Vingaard River.

"I didn't cut it down, I only trimmed the branches that were hanging over my land," said Thom Tregaard, a short squat man with a barrel-shaped belly, long white hair and a matching tapered, gray-white beard.

As the two men blathered on, Soth rolled his eyes and shifted nervously in his high-backed throne chair, searching for that always elusive comfortable position in which to sit. It was the morning of Palast, the one day each week he set aside for the settling of land claims and similar disputes among the people of Knightlund. Sometimes the disputes were of interest to Soth, such as the ones involving some type of crime, the honor of a woman, or a chivalric sort of challenge between two parties.

But this, this was a squabble between two clucking hens.

"Which you had absolutely no right to do," said Dowell.

"A man's tree is a man's tree. The next thing you'll be doing is cutting down my fence because you don't like the shadow it casts upon your land."

"I'd never damage a fence. And certainly not one that serves well as a border between myself and the likes of you!"

Soth leaned forward and held his head in his hands.

"Not to worry, you wouldn't catch me on that weed-infested patch of soil you dare to call a farm." Dowell crossed his arms and turned up his nose in disgust.

"Oh, so my side of the fence is good enough for your tree, but not good enough for you, eh?" Tregaard's face was turning a deep shade of red and his breath was growing deeper and more rapid.

The two men moved closer, rolling up their sleeves in preparation for a fight.

Soth had seen and heard just about as much as he could stand. Although he was mildly interested in seeing which of the two men would emerge the victor of a fistfight—Dowell having the longer reach, Tregaard possessing a decided weight advantage—he couldn't, in good conscience, allow matters to get out of hand.

"Enough!" he cried, his booming voice shocking the two farmers into silence. When he had their attention, Soth sat up straight in his chair and looked the taller of the two farmers straight in the eye. "Now, Vin Dowell, were some of your tree's branches hanging over onto Tregaard's land?"

The farmer maintained eye contact with Soth for several seconds, then looked away. "Yes, milord." The words were whispered, a mere shadow of the voice he'd used seconds before on his fellow farmer.

"And you, Thom Tregaard, cut down the tree or just the branches?"

Tregaard was quick to answer. "Just the branches, milord."

"And what of the fruit on those branches?"

"They're in his cold storage room—" barked Dowell.

Soth held up his hand to silence the man.

"Well?" Soth prodded Tregaard.

"As he said, they are in my cold storage."

"I see," said Soth, pausing a moment to consider the situation. The trick to finding a solution acceptable to both parties was to give them the illusion that each of them was coming away the winner. But, how to do that?

"Since the branches were overhanging on Tregaard's land, he was well within his rights to cut the offending branches from the tree."

Tregaard's face was suddenly brightened by a big self-satisfied grin.

"However," continued Soth. "Because the tree was Dowell's, the branches should be returned to him lest he should want to use them as firewood, and the fruit that was borne by those branches are *his* property and should be in *his* cold storage room by the end of the week. By Bakukal to be precise."

It was Dowell's turn to beam.

"Now, shake hands like gentlemen, and return to Tyrell as good neighbors."

"Yes milord," said Dowell.

"Thank you, milord," said Tregaard.

Both men sounded grateful, but nevertheless defeated.

"Very well, then," said Soth. "This matter is closed."

As spectators and other interested parties began to file out of the throne room, Soth breathed a sigh of relief. His role as Knightlund's chief justice was done for yet another week and the next dreaded Palast morning court was a blessed seven full days away.

Soth had thought he would have enjoyed some of the more mundane aspects of ruling Knightlund, but just two short months after his wedding and ascension to the Order of the Rose, he had come to realize that that simply was not the case. He yearned to draw his sword in battle, to feel its honed edge cutting into the flesh and cracking the bones of his enemies. It was what he had been trained to do. But, here he was a Knight of Solamnia, a Knight of the Rose, performing the duties of a common clerk.

For a brief moment he admired his father's ability to oversee Knightlund so capably, and so happily, for so many years.

He rose from his throne, wondering what unremarkable task would require his attention that afternoon when suddenly—

"Milord, milord!" The voice was that of the squire stationed as a lookout on the top level of the keep.

Soth remained standing, waiting almost impatiently for the squire to appear. At last he ran into the room, out of breath and obviously excited.

"A rider," he said, taking a breath. "A lone rider approaches from the south, at full gallop."

Soth felt the hair on his arms bristle with anticipation. Clearly the rider was on a mission of great urgency.

"Is he flying any colors?"

"Red."

"Prepare to lower the bridge!" he bellowed, his words echoing throughout the keep. Soth followed the squire out of the room and made his way outside, where the rider was bringing his horse to a stop in the center of the entrance area just inside the keep's gatehouse. A small crowd of knights, squires and others had gathered about, all curious to learn what was afoot. The rider had entered slowly, his horse appearing to be on the brink of exhaustion. Even now that his ride had come to an end, the rider seemed no better off and looked rather ragged and sore after what was obviously a long, hard ride. He was helped from his mount slowly, his movements suggesting each movement of his arms or legs was painful to make.

When he finally had both feet on the ground, footmen took hold of his shoulders and helped him over to where Lord Soth waited.

After letting himself down onto one knee, the rider looked up at the lord of the keep and grimaced to fight off a fresh stab of pain. "Ogres," he managed to say, still slightly out of breath.

Soth stepped closer to the rider, noticing for the first time that there were bruises on one side of his face and down along his neck to the shoulder, wounds likely made by an ogre's vine bola or cluster ball. "Where?"

The rider had managed to catch some of his breath and was now composed enough to manage something resembling coherent speech. "I've come from the village of Halton. The ogres have moved north upon us from Throtyl, commandeering our stores and laying siege to the village. Several villagers have been killed, some others have been wounded. I only managed to get away by acting as if my wounds were fatal, then stealing a horse at nightfall."

Soth nodded. Halton was a small but vital agricultural center south of Dargaard Keep on the western foot of the Dargaard Mountains. It served as the initial trade center for much of the annual fall harvests in the region and was often called "Harvest Home" by people all across the plains and throughout southern Solamnia.

Throtyl, on the other hand, was a pocket of lawlessness in the southern tip of the Dargaard Mountains. It was situated in a small forest which opened upon a broad marshy plain called Throt. To the east of the plain lay a passageway through the Dargaard Mountains called the Throtyl Gap. The gap was a place infested with marauding bands of outlaws, barbarians and ogres who made their living smuggling goods through the gap, charging heavy tolls for safe passage, or simply by preying upon unsuspecting travelers. For years Soth had been satisfied to look the other way because the ogres were relatively few in numbers and generally kept to themselves, and because most travelers of Ansalon knew to keep well clear of the gap. Finally, he tolerated them because they were so well entrenched in the forest that any expedition he might mount would likely cost the lives of too many knights and gain far too little in return to make it worth the effort.

This however, was another matter entirely. People of Knightlund had been killed and wounded. His people. And still, many others remained in danger and would be without food through the winter if nothing were done to vanquish the ogres.

"You've done well," Soth told the rider. "Get some food in you, and a change of clean clothing. Then we'll meet in the Knights' Chambers to discuss our battle plans."

He turned to address the rest of those present, perhaps even the entire keep. "Begin preparations," he barked, sending squires and footmen scurrying. "We shall be leaving as soon as possible."

Soth placed a hand on the hilt of his sword. It felt good in his hand, and it would feel even better being swung against an opponent in battle.

Whenever they might be leaving the keep, it wouldn't be soon enough.

* * * * *

Soth found Lady Korinne alone in their bedchamber. She was sitting by the window reading one of the thirty-seven volumes written by Vinas Solamnus which outlined the Measure of the Knights of Solamnia. She had begun reading the volumes that were housed in the keep's library shortly after their wedding and had dedicated most of her waking hours to reading every word in every volume so that she might better understand the laws of conduct to which her husband was bound.

Curious about his wife's progress, Soth checked the number of the volume—twenty-six. Soon she would be as familiar with the Measure as any knight, perhaps even more so. It was a generous gesture, one which endeared his wife to Soth—if it were in fact possible for him to love her any more than he already did.

"There is trouble to the south," said Soth, kneeling by

his wife's side and placing his hands in hers.

"I've heard as much."

"It pains me to leave you here, but the people of Halton need me. Several have died, and more will certainly perish if we don't make haste."

Lady Korinne smiled lovingly and shook her head. "Dear Loren, how sweet that you feel you must tell me lies to protect my feelings."

Soth was somewhat taken aback by his wife's assertion. "I am certainly not telling you lies."

"Oh yes you are," she said, her voice still soft and loving. "You said you can't bear to leave the keep, but I know there's nothing your heart yearns for more than to be traveling Solamnia with your knights at your side, battling Evil."

Soth returned her smile. "You know me too well, then."

"Oh, I doubt that," she said. "I just know that for you, or any Knight of Solamnia, there is no choice between the drudgery of keep life and an all-out battle against Evil."

Soth smiled. "In that you are correct," he said, realizing his wife clearly understood what was needed most from the wife of a Knight of Solamnia—understanding.

She placed a hand on his shoulder. "But please, promise me one thing."

"Of course, anything."

"When you leave the keep, think not of me, but solely of the task ahead of you. I don't want your battle instincts dulled by any sentimental thoughts of me."

"You are as unselfish as you are beautiful, my love."

"Perhaps, but I can think of no other way to ensure that you will return to me quickly and unharmed."

Soth nodded. "As you wish." He leaned forward, took her in his arms and kissed her deeply.

* * * * *

"It was hard to know exactly how many ogres there were in total since they were so spread out over the entire village," said the rider from Halton as he sketched a rough map of his home village on a sheet of pale leather laid over a table in the knights' chambers.

"If you had to guess?" asked Caradoc, standing to the left of the rider.

The rider was silent, deep in thought. "I really can't say." The rider shook his head, apparently frustrated. "We're a village of peaceful farmers. We've relied so much on the protection of the Knights of Solamnia that few of us even have weapons with which to defend ourselves."

"A guess?" Caradoc prodded, a little forcefully.

The rider shook his head. "Perhaps there were no more than ten or fifteen of them."

A ripple of nervous laughter coursed through the knights who stood around the table. That many ogres wouldn't be too hard to handle, especially for such a seasoned warrior as Lord Soth and his company of thirteen loyal knights. No, the problem with liberating the village wasn't so much with the ogres who had besieged it, as with the villagers and trying to keep them out of harm's way during the battle to free them.

"Do you know where most of the ogres are located within the village?" asked Soth, standing to the rider's right and carefully looking over the sketch of the village.

"I can't be sure," said the rider. "But perhaps I could sneak back into the village when we get there and find out."

"Yes, that would help. The more we know about the village and the ogres the better it will be for us," said Soth. "But, we can do nothing until we arrive in Halton." He began rolling up the length of leather. "We leave within the hour."

* * * * *

Soth adjusted his breastplate so that it rested comfortably across his chest. The breastplate, bearing the symbol of the rose, was still unmarred by battle. It gleamed brightly against the light shining through the open entrance to the keep and did justice to the pride Soth felt in wearing it. When the plate was set into position, he checked the armor plates over his shoulders, and on his thighs and shins, making sure they were all properly placed and secured.

Like most of the knights on this expedition, Soth had opted for medium-weight armor with steel plates covering the vital areas like the head and chest, while the extremities were left to the protection of chain mail. The combination of the two types of armor would allow him more freedom of movement, which was vitally important when fighting the much stronger, but slower-moving ogres.

Satisfied with his armor, Soth held out his hand for his sword. The two footmen who had been busy sharpening its blade carried it toward him wrapped in a heavy cloth. They presented it to him hilt first. Although the sword was designed for two-handed use, Soth was a big man, easily strong enough to wield the weapon with only his right hand.

The footmen remained where they stood, waiting for Soth's appraisal of the weapon and his verdict on its suitability.

Soth cut a swath through the air with the sword to check its balance, then raised it up to take a closer look at the cutting edges of the blade. That the footmen had spent all of their time since the arrival of the rider honing the weapon was obvious. Both its edges were as sharp as knives and the tip of its point was needle-thin. He looked at the footmen and nodded appreciatively.

The two footmen smiled at each other proudly, then the taller one said, "Slay one of them foul beasts for us, milord."

"Consider it done," said Soth, placing the sword neatly into its heavy leather sheath.

Next, he took hold of his helm. It was made of bare silver-gray metal with only certain parts of it adorned with decorative roses. The visor was up and the horse's tail that sprouted out from the top center of the helm was as long and black as Soth's own flowing mane. Like the rest of his armor, the helm was of medium weight. Some of the knights had opted for their heaviest helms, but Soth had decided that not even the strongest helm could protect him against a direct blow from an ogre's club or long sword. To Soth, it was far better to die bravely in battle than to be seriously injured and unable to continue his life as a knight.

He balanced the helm between his hands and prepared to place it over his head when he heard a voice calling him.

"Milord! Milord!" It was a woman's voice. He turned around and saw Lady Korinne approaching. While she usually called him Loren, they had decided on using the more formal address in the presence of others.

"Milady," said Soth, nodding his head graciously.

"I wanted to give you one last kiss before you go."

Soth bent forward and the two kissed deeply.

"And to tell you this . . ."

Soth's eyebrows arched expectantly.

"Fight for the cause of Good, and when you're done, hurry home. Hopefully upon your return I will be able to reward you with the news that I am with child."

Soth's mouth fell open and remained that way for a moment. While he was glad to hear the words, he was somewhat confused by them. A short time ago she'd played the part of a knight's wife to perfection, instructing him not to think of her while on the journey. But now she was speaking more like a young bride, teasing him with words of a child in order to ensure that his thoughts were never far from home—no matter where he might be.

A child, he thought, perhaps even a son. Soth's heart raced at the possibility. "That would make my return to Dargaard Keep a truly triumphant one," he said.

He moved to kiss her again, but she stepped away from him and shook her head, once again playing the role of the steadfast lady of the keep. "Go," she said. "Your people need you."

Soth looked at his wife a moment, his heart full of love and pride, then gently slipped his helm over his head. He turned and mounted his horse, a huge animal, char-black from head to hoof, which despite Soth's size and weight, did not seem to be burdened by its new load.

He took one final look around, saw that his knights were ready, and drew his sword. Then he raised it over his head and shouted, "Est Sularus oth Mithas."

A cheer rose up.

Soth's mount surged forward.

And the knights followed him out of the keep.

Chapter 5

After the exhilarating charge out of the keep, the thirteen Solamnic Knights loyal to Lord Soth settled down to a somewhat more relaxed pace which would allow them to travel the maximum amount of distance in what was left of the day.

After night had fallen, they continued on in the darkness for several hours and would have ridden through the night had Soth asked it of them. But of course, he would never think to do such a thing. For although it was imperative they get to Halton as quickly as possible, Soth refused to compromise his knights' fighting ability by bringing them to the point of exhaustion before they'd even arrived at the battle. When they passed the halfway point between Dargaard Keep and Halton, the decision to stop for the night was made easy for Soth when the passage through that part of the mountains proved too treacherous to complete under the cover of darkness.

He stopped the procession and the knights dutifully, if not gratefully, dismounted and stretched their limbs. Soon after, Caradoc had arranged a watch rotation and the knights set about eating what little provisions they had taken with them. In a day or so the squires would catch up to the group and there would be plenty of time to feast, but for now they had to travel as lightly and as quickly as possible.

A chill wind blew down from the mountains, but fires were obviously out of the question. And so, they ate cold food in the dark, and after they'd staved off their pangs of hunger, at least temporarily, the knights silently made themselves comfortable wherever they could.

Finally, they closed their eyes for a few hours' rest . . .

And dreamed of the battle ahead.

* * * * *

Soth looked up and saw the rocks tumbling down the mountainside. He ducked beneath an overhang and watched the stones and boulders roll past, then crash heavily into the soft valley floor below.

He waited another few seconds, listening to the flap of the dragon's wings as it flew over the mountain's peak and prepared for yet another pass.

"Father!"

It was a thin, weak voice, yet somehow familiar. Another moment passed and he realized it was the voice of his son.

He was still alive.

Soth ran out from under the overhang and quickly looked left and right.

"Father!" came the call again.

He ran to the left, over the loose rocks that had been dislodged by the dragon's pass. After cresting a slight rise, he saw his son standing in the middle of a clearing. He was looking around, his steps tentative and cautious.

He was a young and handsome man, with all the size and strength of his father. He was dressed in shining plate armor, dented and scratched in spots in evidence of the fierceness of battles past. He held his sword stiffly before him like a pathfinder, lighting his way in the dark.

Soth ran toward his son, but stopped when he noticed the boy's eyes. They were two large white spheres absolutely without color. The young man was blind, wandering aimlessly over the mountainside, in search of . . .

"Father, are you there?"

"Yes!" cried Soth, moving toward the boy.

But the dragon was back, plunging down toward them, so close now that Soth could feel the rush of hot wind against his body as it approached.

He drew his sword to face the beast. It was a red dragon, its head and snout crowned by great spiny horns and its body covered with large red diamond-shaped scales. Such a powerful and evil enemy, even Soth felt a shiver of fear run through him.

"Father, help me!"

The dragon swooped closely overhead, then rose up in a slow, wide arc in preparation for another pass.

Soth turned toward his son, but a rock rolled in front of him and he was forced to jump back . . .

Directly into the path of another, larger rock. The great stone slammed into him, knocking him down and pinning him to the ground. Desperately he tried to move, but both his legs had been crushed, and the rock—more like a boulder—was far too heavy to move.

"Father? Are you there?"

Soth tried to speak, but the words would not come to his parched throat.

The red dragon had circled back once more, this time coming in to land on the side of the mountain no more than fifty paces from the boy.

"Is that you?" The younger Soth turned his head toward the dragon, listening to the sounds of movement around him.

The dragon moved closer, a wide villainous smile forming on its hideous snout. It began to inhale, gathering its breath. Then, slowly it opened its mouth wide.

Soth felt the blood drain from his face. His heart fell into the pit of his stomach. He opened his mouth to scream, but could not make a sound.

The red dragon exhaled a cone of white-hot flames.

"Father, please . . ."

The boy's sword and shield began to melt in the wash of fire.

"Help me!"

And a moment later the young Soth was also aflame, his armor and body being incinerated by the intense heat of the dragon's fiery breath.

"No!" Soth cried, this time managing to say the word.

The dragon closed its mouth and turned to face him. Thin white tendrils of smoke wafted up from its nostrils and the corners of its mouth as it took several steps in his direction.

Soth began to thrash from side to side, pulling at his ruined legs, trying to get them free.

The dragon inhaled again, then opened its mouth and . . .

"Milord!" whispered Caradoc.

Soth's eyes fluttered open. "What?" he gasped. "What is it?"

"Are you all right? It sounded as if you might be in pain."

Soth fought to catch his breath. He looked around. It was still dark out. Slowly, he remembered where he was, and realized he'd been having a dream.

A bad dream.

A nightmare.

"No, I'm . . . I'm fine," he said. He looked down at his legs, and saw that his feet had become entangled in his cloak. He kicked the cloak away. "Is it my turn to keep watch?" he asked hopefully. Anything to keep him from returning to the nightmare of the dream.

"No, milord," said Caradoc. "It is time to go. Your turn to keep watch came and went some time ago. You were sleeping so soundly we decided it was best not to wake you."

Soth said nothing to this. He could reprimand his knights for not waking him, but he knew the fault lay within himself. After all, the squire's first rule was that knights who slept too deeply did not live very long. It wasn't like him to forget something like that, but he had. Perhaps it was best not to dwell on it. In fact, the less he reminded himself about his ghastly nightmare the better.

"Very well," he said at last. "But, don't let it happen again."

"Yes, milord."

Soth rose up off the ground, stiff and sore, his clothes cold and damp with sweat.

* * * * *

The knights were well on their way as the sun broke over the tops of the Dargaard Mountains. After a cold night and its legacy of stiff joints and sore bones, the sun's warmth was a more than welcome relief for the knights.

Soth took his customary position at the head of the group during the early hours, but as they neared Halton, he allowed the rider who'd come from the village to take the lead position given that he was more familiar with the surrounding terrain.

When the village at last came into sight, Soth moved the knights slightly up the mountain slopes in order to avoid detection as the ogres would no doubt have one or two guards watching the surrounding lands and especially the approach from Dargaard Keep.

As they made their way through a shallow gully, one of the knights let out a birdlike cry. Soth immediately halted the knights with an upraised fist. The procession stopped and went silent as Soth waited for the knight who'd called out the warning to offer a report.

The knight turned out to be Colm Farold, Knight of the Sword. "Voices, milord," he said. "Coming from over there." He pointed with a subtle gesture at a thick patch of fireweed growing close to the ground some yards off.

Soth nodded, and listened closely. Indeed there were faint sounds coming from somewhere to his left. He gestured to Farold with his head, then pointed to two other knights. The selected knights immediately dismounted.

"Nothing here, men," said Soth, moving forward through the gully, leaving the three knights behind. "I think it's best we be moving on."

Once they were through the gully, Soth doubled his men back around in a wide arc and minutes later they were once again traversing the gully.

Except this time, Farold and the other knights were there waiting for them, swords drawn and two prisoners in hand.

"Hender and Pike!" exclaimed the rider.

"You know these two?" asked Soth.

"Indeed, milord. One is my cousin, the other his neighbor."

Soth looked at the men flanked by the trio of knights and recognized them from their manner of dress as being simple farmers.

"We found them cowering in the bushes almost with their heads buried in the ground," Farold explained.

"We were afraid you might be more ogres," said the older of the two, the one the rider had identified as Hender. He was a man with thin gray hair, a long white beard, and the red neck and thickly calloused hands of one who tills the land.

If the man hadn't been so terrified, Soth might have considered his words an insult. And if their task wasn't so urgent, he might have taken the time to make a comment about them. Instead, he decided to concentrate on the matter at hand. "How long ago did you escape from the village?"

"This morning," said the other farmer, a somewhat younger man who was obviously the one named Pike. "Before sunup."

Soth wasn't surprised by this. It was just like ogres to take over a village, then get careless about keeping it while they indulged on food, ale and wine in celebration. Fortunately for Soth and the people of Halton, it simply meant that the ogres' celebration would be short-lived.

"Did you get a chance to learn where the ogres are located?" asked Soth.

"Most of them, milord," said Pike.

"I saw some too," offered Hender.

"Excellent," said Soth. Then in a slightly louder voice. "We'll break for a short rest here. When we mount again, we'll be riding into battle."

He dismounted and began studying the map the rider had drawn back at Dargaard Keep. In comparing it to what was known about the ogres by Hender and Pike, it became clear that, despite what the rider had said about them at Dargaard Keep, these ogres preferred to stick close together.

According to Hender, most of the ogres had gathered in the middle of the village around the open meeting place called Center Square. From there, four pathways led out in four basic directions: north, south, west and east. The pathway leading into the village from the north was the largest of the four and could easily be considered a road. It was the village's main connection to Dargaard Keep to the north and the path most often traveled by villagers. The path heading west was also fairly wide and well maintained. This was the path that hooked up with the trail that led to Vingaard Keep, another stronghold of the Knights of Solamnia. The path south was thin and seldom used, stopping at the edge of Halton Wood, a thick, dark forest that had, up until now, served as a buffer zone between the farmers and the ogres living in Throtyl to the south. The path leading east was also a short one, leading to a single farmhouse and a trail that led up the side of one of the Dargaard range's more majestic peaks.

It was this path that the knights decided on utilizing. It was likely that the ogres had posted guards on the main north-south road, so they would gain some measure of surprise by coming at them out of the mountains from the east. It was also a safer plan for the villagers given that most of them were being held up in the two large homes on the west side of the main road. If the knights were successful, they'd be able to overpower the ogres long before they had a chance to harm any of their prisoners.

So, armed with a rough battle plan, they set out around midday, riding halfway up the slopes of the Dargaard Mountains in the hopes of remaining unseen by any scouts or guards the ogres might have stationed around the perimeter of the village. As they got closer to Halton, however, it became more and more apparent that the ogres didn't perceive there to be much of a threat from outside forces. There were no guards, no sentries, nobody on the rooftops overlooking the countryside. Nevertheless, Soth kept the knights hidden on the mountainside in order to assure they retained the element of surprise.

"Is this the path?" Soth said in a whisper, even though such precautions were proving to be less and less necessary.

"Yes, milord," said Pike. "It curves a little to the right before joining up with the others in the center of town. There is a farm house on the right of it halfway between here and the center of town. On the left there's a small creek that feeds into a large pond which is where the farmers get most of their water during the dry summer seasons."

"Very good," said Soth. He took a look around him to see if all of the knights were close at hand. They were. "Farold!"

"Yes, milord," came the curt, matter-of-fact reply.

"You will take your men across the field there," said Soth, pointing to the open field below. The grain was nearing harvest and stood as tall as a man, if not taller. "Leave your mounts behind and secure the trade post and mercantile before joining me in the center of town."

Farold nodded and dismounted. The three knights under his command also dismounted, leaving their horses to the villagers. In a minute the knights were out of sight, heading toward the village.

"Caradoc!"

"Milord."

"You will continued skirting the mountains and come at the village from the south. I don't expect you'll come up against much resistance, but you might run into several ogres on the run."

Caradoc grinned at the thought. "Yes, milord."

"Take Knight Kern with you," said Soth. "Be careful through the mountains, but move quickly."

Caradoc nodded.

Kern followed, nodding to Soth as he passed.

That left Soth and six other knights, including Sword knights Darin Valcic and Zander Vingus, for what would basically be a full-frontal attack.

Soth took a deep breath. After all these years as a knight and the countless battles and adventures he'd been a part of, he still felt the same excitement beginning to build within him. It was a nervous sort of tension, an almost euphoric sensation that would continue to build until it all but disappeared upon the onset of battle. Then, his knightly instincts and years of training would take control and he would fight like a man possessed, not stopping until the last of his foes had been vanquished.

But that would all come later. For now, he savored the sweet feeling of anticipation, struggling with himself to keep it in check lest it overtake him too early. He still had a responsibility to his men to lead them safely into battle, for if one of them should die during the fight, a little piece of him would die along with that knight.

He drew his sword, held it at the ready and gave his mount a gentle squeeze with his legs. The horse began moving forward.

The rest of the knights followed.

Soon after they set out, the path curved to the right as it followed the bend of the river feeding into the pond. There was a small farmhouse on the right of the road. Soth sent two knights to inspect it, but it proved to be empty of either villagers or ogres.

They continued on, Soth in front and three knights to either side of him in a loose V shape. As the path straightened out, they were able to see Center Square. Apparently, Paladine was smiling favorably on their expedition because they'd arrived just as the ogres were packing up their booty and preparing for the trip back to Throtyl. As the knights watched, several of them were casually inspecting their loads unaware of their impending demise.

Soth gauged the distance between his men and the ogres. He was close enough that any thoughts in the ogres' minds about running for cover would be out of the question. The knights would easily be upon them before they reached safety.

No, Soth's attack plan had left them only one option, stand and fight.

Soth raised his sword high above him and kicked at his mount. The horse surged forward and in seconds the air was full of the sounds of charging hoofs.

The first ogre to see Soth stared at the knight for a moment as if he were looking at death itself. He moved left, then right, then finally picked up his nearby club and took up an improvised battle stance, ready to fight.

Soth continued to charge, leaning right and swinging his sword, the length of which outdistanced the ogre's club by half. The leading edge of the blade cut through the ogre's midsection, spattering Soth and his horse with blood. The ogre stood upright a moment, then doubled over before dropping heavily to the ground.

Quickly, the rest of the ogres became aware of the oncoming knights. Some decided to flee, heading north or south in search of cover. The last knights on either side broke off from the main assault to take care of these, cutting them down as they ran. After that, the knights swung around to rejoin the main group, leaving any further runners for the knights positioned to the north and south of the village.

Soth's charge had brought him through Center Square. He stopped his horse and dismounted, preferring to fight the rest of the battle on foot. The other knights had also dismounted and were now involved in close fighting, each knight battling one or more of the ogres who had remained to fight.

Soth approached the fray, eager to even the odds.

* * * * *

"It's not fair," said Farold.

The Knight of the Sword had led his party through the fields unnoticed and now looked across the main road at the two buildings serving as a makeshift prison for the villagers.

"What's not fair?" asked Kris Krejlgaard, a Knight of the Crown who had just returned from inspecting the mercantile and trade center, both of which proved to have been cleared out by the ogres.

"The stupid brutes have posted a single guard outside the prison and that one's asleep on the job."

"Perhaps their victory celebrations went long into the night?" offered Krejlgaard.

"Indeed, they must have."

"But you can't kill him as he sleeps."

"No, of course not," said Farold. It was forbidden by the Measure to kill an opponent whilst unawares. "But I doubt he'll put up much of a fight after I wake him."

"No," said Krejlgaard. "In his condition, I suppose not."

Farold rose up, walked boldly across the street and kicked at the feet of the sleeping ogre.

"Huh? What?" the beast sputtered.

"Surrender, or die at my blade," said Farold.

The ogre threw a handful of dirt into Farold's face, reached for his nearby spike-end club and leaped up from the ground.

Farold was blinded for a moment, cursing as he wiped his eyes. Luckily he was able to recover from the dirty tactic in time to meet the ogre's challenge.

While Farold and the ogre fought, Krejlgaard went to the two buildings on the west side of the road and released the imprisoned villagers. Then he escorted them to the mercantile where the two other knights in Farold's command waited with the small amounts of food, water and other supplies they had carried in their packs.

When Krejlgaard rejoined Farold, the Sword knight was standing over his fallen enemy looking none the worse for the battle.

"That didn't take long," said Krejlgaard.

"I suspect his abilities were muddled by sleep," said Farold, his voice edged with a hint of regret. "That or by last night's ale."

"Perhaps he would have been wise to remember the squire's first rule."

"So it would seem," said Farold, his eyes already scanning the village before him.

Off in the distance, sounds of a much larger battle could be heard.

Without another word between them, the two knights headed south.

*　*　*　*　*

Soth searched the square for an opponent. He found one in the largest of the ogres who was looking behind a grain cart for an unsuspecting knight.

"I'm over here, you ugly brute," said Soth, putting a boot to the ogre's backside and pushing him headfirst into the dirt.

The ogre tumbled and grunted, then looked up at Soth. "Didn't know Knights of Solamnia fought like common tavern wenches."

Soth was amused by the remark and grateful his opponent had a sense of humor. "Only when fighting old maids."

The ogre stood up, and for the first time Soth realized the beast was a full head taller than himself.

They began trading blows and for a while it was all Soth could do to keep up with the ogre. He'd been able to cut his foe here and there, but the opportunity for a death blow had so far eluded him.

The ogre blocked an overhanded swing of Soth's sword, then countered with a punch to Soth's ribs. His armor softened much of the blow, but it still hurt him.

And that's when the ogre made his one fatal mistake.

He became a little overconfident.

"You're not a bad fighter for a human. There must be some ogre blood in you, probably on your mother's side."

The remark enraged Soth, blinding him with fury. The Soth family was a noble one, certainly free of the vile taint of something as disgusting as ogre blood.

With a roar, Soth was upon the beast, his broadsword moving surely and swiftly, making it seem as if there were two or more swords fighting on his behalf.

The ogre fought off Soth's advances, but eventually began to tire. Soth was able to strike him at will, and took great delight in killing him slowly—wounding him on the shoulder, then the leg, stabbing him in the chest, then the stomach.

The ogre fell heavily to the ground, bleeding but still very much alive.

But Soth showed no mercy, continuing to hack at the body, lopping off limbs and cutting deeply into the flesh, again and again until the once formidable beast was little more than a grotesque lump of gore.

"Milord," said a voice of one of the knights.

Soth didn't hear it.

"Milord!" the knight called again.

Soth continued to stab and chop at the dead ogre.

Finally the knight, Darin Valcic, grabbed at Soth's arm. "He's dead, milord."

Soth stopped at last, his sword poised over his right shoulder and his breath coming hard and fast.

"There are still others . . . alive," said Valcic.

"Then let us find them," said Soth, his eyes alight with a dangerously bright glint of rage.

* * * * *

Caradoc stepped quietly through the bush. He'd heard sounds of movement in the distance and was slowly making his way toward their source.

After a few steps he stopped again and listened. It sounded as if someone was breathing hard. Most likely it was an ogre fleeing the battle that was now raging in the center of the village.

Caradoc continued his approach, being careful not to alert the ogre to his presence. Behind him, he could hear the faint footsteps of Wersten Kern as he came to join him. Caradoc turned, faced the knight and gestured that he should circle around the back of their enemy.

Kern nodded and headed off through the bush.

When the younger knight was out of earshot, Caradoc continued his hunt of the lone ogre. He'd traveled several more yards and stopped. The sound of the ogre's breathing was heavy and loud. In fact he was so close now that he could almost smell the beast's foul breath.

Caradoc pulled back a branch . . .

And there was the ogre, his back to Caradoc, no doubt watching the village to see if he were being pursued. The ogre was a large one, a full head taller than Caradoc and with long, wild hair that covered his shoulders and most of his back like a horse's mane. The beast's arms were as thick as Caradoc's thighs and his legs easily reminded one of tree trunks.

Caradoc took a breath and readied his sword. Then he slipped through the few remaining trees and prepared himself for a fight.

And at that moment the ogre turned.

From the look on his face, he was obviously surprised, but no longer inclined to flee. The ogre drew his huge sword and held it before him as he lunged toward Caradoc.

The knight was able to deflect the initial thrust with his shield, but the force of the blow caused a sharp stab of pain to shoot up the length of his arm. Still, Caradoc managed to strike a retaliatory blow against the ogre's naked thigh. It was a glancing blow, but still strong enough to slow the beast down.

After trading several ineffective blows, the two combatants squared off once more, this time as if ready to begin the fight anew.

"Caradoc!" It was the voice of Wersten Kern coming from somewhere deep in the bush.

The ogre turned to face this new threat approaching from behind, and when he did, Caradoc raised his sword and struck the beast in the back of the head.

Dead.

Seconds later, Kern appeared through the bush. When he looked at the ogre lying prone on the forest floor, his eyes opened wide in awe. "Look at the size of him!"

"He put up a valiant fight," said Caradoc, standing over the fallen ogre with one foot resting on its chest. "But in the end he proved to be no match for my blade."

Kern looked upon his fellow knight with an admiring eye, obviously not having seen the underhanded way in which Caradoc had felled the beast. "Well done, Knight

Caradoc," cheered Kern.

"Thank you, Knight Kern," Caradoc said, bowing slightly.

There was a moment of silence between them.

"Well, enough of this," said Kern. "This fight is over, but there is still a battle to be won."

"Lead the way," said Caradoc.

* * * * *

The battle in Center Square was brief.

Several of the ogres had fallen during the initial attack, reducing their force to a more manageable number. Then as the battle continued and more ogres fell, the will to fight in the ones that remained seemed to weaken, opening the way for a virtual rout over the loosely knit army of marauding beasts.

And now, bloody ogres littered the square.

Those who had fled the battle had been taken care of by Farold to the north and Caradoc to the south. It was possible that one or more of the ogres had managed to escape the slaughter and would eventually make it back to Throtyl, but Soth wasn't too concerned about that. If an ogre were to reach Throtyl it would mean he would be able to tell the rest of them what had happened to their party, thereby providing an effective warning to those who might try a similar attack on villages within the realm of Knightlund.

There was also a chance that the ogres would attempt to mount reprisal attacks, but their numbers would be no match for an extended war with the combined forces of all the Knights of Solamnia. This had been little more than an isolated skirmish, and now it was over.

Soth wiped his blade clean on a dead ogre's loincloth, then sheathed the sword and looked around to inspect the damage. Except for what the ogres had consumed while they had been in control of the village, most of their booty—the village's store—was recovered intact. A few villagers would be inconvenienced by having to cart their valuables back to their homes, and others would need time to get over the shock of the ogres' attack, but all in all, everything had gone as well as, or perhaps even better, than Soth could have hoped.

Best of all, not one of his knights had suffered a serious injury. Of course, a few of them had suffered cuts and gashes, and others had been bruised by the ogres, but their pains were nothing a tankard or two of ale wouldn't cure.

Soth detected some movement to his left. He turned and saw Farold approaching the Square from the north. "All clear, milord," he said.

"And the villagers?"

"Safe."

Soth nodded and looked to the south. Caradoc was there with Kern. Soth raised his head, as if asking a question of his seneschal.

"No more ogres in the forest, milord," said Caradoc. "If there are, they're halfway to Throtyl by now."

Soth nodded. His chest swelled with pride at the way his knights had handled themselves, but he was also rightly proud of himself for planning a battle strategy that ensured all of his knights would be able to fight again another day. As their leader, this had been one of Soth's prime concerns.

"Well done, Knights of Solamnia," he said loudly.

"Well done, milord!" the knights cheered in unison.

It was a good day to be a Knight of Solamnia.

When they ventured out into their village and found their streets rid of the dreaded ogres, the grateful villagers of Halton insisted that the knights remain in the town for a celebratory feast.

And, after a day and a half's ride and a short, but intense battle, the knights quickly acquiesced to the offer.

For the feast, all types of food—much of it taken directly from what the ogres had pillaged and loaded onto their carts—was served up on tables set up within Center Square itself. Ale and wine poured freely into what seemed to be bottomless tankards, and music and song from the town's finest minstrels and bards gave the night an almost festival atmosphere.

After the meal, the villagers continued to show the knights their gratitude by offering them a number of gifts ranging from heirloom quilted blankets to household bric-a-brac made from precious metals and rare wood. In a few cases the offered gifts included the favors of several of the more adventurous—not to mention attractive—women of the village. The knights, of course, all remained true to the Oath and the Measure and kindly refused such tempting entreaties.

Especially virtuous among the knights was Lord Soth himself, who despite the intoxicating effect of the ale and the tempting proposition made to him by a pretty and buxom young farm girl, found his thoughts kept drifting back toward Dargaard Keep and his Lady Korinne who waited patiently for him to return.

Chapter 6

"Step forward," said the Kingpriest.

The young woman stepped forward, carrying her bundled infant in her arms.

To the woman's left was a somewhat older female mage dressed in the familiar yellow and white robes of the followers of the Kingpriest.

"Mage Hailerin," said the Kingpriest, indicating the mage standing beside the woman, "reports to me that you have had wickedly evil thoughts about this child."

"I'm not aware of having any evil thoughts your holiness," the woman said, her head bowed, her voice full of humility.

"Mage Hailerin," said the Kingpriest.

The female mage stepped forward. "I was walking along this woman's street late last night when I heard a baby's cry. It was loud and constant and seemed to convey great pain."

The Kingpriest nodded. "Go on."

"I went looking for the source of the cry, a search that

led me straight to this woman's house."

"And what did you see?"

"When I arrived I looked in through the window and saw this woman tending to her child."

"But the child was crying?" asked the Kingpriest.

"He's been colicky of late . . ." the woman said.

"Silence!" said the Kingpriest. "You may speak when the mage is done."

The woman fell silent, but looked to be on the verge of tears.

"She was trying to comfort the child at first, but it continued to cry and would not stop. And that's when she began to shake the child, only a little at first, but then more rigorously."

The Kingpriest's eyebrows arched and he nodded. He leaned forward. "And her thoughts?"

The mage looked at the woman. "Her thoughts ranged from abandoning the child on a doorstep, to bashing its head with a large rock."

The Kingpriest looked surprised.

The woman began shaking her head. "He's been colicky for the longest time," she said. "I haven't had a decent night's sleep in six months. It seems like he's been crying constantly. Nothing I've done has helped."

"Do you deny having these thoughts?" asked the Kingpriest.

"I love my baby," she said.

"Answer the question."

"What mother hasn't had such thoughts at some point in her life?"

"So you admit to having thoughts about abandoning, even killing your infant child?"

"I was frustrated and might have considered it for a second," said the woman, her voice trembling with fear. "But I'd never do such a ghastly thing. I love my son and would never do anything to hurt him."

"But yet you were seen shaking the child."

"I was at my wit's end, I didn't know what else to do."

"Shaking an innocent child is an evil act. If you are capable of doing that, what is to prevent you from enacting your heinous thoughts of killing the child?"

"I love my baby."

The Kingpriest looked away, no longer listening to the woman's desperate pleas. "You are hereby sentenced to death so that your evil thoughts can never become evil deeds. But you need not worry for your child. He will be taken into the temple and raised by members of the clergy. When he is of age, he will be trained as a cleric's apprentice."

The child was unceremoniously torn from the woman's arms.

"No!" she screamed. "My baby . . ."

The child began to scream.

The woman was grabbed by two guards and escorted out of the temple, her cries echoing off the stone walls and down the stone corridors.

The child was taken in the other direction, its cries as chillingly piercing as its mother's.

The Kingpriest looked at the mage, smiled and said, "Well done, Mage Hailerin. Well done."

Chapter 7

Dargaard Keep was dark.

Silent.

Soth's steps echoed off the cold, hard bloodstone, sounding like drops of water falling into a deep dark well. He climbed up the staircase toward the master bedchamber.

He'd been away for weeks, leading his loyal knights in the fight against the forces of Evil. He had returned a hero, but without warning, and therefore had arrived without fanfare, without a proper hero's reception.

But all that was unimportant. All he really wanted was to see his lady love. To embrace her and love her over and over again, to somehow make up for the long chill nights he'd left her alone while he traveled the dark and lonely plains.

He neared the bedchamber.

And heard the voices.

They were soft, whispery voices. The kind of voices lovers use to exchange secrets and fondest desires. One of the voices belonged to Lady Korinne, the other . . . The other was deeper in tone and louder. It was the voice of a man. Soth suddenly inhaled.

A man's voice in his lady's bedchamber in the middle of the night. It could mean only one thing.

Soth felt anger roil within him as his muscles tensed like iron bands. He drew his sword and pounded on the door.

There were hurried sounds coming from inside. Bedsheets ruffling. Hushed whispers.

Again Soth pounded on the door, this time with the hilt of his sword.

"It is open," came of the voice of Korinne. It was soft and sweet, as if she'd just awakened from a pleasant dream.

Soth turned the handle and pushed the door open.

Several candles lit the room and moonlight beamed in through the open window. Korinne was smiling. "Loren," she said, stretching her arms out to him.

Her smile angered him even more. How could a woman who had proclaimed her love so passionately suddenly become so treacherous and unfaithful? He wanted nothing more than to shout his words at her, to let his anger be known, but he found he could not utter a single syllable.

He moved toward the bed, ignoring the pleading words of his wife. Then he raised his sword above his head, both hands wrapped tightly around the hilt, blade pointed downward . . .

And brought it down with force, running the pointed tip through the shape that cowered beneath the covers next to Lady Korinne.

There was a loud grunt.

Dark stains began to bloom outward around the sword.

He reached down, pulled back the cover and saw a face familiar to him.

His own.

Korinne simply laughed.

Soth awoke abruptly, covered in sweat and shivering. His breath came hard and fast as if he'd been running for hours. He sat up on the bed, an extra large one belonging to the Mayor of Halton, and glanced around him. The room was empty and dark. The night was still and quiet. By the position of the moons it looked as if sunrise was several hours away. Soth lay back on the bed, thankful that no one had seen him awaken in such a state.

Such a horrible, horrible dream.

A nightmare of his own design.

He had no reason to distrust Lady Korinne, and even if he did, no one would be fool enough to covet the wife of Lord Soth of Dargaard Keep, Knight of the Rose.

He took a deep breath and chased all thoughts of the distressing dream from his mind. One last shiver coursed through his body, then he took a final deep breath. He closed his eyes and tried to return to sleep, but fitfully tossed and turned until dawn.

* * * * *

"How did you sleep?" Caradoc asked.

Soth looked at him. "Like a fallen tree," he lied.

"As did I," said Caradoc. "As we all did no doubt."

"Indeed," replied Soth, turning away from his seneschal to hide his yawn while he busied himself in preparation to leave the village.

The villagers had made sure the knights were served a grand breakfast, and while they ate, had loaded up their horses with all manner of provisions for the journey home. The provisions were unnecessary because the knights would be meeting up with the party of squires and footmen mere hours after leaving the village, but no matter how Soth told them this, the villagers would not accept the refusal of their offerings.

And now as the sun rose higher in the morning sky, the villagers lined the main road leading north in order to give the knights a rousing final send-off.

Unlike the knights' charge out of Dargaard Keep, this departure was slow-paced and festive; the knights almost lingered in the village, not wanting to leave.

Soth saw this as a good sign, ensuring that there would be no shortage of volunteers to relieve the three knights he was leaving behind to keep watch on the village.

When they cleared the northern edge of the village, the knights continued on at a leisurely pace. They were all enjoying the freedom of the plains and none of them were in any particular hurry to return to the cold, bloodstone walls of Dargaard Keep.

Even Lord Soth, whose mind had been filled with thoughts of Lady Korinne, was now of a mind to spend a little more time away from the keep to clear his head of the dreams which had been haunting him. Besides that, more time away would make their hearts grow fonder, assuring that their reunion would be a passionately amorous one.

They met up with the party of squires and footmen just after midday and decided to make camp there on the plains. Several of the knights who had been wounded during the brief battle had been treated in Halton, but some of them had wounds that were best treated by the keep's healer who had joined the squires on the journey. These knights were quickly attended to while the rest took the opportunity to remove battle armor and change into fresh clothes.

And as the day wore on and food and drink were consumed in abundance, the knights began to relax. While they had had the opportunity to rest inside Halton, they were still required to maintain the dignified appearance expected of the Knights of Solamnia. But here, among their fellow Sons of Paladine, the mood was considerably more boisterous as they truly celebrated their victory.

"How on Krynn did the ogres think they could actually get away with such an insane expedition?" asked Petr Hallis, a squire assigned to the Knights of the Sword.

Soth considered the question as he and several of the knights sat under the shade of a tree late in the afternoon. "Ogres aren't known for their ability to think a plan through to its end," he answered. "They more than likely found themselves short on supplies for the coming winter and their only thought as to how to procure supplies was to steal them from those who had them in reserve. It's unlikely that thoughts of purchasing supplies or bartering for them with goods of their own making ever entered their mind."

"Why did they think they could get away with it? Halton has been protected by the Knights of Solamnia for years."

Soth looked at the young squire. "Criminals seldom think that they will fail. Their thoughts are almost always concentrated on the success of their venture, not on the repercussions of being caught in the act."

The young squire nodded in understanding.

Soth's eyes caught Caradoc's glance and for a moment he was reminded of his own past deeds. He imagined what might have happened if they had been caught, or implicated in any way in the murders of his half-siblings. A slight shiver ran through his body.

"But enough of this," said Soth. "Ogres are little more than bullies at heart. Bullies who quickly turn out to be cowards when confronted by those unafraid of their size, strength and most odorous smell."

A laugh rose up from the group surrounding Soth.

"A toast to a victory for the Knights of Solamnia." He raised his tankard. "A small victory for us, but none were ever larger or more important to the good people of Halton."

"Cheers!"

Wine and ale flowed well into the night and the minor cuts, wounds, aches and pains obtained during the fight were slowly, and easily, forgotten.

A dozen knights, squires and footmen gathered around the fire, telling stories as a way to keep them all amused. Although some of the tales concerned the exploits of bawdy women, most of the tales featured Knights of Solamnia both real and imagined and ranged from humorous anecdotes illustrating the stupidity of ogres, to more somber tales illustrating the wisdom of Paladine, or the benevolence of Mishakal.

Currently the young squire Arnol Kraas was telling a tale, one he'd no doubt recently learned as part of his studies as an aspirant knight.

"A young Knight of the Sword ventured upon the road to visit his friends in Vingaard Keep," the squire began. "Along the way he came upon a young woman lying by the side of the road, weeping. Quickly, the knight dismounted and went to her side. When he lifted her up he saw that she had been severely beaten."

All of the knights were familiar with the tale, having studied it as squires themselves. Nevertheless, none interrupted him. The telling of the tales, even the most familiar, reminded them all of the lessons to be remembered.

"When he asked the woman's name, she told him it was Stalen Lamplight. The knight was shocked. He knew Stalen Lamplight, and truth be told, had loved her from afar for many years, had considered many times asking her to be his bride. Her beauty had been well-known throughout the land, but now it was gone, taken away by the weapons of the ogres who resented all beauty, whether it be in humans or their Irda brethren.

"The knight took the young woman in his arms and prayed to Mishakal to restore Stalen's beauty, promising to marry the woman and protect her for the rest of her days if she would only grant his wish. Mishakal answered the knight's prayers, appearing before him as a glowing ball of soft white light.

" 'I will restore her beauty,' Mishakal told the knight, 'but I will leave it up to you to decide whether you wish her beauty to return during the daylight hours when others might see her, or during the dark of night when you alone will be by her side.'

"The knight was unsure which of Mishakal's offers he should accept. Certainly he would want her to be beautiful as she lay by his side, but then again he couldn't force her to show her hideously scarred face as he presented her as his wife during daylight hours.

"In the end, he could not decide. In fact, he wasn't even sure if it was his decision to make. And that is what he told the Healing Hand. 'Mishakal,' he said. 'I can not decide the woman's fate for her. I leave the decision up to her, and will stand by my offer of marriage whatever she decides.'

"The glowing light that was Mishakal shone brighter. 'You have chosen correctly,' she said. 'It is not up to you to decide another's fate, but to allow her to make her own choices in life. As a reward, she will have her beauty restored . . . both night and day.' "

His story finished, Kraas looked around. The knights, who were expecting a more polished ending to the tale were caught slightly off guard, but recovered by giving the young squire a polite smattering of applause.

Kraas seemed satisfied.

Soth took the opportunity to put another piece of wood on the fire. The familiarity of Kraas's tale had calmed the knights. Perhaps it was time to make their blood run faster. "How about a tale from you, Knight Grimscribe?" asked Soth.

"Yes." "How about it?" chimed the knights.

Derik Grimscribe was a Sword knight originally from one of the small villages surrounding Dargaard Keep. A knight of average skill on the battlefield, Grimscribe was a master of words, able to tell stories or negotiate between warring clans with equal amounts of tact and skill. A story from Grimscribe was a treat to be sure.

"Very well then," said Grimscribe, moving closer to the fire to give his face an eerie sort of otherworldly glow. "A new story . . . of terror." He looked around at the knights, his face a mask of twisted light and shadow.

"A long time ago, before your grandfather had finished suckling his mother's breast . . ." he began in a low voice.

The knights rolled forward to listen more closely.

". . . a Rose knight of Solamnia had lost his way after a long and exhausting battle with an especially foul blue dragon."

"A battle he no doubt won," quipped a footman.

"Yesss," hissed Grimscribe, "but as the knight left the dragon for dead, the evil blue spoke words in an ancient tongue, placing a powerful curse on the knight."

The knights were silent. Although there were no longer such things as dragons, all of the knights respected the power they were credited with in the stories told of the great dragon wars.

"So, the knight entered the Darken Wood in search of his fellow Sons of Paladine. But the forest was so dark, even in the middle of the day, that it wasn't long before the brave knight was utterly lost.

"Still he carried on through the darkness, hoping to come upon one of his fellows, but after a few hours he finally conceded that he was indeed hopelessly lost." Grimscribe paused after the word to let the thought sink in.

"But just then," snapped Grimscribe, making several squires jump in surprise, "he came upon what looked to be a mounted knight. At first he thought he'd found a fellow Knight of Solamnia, but as he got closer to the figure it was obvious that the stranger's manner of dress was unlike that of any knight he'd ever seen before, Solamnic or otherwise. He was dressed in a deep-blue, almost black, cloak that went from the top of his head and on down past his feet. His horse too, was blacker than any knight had ever dared to ride. The Rose knight was leery about asking such a stranger for help, but he was lost and any help was better than none at all."

The knights were silent, but judging by their faces some were obviously skeptical about this last bit of wisdom.

" 'Excuse me,' the Rose knight called out. But there was no answer from the stranger, who kept on riding as if he hadn't heard a word. The knight then brought his horse to a trot and quickly caught up to the dark traveler. 'I beg your pardon, sir,' he said, this time tapping on the stranger's shoulder to get his attention. Still, there was no response.

"Becoming somewhat frustrated, the knight reached

over and grabbed the man's cloak in his hand and pulled on it. 'I'm talking to you!' he said forcefully. At that moment the cloak fell away from the traveler's head."

The knights were silent. Several held their breath.

"The traveler turned around and the knight suddenly saw that the traveler's face wasn't human, but that of the blue dragon."

Gasps all around.

"Well, even though the Rose knight and his mount had been tested countless times in battle, they were terrified by the unexpected sight and ran off into the darkest part of the woods, never to find their way out again."

Soth smiled and looked around at the somewhat apprehensive faces of the knights. "Well done, Grimscribe," he said. "An excellent tale for such a dark and frigid night."

"How about one from you, Lord Soth?" asked Grimscribe.

"Oh, I don't think—"

The knights quickly joined together in prodding Soth to tell a story and at last he agreed. "All right, all right, but I doubt my story will be told as skillfully as Knight Grimscribe's."

"Whose are?" someone shouted, the words followed by soft laughter.

"Very well, then," Soth said. He knew few tales, but at last chose one he knew well enough to relate orally.

"Before Vinas Solamnus organized the Knights of Solamnia, he was employed by the Emperor of Ergoth as commander of the palace guard in the capital city of Daltigoth."

A soft murmur of hushed voices circulated around the fire. This was a story that deserved to be told over and over again. Especially in such select company.

"Vinas Solamnus was a pious man, a gallant warrior and a leader truly beloved by his men. He was also loyal to the emperor and provided him with a palace guard which no single army could rival. Meanwhile, on the northeastern plains of Ergoth, the people there—proud, noble and independent folk—had grown tired of the emperor's iron-handed style of government and, joining forces, mounted a rebellion.

"Solamnus and his knights were dispatched to the region to quell the uprising. After several fierce battles, Solamnus grew to respect and admire the rebel fighters for their tenacity and courage. He also realized that there must be some truth to their claims in order for them to fight so fiercely for what they believed to be right and just. And so, Solamnus agreed to meet with the rebel leaders so that they could tell their side of the story. The great knight listened patiently to the people detail their grievances. Solamnus was moved by their plight and investigated their claims. To his surprise and dismay, he discovered that the rebels had been telling the truth. But worst of all for Solamnus was the realization that his loyalty to the emperor had left him blind to the injustices being done to the people. Solamnus immediately called his followers together, much in the same way you are gathered here, and presented the people's case to them.

"When he was done, he gave his knights a choice." He gave a nod to Arnol Kraas, connecting the lesson learned from his tale to the story he was telling now. "Those who believed in the rebels' cause were welcome to stay. Those who did not were given leave to return to Daltigoth.

"Most of the knights chose to remain loyal to Vinas Solamnus, even though it would mean certain exile from Ergoth for them, and quite possibly death. Those who returned to Daltigoth gave Solamnus's message to the emperor—correct the wrongs being done to the people, or prepare for war."

Soth paused to wet his throat. The knights remained silent, listening intently. Even though they knew this story well, it must have sounded different coming from a knight such as Soth.

"Of course, the emperor denounced Solamnus as a traitor, stripping him of his lands and title. The people of Daltigoth prepared for a war which would eventually come to be known as the War of Ice Tears because that winter was the most severe in Ergoth's recorded history. But despite the cold, Solamnus was able, with the loyal and steadfast support of his knights"—Soth put extra emphasis on these last few words for obvious reasons— "to lay siege to the city, destroying its food supplies and spreading the news of the emperor's corruption. All the while the emperor himself remained hidden like a coward deep within the bowels of his palace."

Several knights let out mild *harumphs* of contempt.

"In two months the capital fell and the emperor was forced to sue for peace. As a result, the northeastern part of Ergoth gained its independence. The people named it Solamnia in honor of their new king, Vinas Solamnus. And although Solamnia never achieved its greatness and power until long after the death of Vinas Solamnus, it quickly came to be known as a land populated by people who possessed great amounts of honesty, integrity, and fierce determination."

The knights remained silent for several long moments and all that could be heard was the snap and crackle of the slightly greener wood on the fire.

And then a voice.

"May our loyalty to you, milord," said Colm Farold, "someday be compared to that of the knights who served Vinas Solamnus so well."

"Hear, hear!" the rest of the knights said in unison.

"I have no doubt that it will," said Soth, nodding graciously.

After the tales had ended, the fire burned through the night, providing some warmth against the cool nocturnal winds that blew across the plains.

There was little danger of reprisals from the ogres of Throtyl who would no doubt think twice in the future before attacking soil under the protection of the Knights of

Solamnia. And, other than a few wild animals, there was little else to be wary of in this part of Knightlund. So the knights had all drunk their fill and set about to get a peaceful night's sleep under the stars.

All except for Soth.

He did not look forward to the night. Considering the dreams he'd been having of late, sleep was something to be avoided or at least put off until absolutely necessary. For that reason, he wandered around the perimeter of the camp under the pretense of keeping watch.

"Milord," said Meyer Seril. "It is my turn to keep watch. And with all the squires here I don't think you are even scheduled to take a turn."

Soth turned and looked at the young Crown knight appreciatively. "I'm not very tired," he said. "I might as well keep watch if I'm going to be awake. You go to sleep, Knight Seril. You fought well, and you deserve to get some rest."

"Thank you, milord," the young knight said, proud to have been noticed by his lord.

"Go now," said Soth. He had no idea how Seril had fought because the battle had been so brief, but it didn't hurt to tell him he'd done well. Nor did it hurt for him to take the watch when he wasn't required to. Such a thing did wonders for the knights' morale and loyalty, not to mention their opinion of him as a leader.

With Seril gone, Soth walked around the encampment and looked north toward Dargaard Keep. The pinnacle of its rose-shaped silhouette was just discernible against the dark night sky. As he stared at the keep, he marveled at how black its form appeared even in the dead of night.

The sight chilled him.

And, as he wrapped his cloak around himself to stave off the chill shiver that ran through him, he suddenly looked forward to morning, and the coming of the sun.

Chapter 8

The knights broke camp early the next morning and rode across the plains with the outline of Dargaard Keep constantly before them, rising up from the horizon like a rose-shaped beacon. By midday they were close enough to make out details in the keep's walls such as windows and battlements, and by late afternoon they had begun to discern the individual blocks of bloodstone.

Given that their approach would have been monitored throughout the day from one or more of the keep's towers, the knights fully expected that their return would be accompanied by a suitable amount of fanfare.

They were not disappointed.

Residents of the keep and those employed in and around it all came out to welcome the triumphant knights. Men, women and children lined the path of their approach, all happy to see them returning so soon after their departure and in good health.

As the knights neared, the wooden drawbridge was lowered over the chasm that surrounded the keep and the heavy steel portcullis rose up like a welcoming hand being offered in greeting.

Gared Kentner, the keep's quartermaster, counted the number of knights on horseback and asked Soth with a grave voice, "Casualties?"

Soth slowed and looked down at the clerk. "None. I've left several knights in Halton as a precautionary measure."

"Excellent," said Kentner, who was probably thankful that he wouldn't have to process any personal belongings or make adjustments to the bunk allotments.

Soth continued on into the keep.

Heading up the welcoming party inside was Lady Korinne. As Soth rode toward her he noticed that she had donned her finest robes and jewels in order to greet him. He held his breath a moment. She looked even more beautiful than he remembered.

Feeling his heart gathering up in his throat, Soth quickly dismounted and approached her. He took her hand in his.

She said, "Milord."

Soth removed his helm, leaned forward, took her in his arms and kissed her. There was passion in her kiss to be sure, but there was also something else to it, something that was keeping her from giving herself up to him completely.

For a moment Soth's mind raced back to the dream he'd had during his night on the plains. Had she been unfaithful? He immediately broke off the kiss and pulled himself away from her. "Is there something you must tell me?" he said, his voice even and devoid of emotion.

She looked up. Tears began to well in her eyes.

Soth feared the worst.

"I . . . I am not with child as we had hoped." When she finally said the words, they escaped her lips in a rush, like water gushing from a broken damn.

Soth was simultaneously hit by waves of relief and disappointment. Korinne had not conceived, but his dream and subsequent fear over her infidelity had been little more than folly on his part.

As he looked at her, he made sure his face betrayed none of his emotions. He simply gazed into her pale green eyes and said, "Then we shall have to try again." He allowed a loving smile to creep onto his face. "And often."

Upon hearing the words, Lady Korinne let out a long sigh.

Obviously she had feared his reaction would be more severe. But what could he do? Draw his sword and threaten her with it until she produced an heir? It was a popular tactic with barbarians, but there was no proof that it actually worked. No, this was just as difficult for her because she wanted a child just as much—perhaps even more—than he did. Soth felt it best that they try to ease each other's pain rather than add to it.

"Perhaps we should even try . . . right away. Right now," said Soth.

A girlish sort of smile broke over Korinne's face.

He took her by the hand and led her up the stairs toward their bedchamber.

* * * * *

The passionate nights Soth spent by Lady Korinne's side continued throughout the winter, keeping them both warm and protecting them from the chill of the winter months—Frostkolt, Newkolt and Deepkolt.

But the winter's icy cold lingered despite the coming of spring when Dargaard Keep was rocked by the news of Lord Reynard Gladria's death at his home in Palanthas. Although he had been ill for many months, his death still came as a shock to Lord Soth and Lady Korinne. Indeed, all of Solamnia mourned the man's passing. But what made it doubly painful for Korinne was that she hadn't given her father a grandchild before his passing. For this reason, Korinne long considered herself to be a failure and no amount of words from Soth, family or friends—however kind—could bring her out of her state of despondency.

After journeying to Palanthas for Lord Reynard's elaborate public funeral, Soth remained in the city for several weeks while the slow passage of time gently eased Korinne's pain. Then as the month of Brookgreen came to a close and Soth felt he'd neglected his knightly duties long enough and was compelled to return to Dargaard Keep, he offered to let Korinne remain with her mother in Palanthas and return to the keep only when she felt she was ready.

Korinne refused.

With a loyalty and honor worthy of a Knight of Solamnia she told Soth, "My place is by my husband's side. I will return with you to Dargaard Keep." And with that they returned to Knightlund with renewed hopes of birthing an heir before Korinne's mother Leyla also passed away.

But Yurthgreen also came and went, and despite the flowering of the plants and the greenery beginning to sprout on the trees around the keep, Korinne once again came to Soth with the now agonizingly painful news.

This time Soth simply raised his eyebrows expectantly, having used words to ask the question far too often.

Korinne shook her head.

Soth let out a sigh, his chest aching. He'd been able to remain optimistic by believing that when Paladine (the Great Dragon and the God of Good) wished him to have an heir, he would bless the couple with one. After all, were not the Knights of Solamnia also called the Sons of Paladine? Surely, a new "Son" for the Soth household was only a matter of time. Still, the wait grew more and more painful with each passing month.

Korinne's eyes welled up with tears. She looked away from Soth as if ashamed, then turned and quickly left the room.

Soth remained where he was, his words on the matter— no matter how kind—having been unable to ease her pain for many, many months now. He tried to busy himself with some task, but could not.

Korinne's sobs could be heard echoing too loudly through the keep.

* * * * *

The forest was burning.

Soth looked around him and saw nothing but flames eating up the trees. He was being pushed northward, the fire at his back leaving him no other choice.

He must have been running for hours. His legs had become heavy and leaden, each step becoming that much harder to take. At last, he could not go on.

"Father?"

The voice, it was the same one as before. It belonged to his son.

"Father? Are you there? Help me!"

Soth tried to run, but his legs had grown far too tired, his body exhausted from continually running from the flames. He took two more awkward steps and fell to his knees.

"Father, why don't you help me?"

He searched the smoke that hung over the forest like a pall and discerned movement in the distance.

It was his son, younger than before, dressed in the garb of a squire. His eyes were closed, no doubt seared by the heat and smoke of the fire. He was wandering the forest aimlessly, stepping over fallen trees and smoldering ashes, even walking at times directly toward the fire itself.

Soth opened his mouth to call out to the boy, and suddenly realized he did not know what to call him.

He didn't know his own son's name.

"Father! Save me!"

Soth opened his mouth once more and gagged on the thick black smoke enshrouding him like darkness incarnate.

"Father, are you there?"

He gagged and coughed on the acrid smoke. He wanted to call out, but before he could make a sound a burning tree toppled, crashing down onto the younger Soth, knocking him to the ground and setting his clothes ablaze.

As he watched the flames eat away at his son, his own flesh and blood, Soth heard the boy's final words.

"Father, it hurts . . ."

Soth's eyes shot open and he coughed to clear his throat of phlegm. He looked over to where Korinne lay. Thankfully, she was still asleep, the slight smile gracing her visage proof that she'd remained oblivious to the horrible nightmare that had haunted him yet again.

Soth rubbed his fisted hands against his sleepy eyes. It had been months since he'd had such a dream, not since he had been on the trail toward Halton. At the time he'd dismissed it as simply a product of his eagerness to do battle. But now, there had been months of calm and peaceful existence within the keep. Even the citizens of Knightlund had been cooperative, settling their minor squabbles and arguments themselves rather than wasting the valuable time of the lord of the keep.

Then what could have brought it on?

He rose from the bed, careful to leave Korinne undisturbed. Then he quickly got dressed in leggings and a tunic, and slipped into a pair of soft-soled boots so as to not make any noise as he wandered through the keep.

It was still quite early in the morning and few in the keep would be awake yet. Even the roosters had yet to begin crowing the dawning of a new day.

He slipped out of the room and ventured down to the keep's gatehouse. The drawbridge was already down in preparation for the morning's deliveries. Soth asked the footman on watch to raise the portcullis enough to allow him to get outside of the keep and wander the grounds.

"Alone?" asked the footman.

Soth merely glared at him. Even though it was customary to have a knight or footman accompany anyone venturing out of the keep on foot, Soth wanted very much to be alone.

The footman looked at Soth for several seconds waiting for an answer. Then, realizing he wouldn't be getting one, he said, "Yes, milord." He began turning the winding gear that slowly lifted the portcullis. Soth crouched down and ducked under the still-rising portcullis, then walked across the heavy wooden bridge, his feet making no sounds against its planks.

He stopped at one side of the bridge and looked down into the chasm below. It was dark and foreboding, like the open maw of a dragon might appear when viewed from close up. There were several pebbles on the bridge. Soth nudged one toward the edge and finally over the side. He listened carefully, but did not hear the stone hit bottom.

He moved on, crossing the bridge and heading toward the small garden kept on the grounds. After the wedding, flowers and trees and shrubs had been planted on the site and now, almost a year later, the plants were beginning to bloom. The garden was awash in bright yellows and oranges, and rich blues and greens. It was still too early for the roses, but the groundskeepers had assured him they would be a brilliant spectacle of red, white and yellow when they bloomed in a few short weeks.

The stunning rebirth of nature did little to improve Soth's state of mind. The blossoming of new life only served to remind him of his and Korinne's inability to do the same.

It just didn't make any sense.

If his father, Aynkell Soth, had been able to create offspring so often—and with such apparent ease—then why not him as well? Was he not of the same flesh and blood?

And what of Korinne? Hadn't Lord and Lady Gladria given birth to a large family, providing Korinne with several brothers and sisters, each of them with several children of their own? Why hadn't such fertility been passed on to her as well?

For the first time since the wedding, Soth's mind was infected by doubt.

Perhaps I've made a mistake in marrying Lady Korinne.

The thought hit him like the slap of a hand encased in cold, hard mail. *How could I have thought such a thing?* And yet it continued to haunt him, like the dreams.

He walked through the garden, smelling the flowers in the hopes that the devilish thought would fade from his memory. But instead it lingered.

He approached the small gazebo positioned in the center of the garden. It was closed off by a small gate and the gate was kept closed by a latch. Although the latch was made to accommodate a lock, it was without one. Soth opened the latch and stepped into the gazebo. As he closed the gate behind him he was reminded of a kender saying.

"Why insult a door's purpose by locking it?"

Indeed, and why would Paladine allow them to build a nest of such love if its destiny was to be barren? Soth still believed Paladine was waiting for the proper time to give the couple children, but he was beginning to question why the Great Dragon was making them wait so long.

As he sat down on the bench inside the gazebo and watched the morning sun begin to crest the peaks of the Dargaard Mountains to the west, he felt he had an idea of what the answer might be.

Perhaps Paladine was making him pay the price for his father's indiscretions and his own concealment of them.

The sins of the father.

They would be with him.

Always.

Soth felt a breeze blow heavily down from the mountains. It was a cool wind and it made him shiver.

"Milord."

Soth turned to his left. Caradoc slowly appeared out of the garden's shadows.

"Is everything all right?" asked Soth's seneschal, concern for his lord apparent in his voice.

"Yes, everything is fine," said Soth. "It's just that there's a chill in the air this morning." He pulled his cloak more tightly around his body to stave off the cold. "Can you feel it?"

Caradoc looked at Soth strangely. "No milord, I can't."

Chapter 9

The elderly mage walked casually through the streets of Istar, his yellow and white robes flowing behind, swirling over the cobblestones. Every once in a while he would glance into a store front or shop window looking at everything, but nothing in particular.

It was a strange feeling.

He had been empowered by the Kingpriest to read the minds of the people of Istar so that he could discern their evil thoughts. But, what was he to do about those evil thoughts after they'd been found out, and how was he to prevent them from becoming evil deeds?

On this subject the Kingpriest had been vague, leaving the matter up to the discretion of the individual mages.

Earlier in the day the mage had watched a business transaction being conducted in the marketplace on the city's west side. A fisherman from the coastal down of Cesena had brought baskets of fish to trade for grain, sugar, spice and other necessities of life. In this particular transaction he had exchanged twenty-four fish for two bushels of grain, a poor trade given that the fish were quite fresh—even packed in ice—while the quality of the grain was rather dubious. But grain at this time of year was hard to find, especially high quality grain, so the fisherman was forced to make the trade or else do without.

After the deal had been made and the two men shook hands, the mage read the minds of each. The grain dealer was obviously happy, but the fisherman was frustrated by the deal, knowing he had given up more than he'd received.

And then . . . something of an evil thought.

The fisherman wished that the grain dealer would be similarly cheated in another transaction later in the day.

As he'd watch the two men part, the mage considered the fisherman's thought.

Had it been evil?

At length, he decided it was not. It was simply wishing that the trader eventually got what he deserved. That had not been an evil thought, but rather, merely fair.

Now as he walked the streets of the industrial district, the mage stopped by the open window of a blacksmith's shop and watched the smith as he worked.

The interior of the shop glowed orange from the light of the fire burning hotly off in one corner. Judging by the several decorative swords leaning against the wall in a neat row, the smith was busy hammering out items to be hung in one of the halls within the Temple of the Kingpriest. The hilt ends of the swords were of an elaborate design and considering the amount of effort the smith was putting into the sword currently on the anvil, quite difficult to fashion.

The mage decided to read the smith's mind.

Little more there . . . Too much . . . A curve here . . . More . . . More . . .

The thoughts seemed to correspond with the blows of his hammer.

Again . . . Harder this time . . . More . . . Too much!

But in addition to the simple thoughts that went along

with each blow, there was also an underlying current of anger. Anger against what or whom, the mage couldn't tell, but it was there just under the surface, ready to break through at any moment.

Too much work for so little pay . . . Flatter . . . Harder . . . Again . . .

Suddenly the sword the smith was working on cracked, sending pieces of hot metal flaring away like comets before sizzling against the damp stone floor of the shop.

More time and money gone . . . Too much work, even for the Kingpriest . . .

The smith lifted the broken sword away from the anvil and inspected the crack, and then its sharp, pointed tip.

Perhaps it's just sharp enough for the Kingpriest . . . Straight through the heart and a quick turn for good measure . . .

The mage gasped at the wickedness of the thought. To kill the Kingpriest was unthinkable. The mage simply could not allow such evil thoughts to fester in the smith's mind. And there was only one sure way to put a stop to them.

The mage closed his eyes and began to mumble a string of unintelligible words and syllables.

And as he did so, the smith began to sway as if he were beginning to feel dizzy. The smith shook his head slightly and closed his eyes, but still continued to sway.

At last the mage fell silent.

The spell had been cast.

The smith fell forward still holding the sword in his hands.

The hilt hit the floor and the sharp point pierced his throat, choking off his breath . . .

And putting an end to all his evil thoughts.

Chapter 10

Sunshine-filled days and rain-swept nights provided the perfect conditions for farming, and the farmers of Solamnia were already thanking Paladine for what they expected to be a bumper crop and bountiful harvest.

But for Lord Soth, the month of Holmswelt meant something else. Every summer the Knights of Solamnia traveled across Ansalon to meet and confer about everything from the training of squires, to the retirement of elderly knights, from the latest developments in weaponry and armor to scholarly studies of the Oath and The Measure.

The previous year, Soth had missed the annual meeting because of preparations for the wedding and the transfer of rule of Knightlund from his father to himself. This year however, Soth had to attend because, as a leading member of the Order of the Rose, he would be more than conspicuous by his absence.

And so, on the first day of Holmswelt, Soth and six of his loyal knights prepared for the three-day journey across the Solamnic plains to Palanthas, the great port city and the jewel of Solamnia.

Soth had chosen to take only six knights with him—Crown knights Caradoc, Kern and Krejlgaard, and Sword knights Valcic, Vingus, and Farold—the journey being something of a reward for their outstanding conduct over the course of the past twelve months. Soth took everything into consideration when making his choices, from bravery in battle against the ogres in Halton to keeping spirits and morale high throughout the long, cold winter. He might have been able to bring more knights with him, but with a limited number attending the meeting, that would have come at the expense of other Knights of Solamnia stationed elsewhere on the continent.

Besides, the system currently in use had proved best in terms of educating the entire knighthood. When Soth's six knights returned to Dargaard Keep, they would instruct the others in what they had learned. In this way *all* the Knights of Solamnia could grow stronger while those in Palanthas wouldn't have to scramble in order to accommodate every knight who wished to attend.

Out of respect for the hot summer sun, Soth dressed for the journey by wearing a light tunic and leggings and covered that with lightweight leather armor. He expected little trouble on the way and indeed there had only been a few uprisings (such as the ogre attack on Halton) ever since the Kingpriest of Istar's Proclamation of Manifest Virtue. The proclamation, made many years ago, had dealt a death blow to the minions of Evil still brave (or perhaps mad) enough to show themselves on the continent of Ansalon. At times Soth felt the Kingpriest was becoming too powerful for his own good, but that was something for clerics and politicians to decide. He was a warrior, and fought for the cause of Good in whatever guise it decided to manifest itself.

The six knights were already mounted upon their horses and waiting patiently while Soth said goodbye to Korinne. "The Knights' Meeting runs seven days. I will likely be gone twice that length of time."

"Take as much time as you need," said Korinne. "No more, no less."

Soth nodded. Korinne was a strong woman and had proved to be an excellent wife in all but one crucial area.

She looked at him with a glimmer of hope in her eyes. "Perhaps by the time you return—"

Soth cut off her words by placing his right index finger to her lips. He shook his head. "It pains me to continue to be so hopeful," he said, knowing the words would hurt Korinne, but not knowing any easier way to say them. "Perhaps it would be better for both of us if you would talk to me about children only when you are truly with child."

Korinne looked up at Soth, her lips pressed together to no doubt keep them from trembling. Her eyes looked wet and glassy, on the verge of tears. "Yes, milord."

He leaned forward to kiss her and felt her dry lips press against his cheek. He straightened up and looked at her for several moments wanting to say something but not knowing what. Finally, he turned away and mounted his horse.

"To Palanthas!" he said.

He led the knights slowly through the gate, under the portcullis and over the drawbridge leading out of Dargaard Keep. Although the portcullis remained up until they were well on their way and nearly out of sight of the keep, Soth never once looked back.

* * * * *

"A honed broadsword, a sturdy shield and a little plate armor is all a good Knight of Solamnia ever needs in battle," said Caradoc, riding alongside Soth as they neared the end of the first day on their journey to Palanthas. They had already discussed life in the keep, prospects of a good crop, and the charms of certain women Caradoc found "interesting." And now they were talking about weaponry, a subject that would have much attention paid to it when they reached the Knights' Meeting.

Soth was of a mind that there was more to weapons than simply a broadsword and shield. While they would always be the chosen weapon of the Knights of Solamnia for close man-to-man fighting, there were other weapons in development across the continent that would prove most effective should there ever be another large-scale war.

"A broadsword is a fine weapon," said Soth. "No doubt about it, but the great Huma Dragonbane proved that battling certain enemies requires specialized weaponry."

"Perhaps," said Caradoc, obviously not ready to fully concede his point.

"Take elven weapons for example," Soth continued. There were still many long hours ahead of them and conversations didn't necessarily have to end just because the other party was partially in agreement. "I hear talk that they have developed several types of arrowheads for use with their crossbows: a narrow spiked head for piercing armor; a heavy ironwood head for bashing; a razor-sharp Y-shaped head for cutting ropes, banners, legs and arms; a flanged leaf-shaped head for inflicting the maximum amount of damage; and a "singing" head that is fitted with a hollow tube that creates a piercing shriek when it's fired."

"Really?" Caradoc's eyes opened wide, perhaps in terror of the weapon, perhaps in amazement over its ingenuity.

"Yes, a dreadful weapon if there ever was one."

"I would be interested in seeing such a weapon."

"Eiwon van Sickle has told me that there will be examples of them on display in Palanthas. Demonstrations are scheduled as—"

Soth's words were cut off by a scream.

A woman's scream.

Instinctively, all the knights stopped in their tracks and listened for the sound again.

Moments later there was another scream, this one more faint and less sharp than the first. It was coming from somewhere up ahead and to the left. Soth looked in the direction and saw that the trail crested slightly in the distance. On the left of the trail the tops of several trees could be seen peaking over the horizon. The dip on the other side of the crest had to be fairly deep considering that the valley had given rise to a small forest in the midst of the plain.

There was yet another scream, this one different from the first two. Obviously there was more than one woman in peril.

Without a word, Soth gave his mount a kick in the ribs.

The large, black horse shot forward and was quickly running at full speed toward the forest.

And without even losing a step, the knights were right there with him, three on each side.

Soth slowed as he came over a crest. Below he could see what looked to be an encampment. It was a small clearing at the edge of the forest, a place where many travelers had rested on the road between Palanthas and Dargaard Keep. Except these travelers were not resting. Judging by their screams, it sounded as if they were being tormented.

But by whom?

Soth cut to the left and headed for the edge of the forest in the hopes that the knights could reach the woods without being seen. After slowing to assess the situation, he stepped up the pace again. Time appeared to be of the essence.

Upon reaching the edge of the forest, Soth gestured to Colm Farold to take two knights around the other side of the woods while Soth and the three remaining knights went to investigate what was going on in the clearing.

The forest was small and in no time Soth and his knights had circled back to the clearing. When the camp came into view, things suddenly became clearer.

Much clearer.

Whoever had made camp had been ambushed by a

small party of ogres. Soth could see one of the brutes, holding someone to the ground. The screams coming from the person beneath the ogre sounded muffled, yet the terror contained within the scream was real.

Soth dismounted and ran to where the ogre wrestled to subdue his victim. Drawing his sword as he approached, he gave the brute a kick to the ribs to announce his arrival.

That seemed to get the ogre's attention.

He rolled off his victim and onto the grass. An elderly elf-woman lay on the grass, eyes wide with fright, body trembling in fear.

The ogre held his midsection tightly and struggled to catch his breath. When he looked up and saw Soth towering over him, he searched the ground for his weapon, but it was too far away to be of any use. Quickly he stood up and prepared to fight Soth with his bare hands.

Soth wasn't about to battle an unarmed opponent with his broadsword, but then what constituted a fair fight with an ogre? Thankfully, the ogre settled the matter himself by picking up a sturdy nearby branch, using it as a pike.

The ogre thrust the branch forward, but Soth was able to deflect the blows with his shield. Then the ogre decided to sweep the ground with the branch hoping to knock Soth off his feet. Soth was able to step quickly enough to avoid the sweeping branch, then managed to go on the offensive while the ogre was bringing the branch back into position.

Wielding his sword with a single hand, Soth brought it straight down upon the ogre. But instead of splitting the beast in two, the blow was blocked by the branch, which only chipped and splintered.

After several near misses for each of the combatants, Soth was able to execute another overhanded blow. Again the ogre protected himself with the branch, but this time the blow broke it in two, giving the ogre two too-short clubs and rendering him once again weaponless.

This time, however, Soth had no qualms about battling

an unarmed ogre. While the ogre was still looking dumb-founded at the broken wood in his hands, Soth lunged for-ward running the beast through with his sword.

After crying out in pain, the ogre looked at Soth with a mix of shock and terror for several long moments before Soth wiped the look from his face with a backhanded swipe of his shield. The ogre's eyes suddenly glazed over and turned upward as he fell heavily to the ground.

Dead.

Wasting little time, Soth ran to the elderly elf-woman who had been helped off the ground by Darin Valcic and Zander Vingus. Apparently, as Soth had been finishing off the ogre, they'd made sure she wasn't in any danger, then ventured into the forest in search of more of the foul beasts.

"Are you all right?" Soth asked, seeing a thin line of blood running down from her pointed left ear.

"I think so," she nodded, her eyes staring blankly before her. "We're on pilgrimage to Palanthas," she said. "To become Revered Daughters of Paladine." A sigh. "We stopped here for the night. We were just about to begin our prayers when . . . when . . . they came."

"How many ogres were there?" asked Soth, his voice as calm and soothing as he could make it under the cir-cumstances.

"Five or six. Maybe more. It was so hard to tell, they all look so much alike. Hideous, horrible . . ." The shock of her ordeal was beginning to settle in and she began to weep.

Soth had to know one last thing.

"How many in your party?"

"Five. Myself and . . . four young maidens." She drew in a sudden gasp in realization. "Oh merciful Mishakal! What's become of them?"

Soth knew the woman needed further comfort, but there were others in greater danger. If there were ogres in the forest, his six knights would need all the help they could get in finding and defeating them.

"Will you be all right on your own for a short while?"

The question seemed to give the elf-woman reason to compose herself. She sniffed once and nodded. "Go find the others. I'll be well enough."

"Good," said Soth, rising up and heading into the forest.

* * * * *

"There's two of them over there," said Colm Farold, pointing to a small clearing just through the trees.

"Three," said Wersten Kern, pointing to the right side of the clearing.

"So there are."

Kris Krejlgaard came up behind the two knights after circling the clearing. "It looks as if they've captured a group of elf-maidens. Two of the women are tied to trees just past those bushes. They appear to be unharmed, but it's hard to tell from a distance."

"Any other ogres?" asked Farold.

"Not in the immediate area," answered Krejlgaard. "I heard some voices in that direction, but Caradoc was over that way and further along should be Valcic and Vingus."

"Very well then," nodded Farold. "We'll sweep through the woods in that direction once we're done here. Did you see any weapons?"

"A few clubs and swords, maybe some daggers. Nothing out of the ordinary for ogres."

"Anything else?"

"There's a formidable foul stench downwind of them. It burned my eyes and seared my throat."

Farold turned to Krejlgaard and gave a little smile. "All right then. There are some maidens in distress. Let's save them, shall we?"

The three knights rose up proudly, drew their swords and rushed into the clearing with a loud, sharp battle cry.

* * * * *

There was the sound of running water up ahead. That seemed strange to Caradoc because he hadn't seen any creeks or streams cutting through the forest.

He took two more cautious steps forward, using his broadsword to part the overhanging branches ahead of him.

And then there he was.

An ogre.

Relieving himself against a tree.

The ogre's weapons were lying on the ground several feet away. Caradoc laughed inwardly at the sight. Such a vulnerable position for an ogre to find himself in—for any warrior to find himself in for that matter.

He took a few more steps toward the ogre and smacked his hairy behind with the flat side of his broadsword.

"Ow!" cried the ogre, turning around to see which of his fellows had been so brazen. When he saw Caradoc he was suddenly in a hurry to finish relieving himself, but his body didn't seem to be cooperating.

Caradoc couldn't help but laugh at the ugly brute as he struggled to finish his business while he hurriedly tried to collect his weapons off the ground.

"If you were at all familiar with the Oath and the Measure," said Caradoc, a bit of smug confidence to his voice, "you would know that it is against the Knights of Solamnia's code of ethics to battle an unarmed opponent in anything other than a fair fight."

The ogre seemed to be comforted to hear this and calmly went about finishing his business against the tree.

The beast's sudden casual demeanor angered Caradoc. It was obvious that the ogres had attacked innocent and defenseless travelers, robbing and looting them, and Paladine only knows what else. In just a few moments they had turned an otherwise peaceful journey into a nightmare of horrors. And now the ogre thought he'd be getting a fighting chance just because the knights happened to be governed by a strict and chivalric code. Well, it was obvious to Caradoc that the ogres lived by no such honorable code of conduct, so why should he be bound by honor in a fight with one of them?

"But since you've probably never even heard of the Oath and the Measure," Caradoc continued, his voice now edged with a hint of contempt. "I see no good reason why I should remain bound to it."

Caradoc immediately raised his sword and swung it from left to right, the sharp cutting edge leading the way.

Almost at once, the ogre's head became separated from its shoulders. It spun in the air and hit the ground with a thud, its mouth open and its eyes wide in a look of utter surprise.

A moment later, the ogre's great body fell to the ground like a tree, covering the upturned head and face with its trunk.

"Stupid savage," said Caradoc, wiping his bloody sword on some of the leaves around him.

Just then, a loud call came from somewhere to his left. He headed in that direction, the pointed tip of his sword leading the way.

* * * * *

After leaving the elderly elf-woman behind, Soth quickly came upon two more ogres, one a black-haired giant standing a head taller than Soth himself, the other red-headed and somewhat shorter than the first, perhaps even equal in height to Soth.

The black-haired ogre was holding an elf-maiden in his arms, moving his great thick-fingered hands over her seemingly lifeless body. If the elf-maiden was dead, Soth vowed, the ogre's death would be slow and painful. The red-headed ogre seemed to be asleep on the ground on the other side of a large log. He was of little concern to Soth.

Soth decided to battle the black-haired ogre first and charged headlong in that direction.

Seeing Soth approaching, the ogre dropped the elf-maiden onto the soft layer of humus covering the forest floor. In another second he was up on both feet, sword before him and ready to fight. The ogre wielded a heavy clabbard style of sword, a type of weapon most often used by minotaurs, but just as easily wielded by large and powerful ogres. Soth noticed the weapon, saw the cutting edge backed with a serrated saw-toothed edge that could cut through his leather armor with ease, and suddenly became more cautious. Obviously, these ogres were much fiercer warriors than the ones they'd encountered in Halton. These were nomadic marauders, used to fighting—and *defeating*—an assortment of foes.

That fact was evidenced as Soth realized that this ogre wasn't about to show Soth any amount of respect or proceed with any caution. He lumbered forward, swinging his clabbard sword as easily as Soth might wield a dagger.

Soth held out his sword in an attempt to slow the ogre's progress, but to no avail. The ogre kept charging, forcing Soth to leap to the side. He was almost out of the way, but was caught by the ogre's shoulder. The hard impact sent Soth flying backward through the air. He landed with a hard thump that nearly knocked the air from his lungs.

As Soth clambered to get back to his feet, he felt his clenched hands gather up soft dirt and leaves from the forest floor. For a moment he considered blinding the ogre by throwing the mix into his eyes, but decided the tactic was too foul and very much beneath him. Instead he found a large rock about half the size of a loaf of bread and picked it up. Then as the ogre made a second charge, Soth threw the rock at the ogre's head.

The rock's flight was true, and when it hit the ogre's forehead, the sound it made reminded Soth of solid rock colliding with solid rock.

Following the blow, the ogre stumbled a few more steps then stopped, blinking several times as if unsure where he was. Soth let out a slight sigh of relief and felt pleased with himself at recalling the squire's second rule. Simply stated it was this: No matter how well-armed or armored an opponent is, he can still be killed by a simple blow to the head.

This ogre wasn't dead yet, but he was dazed.

Severely so.

The ogre staggered forward, then back, then forward again. Soth followed his path for a few moments, then decided he'd had enough. With the ogre so incapacitated, it was a simple matter to run the beast through with his sword.

When the fallen ogre was lying still on the ground, Soth moved forward to take a better look at the creature.

He took one step . . .

And was sent hurtling forward by a heavy blow to the small of his back. As Soth tripped over the fallen black-haired ogre, he realized he'd forgotten about the red-headed one sleeping on the other side of the log. When Soth hit the ground, he did his best to roll and rise up to his feet, but several of his ribs were bruised and any sudden movements sent pain shooting up through his body.

Yet despite the pain, he somehow made it onto his feet and managed to turn and face his attacker.

Thankfully the red-headed ogre was the smaller of the two. But even so, Soth would have been hard-pressed to defeat the ogre at the best of times. Now, with his bruised, or perhaps even broken ribs, the ogre would prove to be more than a match for him.

"The forest is full of Knights of Solamnia," said Soth, hoping to scare the ogre off and avoid having to fight him at close quarters. "If you turn and run now, you'll be able to leave this forest with your life."

The ogre simply laughed, a loud mocking call that boomed through the woods. Soth said nothing, hoping the ogre's laugh would rally the knights around him.

But as the seconds passed, Soth began to get the feeling that he was alone in this fight. Very well then, he thought, raising his sword to confront the beast.

The ogre also carried a sword, one that was slightly wider and longer than Soth's own. Usually this would put Soth at a disadvantage, but it appeared that the ogre was unable to wield the weapon without the use of both hands, which might be enough to tip the balance in Soth's favor.

"Only one way to find out," he muttered, moving forward to confront the beast.

Almost at once their swords came together, clanging and singing as they banged and scraped against one another with each mighty blow. Soth quickly realized that it would be impossible for him to match the ogre blow-for-blow. Instead he began moving left and right in order to avoid having to counter as many blows as possible. Soon the ogre began to tire, his movements becoming wilder and wilder with each progressively sluggish swing of his sword.

Frustrated, the ogre held his sword before him and charged at Soth, most likely hoping to get close enough to render their swords useless and to force them to switch to wrestling and barehanded fighting. Needless to say, Soth wanted no part of that, given that he was in no condition to try and kill an ogre with his bare hands.

So, as the ogre came toward him, he ducked down to the ground, falling on his hands and knees and turning himself into an obstacle too large for the ogre to avoid.

Soth winced in pain as the ogre's heavy shins slammed into his side, but the tactic had paid off. Like a tree cut off at its stump, the ogre began to fall.

By the time the beast hit the ground, Soth was already on his feet towering over him. The ogre was dazed by the fall and had even cut himself by falling on top of his own blade. The wound wasn't enough to keep him down however, and Soth had to quickly see to it that the ogre would never be getting up again.

He clasped both hands around the upturned hilt of his sword and drove the point of his blade downward with all his might, through the ogre and into the soft ground beneath him.

The breath came out of the ogre's body in a *whoosh*, and then all was silent.

All except for . . .

Soth listened closely for the faint sound.

There was a low moan coming from somewhere nearby. He looked at the elf-maid the dark-haired ogre had laid upon the ground, but she was nowhere to be seen. More than likely she had run from the scene as soon as she was able.

Who, or what then, was making the sound?

Something caught Soth's attention, a slight movement in the left corner of his field of vision. There seemed to be another maiden, this one fair-haired, lying on the other side of the large fallen log.

Soth pulled his sword from the ground and turned to investigate.

At first he feared the woman dead.

Her face was pressed hard against the forest floor and all he could see was the dirty blond hair that covered the back of her head and shoulders. Her body appeared to be still and without breath. For a moment, Soth cursed the ogres for their deeds, but then came the familiar moan.

Quickly, Soth leaped over the log and rolled the elf-maiden gently onto her side. Then he removed his leather gauntlet from his right hand and wiped the dirt and humus from the maiden's face with the tips of his fingers.

Even through the dirt and grime that remained on her visage, Soth could see that she was utterly beautiful. Anger at the ogres flared within him once more as he thought about what the ugly brutes had done to this lovely, innocent flower and her companions.

He removed the gauntlet from his left hand and eased her body off the ground, sitting her upright against the log. Her body was thin and limp beneath her flowing pale green and brown robes. Still, despite the fact that she was barely heavier than a handful of down, Soth had the feeling she was a very strong woman.

When she was finally sitting comfortably Soth brushed more of her face clean, marveling at the prominence of her high cheekbones, the delicate points of her ears, and the softness of her goose-white skin, skin that had unfortunately been marred in spots by bruises and scrapes.

She was breathing easier now, yet still unconscious. Soth reached down around his waist and opened up a small pouch. Inside was a mixture of sharp and pungent herbs that Soth had used many times to awaken knights who had been knocked unconscious by a blow to the head.

He took a pinch of the mixture and held it under the maiden's nose. When she did not stir, he rubbed the herbs between his fingers, releasing a sharp new aroma into the air.

Finally she jerked her head away. Slowly, her eyelids began to rise. After several false starts, her eyes finally fluttered open. They were hazel in color, indicating to Soth that—considering the color of her hair and complexion of her skin—the party of elf-maidens on its way to Palanthas had probably originated in Silvanesti.

She turned her head to look at him . . .

And Soth felt his heart begin to pound beneath his breastplate like that of a squire sneaking a peek through the window of a lady's bedchamber.

She was strikingly attractive, her beauty perhaps even rivaling that of Lady Korinne. But more than simple beauty was the air of nobility and grace she exuded, a quality that refused to be dulled, even by coming into contact with the rough and jagged edges of the ogres.

"Are you all right?" Soth asked softly, a little surprised to find his mouth dry as dust.

"Yes," she said, the word sounding slightly melodic, as if it had been plucked from the middle of a verse. "I think so. Who . . . who are you?"

Soth eased one knee onto the ground and placed his arms on the other. He slipped off his helm and said, "I'm Lord Loren Soth of Dargaard Keep, Knight of the Rose."

She smiled at him and said, "You saved my life."

Soth opened his mouth to speak, but words would not come.

He gently helped the elf-maiden to her feet and began to lead her through the forest toward the clearing where he expected to find both the knights and maidens gathered. After a few steps it became apparent that the elf-maid had twisted her ankle during her struggle with the ogre. It was at least sprained, perhaps even broken.

"Allow me," offered Soth, scooping the woman up in his arms and carrying her the rest of the way.

"Oh," the elf-maid said as she was lifted off the ground.

"It's easier this way," said Soth, trying to make light of the close contact which might or might not have been necessary. If she had been an ugly old maid, would he have offered to carry her? Probably, but he would have done so a lot less enthusiastically.

"Perhaps I should introduce myself," said the maiden, her voice sounding to his ears like that of a songbird.

"I was curious as to your name."

"It's Isolde," she said, putting her arms around his neck to steady herself as he stepped over a fallen tree. "Isolde Denissa."

"A lovely name," said Soth. "For a lovely elf."

She smiled at that. "So you're charming as well as brave, strong and handsome." She rested her head against his shoulder.

Soth felt warm all over and found himself firming up his grip even though there was no danger of dropping the lithe young elf.

As he stepped into the clearing however, the feeling of warmth vanished as he came under the scrutiny of his fellow knights and the elderly elf-woman.

Did she look too comfortable in his arms? Could his sudden—he tried to think of the right word—*affection* for her be so easily discerned from the look on his face?

"Is she all right?" asked the elf-woman, who had

undoubtedly been charged with the care of the maidens.

The question jarred Soth's train of thought. Of course, with her eyes closed and her head resting upon his shoulder, she appeared to be near death in their eyes. "She's been injured, but"—he paused for a moment as a wild thought leaped forward in his mind, quelling all other thoughts—"it's nothing the healer won't be able to mend." He put her down on the ground to reunite her with her fellow travelers.

"The healer?" asked Colm Farold, looking the elf-maiden over. "She doesn't look to be in need of Istvan."

"On the outside no, but she appears to have suffered"—he hesitated slightly—"internal injuries which might be best left to the healer to remedy. She may very well heal on her own, but it's always best to be sure."

Farold gave Soth a curious look, but dared not contradict his lord twice. "Very well, milord. We can always attend the Knights' Meeting next year."

Soth raised his hand dramatically. "No," he said. "These elf-maidens were on a holy pilgrimage to Palanthas. It is your duty as a Knight of Solamnia to see they arrive there without further harm."

"Our duty?" asked Farold. "You say that as if you won't be coming with us."

"I won't," said Soth. "I will be escorting the injured elf-maid back to Dargaard Keep while you and the others continue on to Palanthas. Deliver them safely so that they may pledge themselves to Paladine, father of all that is good. Then, attend the Knights' Meeting as heroes worthy of the title Knights of Solamnia."

Farold smiled with pride and gratitude. Arriving in Palanthas escorting a group of maidens they'd rescued from ogre bandits would make the knights the talk of the entire meeting, a rare opportunity for the knights to be regarded with the highest esteem by their peers. "Thank you, milord."

Soth shrugged his shoulders. "After she is in the care of

the healer, I'll once again set out for Palanthas and join you there. You must extend my apologies to the grand master, and conduct yourselves with the utmost honor and decorum in my absence."

"I will, milord," said Farold. "*We* will."

Soth nodded, then turned to inform the maidens of their plans.

"My knights will be escorting you the rest of the way to Palanthas," he told the elderly elf-woman. "Meanwhile, I will be taking Isolde Denissa back to Dargaard Keep where she can receive proper aid at the hands of the keep's healer."

The elf-woman tilted her head back and looked at Soth down the length of her nose. "I've looked her over and her injuries seem to be minor. I think she's healthy enough to continue on with us to Palanthas, but thank you very much for your most generous offer."

The elf-woman was probably several hundred years old and had likely seen a great many things in her lifetime. She had acquired great wisdom through her years of experience and for that reason alone deserved Soth's respect. Nevertheless, he couldn't allow her to meddle with his plan.

"It's not an offer," he said plainly.

She looked at him with narrowing eyes. "You mentioned Dargaard Keep before. Who are you exactly?"

Soth realized that their first meeting had been somewhat rushed and they'd never properly introduced themselves. "I . . . am Lord Loren Soth of Dargaard Keep, Knight of the Rose."

A mixture of shock, surprise and embarrassment traversed the old woman's face at the mention of his name. Apparently she had heard of Soth at some point in her long life.

"Excuse me, *milord*," she said, using the word even though she was not required to do so. "I was dubious of your intentions, but now that I know who you are I have no doubt that Isolde will be safe in your care." She finished her words by lowering her head slightly, an unmistakable sign of respect.

"You have my word as a Knight of Solamnia," said Soth. "No harm will come to her."

* * * * *

The ride back to Dargaard Keep was taken at a slow pace as the bump and jostle of a hard ride might further injure the young elf-maid.

For much of the time, Soth trailed Isolde by a horse length to the left. As they rode slowly across the plains he watched her ride, her long thin legs draped over the horse and sometimes made bare by a sudden gust of wind. The wind also played through her hair, making her dirty blond locks dance like flames in the light of the sun.

And even though Soth had never imagined that he'd be so enamored by an elf—in fact he'd never been particularly fond of the race to begin with—he somehow found himself becoming attracted to the maiden. Perhaps it was her mix of youthful innocence and womanly beauty, or perhaps it was the look of awe in her eyes when she spoke and looked at him. Whatever it was, he was enchanted by her. Of that, there could be no doubt.

"I'm becoming weary," said Isolde. "Can we stop for a little while?"

Soth scanned the surrounding landscape. It was barren and flat and the sun beat down on them mercilessly. He would have liked to have stopped by a stand of trees or a rock formation, but he wasn't about to suggest that Isolde continue on if she didn't feel up to it.

"All right, we can stop here. But not for long."

"Thank you, milord."

"You may call me Loren."

"Very well . . . Loren."

They stopped on the trail and Isolde waited until Soth

had dismounted and could assist her from her mount. He reached up, put his hands about her waist and eased her off the horse. Before her feet touched the ground Isolde put her arms around Soth's neck and held him close.

"I wanted to thank you for all you've done."

Soth was surprised by how tightly Isolde held onto him, or perhaps surprised that she was so at ease when there were only inches between them.

"It was nothing, really," said Soth, holding Isolde aloft because she didn't seem in any hurry to get her feet onto the ground. "I did nothing that any Knight of Solamnia wouldn't have done in a similar circumstance."

"Perhaps, but it wasn't just any Knight of Solamnia who saved me, it was you."

"But—"

His words were cut off by a kiss.

A deep soulful kiss, more passionate than mere thanks would require.

Soth hesitated at first, but quickly felt himself giving in to the moment until he returned the kiss with as much urgency as it was given.

It was a long time before Isolde's feet touched the ground.

* * * * *

When Dargaard Keep was well within their sights and he knew he would be seen from the highest of the keep's towers, Soth felt the warm summer's breeze touch the back of his neck like a cold, cold hand.

It had been so easy to kiss Isolde.

It had felt so natural. It was natural, too, that they ride together on his horse, leaving hers to trail riderless behind them.

But now with the red rose of Dargaard Keep blooming on the horizon, his thoughts turned to Lady Korinne and he felt a churning in the pit of his stomach, almost as if he were going to be sick.

Did his attraction to Isolde mean that his love for Lady Korinne was waning? After all, Lady Korinne was herself an attractive woman whose beauty was known throughout Ansalon. Then why had he so easily forgotten about her upon seeing Isolde? What was it about the elf-maid that would prompt him to forget his lovely, loyal and most-cherished wife? What did Isolde possess that Korinne did not?

He couldn't think of anything.

He'd merely been attracted by her appearance. And while she was stunningly attractive, her looks were no reason for him to lose his head and start acting like a lovesick young boy. But while there wasn't anything wrong with lusting after beautiful young women, elf or otherwise, (he was married, not dead, after all) it was another matter entirely if he chose to act upon his emotions.

The kiss had been an aberration, he thought, vowing to have Isolde's injuries taken care of, then send her off to Palanthas with an escort so that she could rejoin her fellow maidens.

"Almost there," he said.

Isolde craned her neck to see the top of the keep over Soth's shoulder. "Where are your chambers?" she asked.

"The second window from the top on the left side of the tower," he said.

"And that's where you sleep?"

Soth considered telling her that it was the room where both he and Lady Korinne slept, but for some reason he did not. Instead, he merely said, "Yes."

* * * * *

"Lord Soth returns!"
"Milord approaches!"
The loud shouts echoed down from the tower's two top observation posts almost at the same time.

Immediately upon hearing the words, Lady Korinne felt her heart drop like a stone into the pit of her stomach.

Something had to be wrong.

The Knights' Meeting was to have lasted seven days and her husband was not to have returned for at least ten, or perhaps for even two weeks, yet here he was returning just two days after leaving. He hadn't even reached Palanthas.

A lump of worry gathered in Korinne's throat as she hurried to the window of her bedchamber. The room was high up in the keep with a view that stretched all the way to the Vingaard River. If the sky was clear, she'd likely be able to see her husband's approach.

She scanned the horizon and picked out two horses far off in the distance making their way toward the keep. There appeared to be two riders, but she couldn't be sure. One was obviously Lord Soth, his size, shape and the deep rose-red color of his leather armor unmistakable even at this distance. The other traveler was much harder to identify. Clearly the rider was not a knight, being too small and slender to belong to any of the orders.

At one point, the two horses turned slightly to one side. At once, Korinne saw that the trailing horse was riderless, while the second rider sat directly behind Lord Soth.

She shifted her gaze back onto her husband. From the way he was riding, it was obvious that he was unharmed.

She was relieved but the lump of worry was still knotted in her throat. In fact, it seemed to have grown larger.

If he hadn't been injured, then why was he returning so early, and in the company of a woman? A woman who rode with her arms wrapped tightly around the waist of Korinne's husband.

BOOK TWO
KNIGHT'S FALL

Chapter 11

By the time Soth reached Dargaard Keep, dozens of people had
gathered just inside the gate to receive him. There was a
buzz traveling through the crowd and speculation ran
rampant with theories ranging from an ambush and
slaughter on the trail, to the discovery of a lost lone traveler brought back to the keep for her own safety.

When Soth and Isolde entered the keep, something of a
stunned silence came over those gathered as they recognized the maiden's beauty to be quite extraordinary.

Soth stopped his horse and dismounted. "Where is
Istvan?" he shouted, his voice tinged with just a hint of
urgency.

"Here I am, milord!" said the elderly healer. In his prime
Istvan had been a short man of stocky build with a full
head of thick brown hair. Now, after more than twenty
years of service as healer, first for all of Knightlund and
now within Dargaard Keep, his dark brown mane had
turned white and flowed down over his shoulders like tattered white threads. He was also thinner and scraggier—

some might even say emaciated—than he'd been in his youth, yet despite his lack of bulk, he was still quite nimble, especially considering his age.

But nimblest of all was his mind, not only in areas of healing, in which he had no rival, but also in areas of keep politics. No one understood the internal machinations of the keep and the knighthood better than he. For that reason he had managed to offend no one in all his years of service and had maintained his position for decades despite changes in rule and shifts in allegiance.

Soth helped Isolde down from her pillion. When her feet touched the ground, much of her weight was placed on her injured ankle causing her to stumble. Soth made an overly dramatic gesture to help steady her and turned to Istvan with a look of grave concern.

"She was injured in an ogre raid on her traveling party. She's in desperate need of your attention."

Isolde grimaced at the pain in her ankle.

Istvan looked the elf-maid over, quickly inspecting her wounds and using what he saw to make a general assessment of the injuries he could not see.

From the look on his face it was obvious to Soth that the healer thought her injuries to be minor, nothing that a few days rest wouldn't cure.

He glanced up at the lord of the keep with a look that asked, "Why are you wasting my time with such superficial cuts and bruises?"

Soth merely stared at him, knowing his steel-gray eyes could be as piercing as daggers when he needed them to be.

In a moment, without a word being spoken, Istvan understood.

"Quickly," shouted Istvan to his assistants. "Take her to my chambers. Prepare the comfrey and yarrow." He clapped his hands together twice and his assistants swung into action, carefully escorting the elf-maid away.

Then Istvan turned to face Soth. "She will recover, milord," he said, his head bowed. "I give you my word."

Soth nodded to the healer. "Well done."

"Thank you, milord," Istvan answered, turning in haste to follow the elf-maid as she was carried to his chambers.

Soth glanced around, noticing that all eyes were on Isolde. Including those of Lady Korinne.

* * * * *

Lady Korinne watched the elf-maid being taken away to the healer's chambers then turned to look at her husband. She was surprised to find his gaze lingering on the doorway the elf-maid had just been taken through, but dismissed it as his simply being concerned with the woman's well-being.

She walked over to him. "Milord," she said when there was still some distance between them. Then as she came closer, "Loren," she whispered.

Soth turned, smiled upon seeing his wife then greeted her with an embrace and a kiss. The kiss was less passionate than Korinne would have liked, but he had been traveling for some time and was probably weary from the journey.

"Are you all right?" she asked.

"Yes," he answered plainly.

"What happened?"

Soth took a deep breath and began explaining how the knights came upon the encampment, rescued the elf-maids and routed the offending ogres. As they walked through the keep, several other people including many knights followed, all keen on hearing the details of his foreshortened journey.

"And her?" Korinne asked when Soth was done with his story, nodding her head in the direction of the healer's chambers.

"Who? Isolde?" said Soth.

Korinne inhaled a slight gasp at her husband's mention of the elf-maid's name. There was something too familiar, too personal about it. "Yes," she said. "Isolde."

"I found her face down on the ground. She'd been savaged by an ogre, or at least the attempt had been made. According to her account of what happened, she put up a respectable fight. And her wounds bear her out."

Korinne suddenly felt foolish for doubting her husband's intentions. Although the elf-maid was quite beautiful and she was instinctively jealous of her youthful appearance—what human woman wouldn't be?— Korinne concluded that her husband had acted as any Knight of Solamnia would have in accordance to the rules of conduct set forth within the Oath and the Measure. It was in his power to help the elf, so he did so. There was nothing more to it than that. "The poor creature," she said at last, her voice edged with pity.

"Indeed," answered Soth.

For some reason, the word sent a chill down Korinne's spine.

* * * * *

"Lord Soth," said the healer. "You may see him now."

Soth rose up off the bench, his legs made stiff from the hours he'd sat there waiting.

Waiting for the birth of his son.

He entered the room. It smelled quite foul, much like a battlefield, tinged with the scent of blood and other bodily fluids. The healer's assistants were busy changing the sheets on the lower half of the bed while the child itself was being cleaned behind a curtain in a shadowy corner of the room. His wife lay still on the bed, sleeping after what was no doubt an exhausting ordeal.

He waited.

His body hummed with anticipation.

At last the healer approached, a small bundle in his arms. He handed the bundle to Soth and the knight fumbled with it as if all his fingers had been replaced by thumbs. When he had the child steady, he raised a hand and lifted the part of the blanket covering the child's face.

Soth awoke with a start, his body shivering despite the fact that several warm blankets were covering him. He looked to his left and was grateful to see that his abrupt awakening hadn't disturbed his wife. She was still sleeping as soundly as ever.

He closed his eyes and reflected upon the dream, then did his best to block it from his mind. He hadn't been bothered by his dreams in months. This one, he decided, had been an aberration. He would not dwell on this dream as he had done with the others in the past.

He opened his eyes once more and slid out from beneath the covers, leaving Korinne to sleep because it was still well before dawn. Then he got dressed and headed down to the keep's kitchen for a quick bite to eat.

He was met there by Meyer Seril who would be joining him on the journey back to the Knights' Meeting. Although it was unlikely that Soth would run into trouble on the way—running into the band of ogres had been an extraordinary circumstance as it was—he preferred to have company on such an extended trip. If the Council didn't like the fact that he'd brought an extra uninvited knight to the event, then they would have to send them both back to Dargaard Keep.

After eating their fill of fruit, eggs and cheese, Soth sent Seril to prepare the horses for the journey while he went to the healer's chambers to check on the condition of the elf-maid.

When he reached the healer's chambers he stepped quietly up to the door and was about to knock when the door suddenly opened up before him.

Istvan was standing there, his right index finger pressed against his lips suggesting that Soth should keep quiet. "She's asleep," he said in a whisper.

Soth nodded. "How is she?"

"She suffered bruises to her body, mainly to the extremities, but I suspect there were also injuries on the inside, ones which I could not see but nevertheless require an extended period of healing."

Soth smiled. His knights suffered such injuries all of the time and were required to get along with their daily routines as best they could while they healed. Obviously, Istvan was making a big deal about the elf-maid's condition, certainly more than was required for her to make a complete recovery.

"You've done well, Istvan," said Soth. "I look forward to seeing her completely healed upon my return."

Istvan looked at Soth for several seconds, running his bony fingers over the coarse white stubble of his beard. And then his face brightened, as if the gist of what Soth was saying had just dawned upon him.

"I understand completely, milord."

"Good," said Soth. "Is there anything you are lacking that I may be able to pick up for you in Palanthas?"

Istvan smiled, then stroked his chin once again. "Let me think," he said. "I've heard they have ground blue hyssop for sale in some of the finer shops in Palanthas."

"Is this a rare herb?" asked Soth.

Istvan nodded. "One of the few I have done without."

"Then you shall have some."

Soth quickly left Istvan and joined Meyer Seril just inside the keep's gate.

"All ready?"

"Yes milord, except for . . ." Seril gestured behind Soth with a nod.

Soth turned. Lady Korinne was standing there, a deep rose-red robe wrapped around her nightdress. Soth went to her.

"You've come to see me off," he said.

"Yes."

"You didn't have to, but the gesture is greatly appreciated." Korinne smiled.

Soth kissed her goodbye.

* * * * *

As she watched her husband ride out through the keep's gate and over the drawbridge, Lady Korinne pulled her robe more tightly around her body. Although it was the middle of Holmswelt, the mornings inside Dargaard Keep were still quite chilly.

She contemplated the good-bye kiss her husband had given her. Like the morning, it had been cold and passionless, a kiss one might expect from a brother, cousin, or uncle.

Was her husband's love for her waning? The thought made her shiver.

As she watched him descend onto the plain heading for Palanthas, she realized that for the first time since their marriage, Soth had left without once asking her if she was with child.

Apparently he'd meant what he'd said about not speaking of children until she was sure.

With that thought, the morning air seemed even colder.

Once Soth and Meyer Seril were out of sight of the keep, Lady Korinne postponed returning to her chambers and made a trip to the healer's chambers instead.

When she arrived she knocked lightly on the wooden door, making sure to be careful not to disturb anyone who was not yet awake. After a short wait she knocked again. When there was still no answer, she tried the door. Much to her surprise, it opened.

Korinne looked down the hall in both directions before entering the chambers. Inside the sunlight that was usually shining brightly through the windows at this time of day was blocked by fabrics that had been draped over the openings. The deep reds and greens of the fabrics gave the room a soft and comfortable glow.

Korinne waited just inside the door for several moments, waiting for Istvan to appear from the shadows as he was sometimes known to do. But as time passed, it became obvious that Istvan was not here. Perhaps he had gone for breakfast, or was preparing some mixture. Whatever the reason, he'd left the elf-maid alone.

It was too good an opportunity to miss. Korinne moved deeper into Istvan's chamber and searched for the elf-maid. She was sleeping on a bed at the far end of the room, covered to the neck by a light-colored blanket. Korinne moved closer in order to get a better look at the maid.

When she was standing next to the bed, Korinne felt her heart sinking like a stone in a river. The elf-maid was beautiful, a stunning example of the sort of elven beauty that had made the race famous throughout Krynn for their grace, comeliness and elegance.

How could a human woman compare to a creature possessing such fair skin and hair, such a lithe and supple form? How could a human woman compare herself to an elf-maid?

Korinne thought of that for a moment.

And let out a little laugh.

How foolish could she be? How *could* she compare herself to an elf-maid? There was no comparison. Surely her husband was aware of that fact. Korinne was still young and it would be many years before her own beauty began to fade. And even if Lord Soth found the elf-maid attractive, she was still his wife and according to the Oath and the Measure that was a bond that was as highly honored and respected as the one linking him to the knighthood.

What's more, Korinne was in the prime of her life, ready and more than willing to produce an heir to the much-heralded Soth family name. It would make their union complete, draw her even closer to him.

Ready and willing, she thought.

But unable.

The worry that had fled her heart and mind just seconds earlier, came back with a vengeance.

She turned to leave the healer's chambers, her hand groping the wall in order to keep herself steady as she walked.

Chapter 12

The city of Istar seemed barren.

Lifeless.

The elderly mage moved through the streets, his thoughts wandering aimlessly, much in the same way as did his feet.

When the Kingpriest first introduced The Edict of Thought Control it had sounded like such a good idea. Indeed, how better to prevent evil deeds than to put an end to evil thoughts?

How better to stop a rose from blooming than to nip it in the bud?

What had sounded good in theory had turned into a nightmare in practice. Since the introduction of the edict, children had lost their parents, wives had lost their husbands, and husbands had lost their wives.

And for what?

For evil thoughts that might or might not have manifested themselves into evil deeds. The edict lacked any consideration for the faculties of human reason and self-control. It was based on the belief that human beings were little more than animals who acted upon every impulse and instinct without consideration for any of the consequences of their actions.

Such was simply not the case.

People were basically good at heart. Sometimes the evil side of them came to the surface, but that was just a part of being human.

But despite all these thoughts, the mage continued to practice his craft on behalf of the Kingpriest in the hopes that the Kingpriest would eventually realize the damage his edict was doing to the people of Istar. Once that happened, surely he would revoke the edict and life would return to something resembling normalcy.

In the meantime, he continued to read minds.

Up ahead in the middle of the street a mother was scolding her child for dropping a bag of fruit onto the ground. This, after the child had assured his mother that he would not let the bag touch the ground until they reached home.

The mage read the mind of the mother. There were no evil thoughts there, just a proper reprimand and instruction so that a similar incident wouldn't be happening again any time soon. She finished her talk with a single slap on the boy's behind, sort of as an exclamation mark to her impromptu lecture.

And then the mage read the mind of the child. To his surprise, the young boy's mind was full of evil thoughts toward his mother.

I hate you . . . And I'm going to hurt you like you hurt me . . . Then you'll be sorry.

Evil thoughts to be sure.

But they were the thoughts of a child, an innocent who understood nothing about what he thought or did.

What then, would constitute suitable punishment for such thoughts?

If the mage reported the boy to the Kingpriest, the lad might be sentenced to death. That had been the punishment prescribed to adults who'd had similar thoughts.

But, to execute a child?

The thought made the mage sick to his stomach.

He watched the mother and child continue on down the street as if the incident had already been forgotten.

He read both their minds once more.

There was love there. Strong love. All the boy's evil thoughts were gone.

His evil thoughts had been . . . harmless.

The mage stood in the middle of the street thinking about what he should do. By order of the Kingpriest, he was bound to report all the evil thoughts he had read. But, he couldn't bring himself to report the boy and have him taken from his mother, a woman who obviously loved him more than anything else in the world.

The Edict of Thought Control was unworkable.

The realization left the mage with only one option. He decided he would take it.

He turned his back on the mother and child, and began walking west.

When he reached the outskirts of the city, he turned south, headed for Silvanesti.

To start a new life.

Chapter 13

"No matter how many times I've seen it," said Caradoc. "Each time I lay my eyes upon it after some time away, I'm always in awe of its beauty."

"Indeed," said Soth. "It is a beautiful sight."

Ahead on the eastern horizon, the deep red outline of Dargaard Keep stood out like a single perfect rose. After ten days at the Knights' Meeting in Palanthas (Soth attended six of those days) and an uneventful journey home, the knights were all eager to return to the keep and relate what they'd learned to their fellow knights.

But for Soth, there were other reasons which made him look forward to his return. For one there was his wife. Dear, sweet Korinne. After such a long time away, perhaps she had some news for him. Even though Soth had vowed not to speak of such matters until she truly was with child, he couldn't stop himself from considering the possibility.

To have a son . . .

Or perhaps even a daughter. He would teach her to fight, make her strong, the first female Knight of Solamnia.

He shook his head, realizing his dreams were getting the better of him.

And then there was Isolde. She would be fully healed by now, her stunning beauty completely restored. There was no real reason for him to contact her—she was merely just another person in the keep now, one of many—but nevertheless, he wanted desperately to see her, to speak to her, perhaps even to . . . touch her.

"The elf-maid you brought back to the keep," Caradoc said idly.

Mention of the maid startled Soth, bringing him back to the plains. Even though he was sure Caradoc's speaking of Isolde had been a coincidence, the uncanniness of it made Soth shiver. "You mean Isolde?"

"Is that her name?"

"Yes."

"Well, Is-olde," Caradoc had some trouble pronouncing the name, "is certainly a beautiful woman, elf or otherwise."

"Yes," said Soth, his voice noncommittal. "That she is."

"Might make a man a fine lover."

Soth turned to look at Caradoc. His seneschal was staring blankly out over the horizon, obviously speaking of Isolde with a sort of wistfulness that he might speak about a well-made sword or a fine bottle of wine.

Soth turned his gaze forward and tried to match Caradoc's pensive sort of look with a similar expression of his own. "That she would," he said, trying to say the words musingly.

* * * * *

When the knights entered the keep they were greeted by dozens of people, most of whom were family and friends. Soth dismounted and was quickly greeted by Lady Korinne who had come to see him dressed in some of her finest red and purple robes.

Despite his mind being clouded with other thoughts, Soth had missed Korinne deeply, and when they came together he took her up in his arms and kissed her passionately on the mouth.

"Did you miss me?" Korinne asked.

"Of course."

"And I you."

Soth smiled. "Then perhaps we should get away from here."

"I thought you might never ask."

Soth gave the reins of his mount to a squire and walked arm-in-arm with Lady Korinne into the tower leading to their chambers. When they arrived, Korinne opened the door and Soth picked her up and carried her inside, closing the door behind him with a backward kick of his foot.

He carried her over to the bed and laid her down upon it. As Soth began to undress, he noticed something different about Korinne's smile. It was as if she were trying to contain herself, holding back some great secret that was mere seconds from bursting from her lips.

"What?" asked Soth. "What is it?"

"I'm glad to see you," answered Korinne. "Is that so wrong?" Already her smile was starting to wane.

"Well, from the look on your face I thought you might have something to tell me."

"Like what?"

"That you're with child, of course."

"Oh."

There was a long silence between them.

"Well, are you?" asked Soth.

Another extended period of silence.

Korinne let out a sigh. "No."

Soth let out a long sigh of his own. He was disappointed, especially because he knew it had been entirely his own fault. He had told her not to mention word of a child until she knew for certain and now he had been the one to ask the question, destroying what should have been a wonderful moment between them.

Korinne rolled onto her side on the bed and began to weep softly.

Soth didn't know what to do. He had slain ogres, defeated whole armies, and performed a hundred other heroic deeds, but here and now he found himself wishing he were somewhere else, somewhere far away.

He was also angered by her inability to bear him a child, but instinctively knew that harsh words had no place in the room at this particular moment.

Korinne's weeping had grown into open sobs.

After another moment's hesitation, Soth crawled onto the bed and placed a comforting hand on Korinne's shoulder. It did nothing to staunch her cries, but it still felt as if it were the right thing to do. He placed an arm around her and held her close.

* * * * *

That night after supper, Soth excused himself from the table on the pretense of wanting to stretch his legs and reacquaint himself with the keep.

After leaving the dining hall, he made a series of twists and turns that brought him to the maids' quarters where Isolde was now staying. He checked in the larger chambers but found the room to be empty except for eight neatly prepared beds, each with its own trundle. He checked a few of the adjoining rooms and finally heard soft music coming from one of the rooms down the hall. He tracked the sound until he found Isolde in the music room playing a harp.

Soth looked up and down the hallway, then stepped into the room, leaving the door behind him slightly ajar so as to not to make any noise that would disrupt Isolde's sweet, sweet music.

He sat down on a stool to her right and listened.

Almost at once he recognized the tune as "The Silver

Moon's Passing," an elven song of mourning. As he listened he could almost hear the emotions in the notes, could almost picture the swaying grasslands of the plains, the love of a young man, and the loss felt by his young bride upon his death.

She finished playing the song without realizing that Soth was in the room. When the last note faded Soth began clapping.

Isolde turned, startled to find him there.

"That was beautiful," he said.

"I didn't realize I had an audience."

"Would it have mattered?"

"No, I suppose not."

"You play very well."

She almost blushed at the compliment. "Thank you, milord. Istvan said I could keep his harp as long as I liked."

"From the way he plays the instrument, I wouldn't be surprised if he were glad to be rid of it."

Isolde laughed, giving Soth reason to smile. Her face was so bright, so alive.

There was a lengthy pause between them. Finally Isolde said, "But you didn't come here to hear me play the harp now did you?"

"No."

She looked at him curiously. "Why did you come here?"

Soth thought about it, and realized he didn't have a good answer to the question. Why did I come here? he wondered. "I wanted to make sure you were all right." A pause. "And perhaps I need someone to talk to."

"Talk? About what?"

Again Soth hesitated. "Family matters."

"I would think your wife would be the best one with which to discuss such things."

"Perhaps, but what if *she* is the topic to be discussed?"

"I see," said Isolde, her eyes darting somewhat nervously. "But shouldn't you speak of such things to one who is closer to you? A family member, perhaps even Istvan?"

"No, I couldn't. This is something that is best discussed with someone from outside of Dargaard Keep. Someone . . . like yourself." This was true. If he let it be known to others close to him that Korinne was unable to conceive, news of it would sweep through the keep in a matter of days, and across Solamnia in mere weeks. For some reason, he instinctively knew that Isolde would speak to no one about the matter, that his secrets would be her secrets.

"All right, then," she said warmly. "Talk to me."

Soth began explaining how, despite all their efforts, he and Korinne had been unable to produce a child. Then he began talking of the pain and disappointment he felt each time she told him of their failure, not just for himself but for her as well. He told her too, how it was beginning to affect their relationship.

Isolde listened in silence, providing him with little response other than a slight nod of her head, or an arch of her brow.

The more he spoke, the more Soth realized that perhaps he *had* come here looking for someone to talk to. He was indeed feeling better, his frustration over the matter somewhat lessened by the mere act of telling someone else about the problem.

And it was a problem.

He was Loren Soth, Knight of the Rose, Master of Dargaard Keep and Lord of Knightlund. He should be the father of many, many distinguished Knights of Solamnia. The Soth family name was a great one with a hallowed history and a grand future, but if he failed to produce even a single heir, the Soth name would die along with him. For a Knight of Solamnia, it was a problem greater than any that could be created by an opponent on a battlefield. And in fact, many times Soth had wished this problem could be dealt with by the sword. But alas, it could not. This was a problem that could be remedied only by the good graces of Paladine, or the benevolence of Mishakal.

* * * * *

"Take these up to the maids' chambers," said the head laundress, a large, stout woman with arms as thick as those of some men. "And these go to the Lord's chambers."

The maid chewed her bottom lip to stop herself from saying unkind words to the laundress. Reminding her not to mix up the stacks was an insult to her intelligence because there was little chance that anyone could ever mistake the two. The stack which had grayed slightly and had been repaired by numerous patches was obviously for the maids' chambers while the newer, whiter linens were surely reserved for the lord and lady of the keep. Even a child could tell the two apart.

Mirrel Martlin, had been a maid in Dargaard Keep for the past year and a half and she was growing tired of being a maid in every sense of the word. While she didn't mind doing the work that was required of her—she was a maid after all—she knew she was destined for better things. Many nights she dreamed of being one of milady's personal maids, or Mishakal be praised, a lady-in-waiting. When she told others of her hopes and aspirations, they simply dismissed them as being the wild fantasies of a young girl. But she remained undaunted by this, knowing in her heart that these aspirations were not fantasies, but dreams. Dreams, she knew, sometimes came true.

Maybe she would be the lucky one.

"Now don't get them confused," said the laundress, already moving onto another matter.

Again Mirrel chewed her bottom lip. "No ma'am."

The laundress didn't answer.

Mirrel carried the linens through the keep and reached the maids' chambers. She heard voices coming from down the hall and wished she had someone to talk to. A friendly presence might make even the task of putting away the linens seem almost pleasant.

When she was done, she picked up the linens destined

for the lord's chambers and walked down the hall in the direction from which she heard voices. She considered entering the room and perhaps greeting the maids inside when she saw that the door was closed.

Or at least, almost closed but for a tiny crack.

Mirrel could now clearly hear the voices coming from inside the room, one female, the other male.

This was curious because men were rarely seen in this part of the keep. She peered through the crack and was surprised to see the lord of the keep sitting next to the elf-maid he'd rescued on the way to Palanthas.

* * * * *

Isolde listened quietly, waiting patiently until Soth had finished. When he was done, she placed her hand on his and stroked it gently. "My good lord," she said. "You are a paragon of virtue, but patience seems to be one virtue you are lacking."

Soth smiled at this.

"Paladine does not abandon those such as yourself who uphold the laws of Good and abjure the forces of Evil. If your heart is pure, the Father of Good will bless you with a child when he deems the time to be right."

Soth nodded at the truth in her words.

"Speaking of Paladine," said Isolde softly. "I'm feeling much better now and I thought that I might be strong enough to resume my journey to Palanthas. . . ." Her voice trailed off, as if she were asking a question instead of making a statement.

"So soon?" asked Soth.

"I've been here for weeks. I really must think about rejoining my friends."

"But you can't," Soth said quickly, his voice walking a fine line between commanding and pleading.

"And why not?" asked Isolde, a thin smile on her face. "I'm better now."

"I need you here," said Soth. A pause. "To talk to."

Isolde's smile widened. She leaned forward and kissed Soth on the mouth.

The move startled Soth, and the touch of her sweet lips on his immediately rekindled his feelings of passion, an emotion which—up until this moment—he'd been able to keep subdued.

Without hesitation, he pulled the maid closer, and returned her kiss.

* * * * *

Realizing she was spying on the two, but too curious to pull herself from the door, Mirrel watched them talk. Although she could not make out their words, their conversation seemed pleasant enough, even if the lord did seem a bit troubled by something.

And then it happened.

The elf-maid kissed Lord Soth.

Lord Soth returned her kiss.

Mirrel slapped a hand over her mouth to cover the sound of her gasp.

Then she looked again, clutching the linen tightly against her chest. After watching the two kiss for several moments she moved away from the door and stood with her back to the wall. She remembered the linen in her arms—linen destined for Lord Soth's chambers.

She would take them there.

And as she set off, she wondered whether she might run into Lady Korinne along the way.

* * * * *

"This isn't right," said Soth, breaking off the kiss.

Isolde looked away. "No, I suppose it isn't." She sighed and placed her hands delicately in her lap.

For several long moments they simply sat in silence,

their eyes avoiding each other as the full realization of what they'd just done settled into their minds.

"You have a wife," said Isolde, sliding a hand onto Soth's well-muscled shoulder. "Just because she's yet to have a child doesn't mean she never will."

Soth nodded.

"Perhaps it would be best if I left soon." She raised her head and looked at him, as if to gauge his reaction.

She was right. He knew that, but he couldn't bring himself to let her go. Not now. Even though he knew it was wrong, he still wanted her. And, truth be told, he really couldn't be sure that she didn't want him, too. He wasn't sure if her words matched her true feelings. "No," he said at last.

"But . . ." she said, her eyes wide and innocent as that of a child.

"I'd still like to visit you from time to time," he said. "I need you . . . to talk to."

"Of course," said Isolde with a smile, her eyes narrowing almost seductively. "I will stay a while longer, milord—if you need me."

* * * * *

When Mirrel arrived at the lord's chambers she took a deep breath and knocked on the door. There was no answer. She knocked again, this time a faint voice responded. "Yes."

"Linens milady."

"Come in," she said. "The door is open."

After a brief moment of hesitation, Mirrel opened the door and entered the room. She'd been inside it only once before and was still somewhat unfamiliar with its layout. On one wall there was a large fireplace that had a small fire alight in its hearth, giving off only a small amount of light and heat. One side of the room was covered by a fanciful design of connected crowns, swords and roses. In the center of the design was the rough likeness of a knight who Mirrel guessed was Vinas Solamnus, founder of the Knights of Solamnia. At the other end of the room was a small chair upon which sat Lady Korinne. She was busy reading something, an old volume by the looks of it.

She stood in the center of the room not knowing where to place the linens. Lady Korinne did not look up from her reading, and Mirrel was left with no other choice but to interrupt her. "Beg pardon, milady."

At last Korinne looked up and smiled.

"Where might I put these linens?"

"I believe there's room in the trunk at the foot of the bed."

Mirrel nodded and went to the trunk. There was more than enough room inside. She placed the linens neatly inside and closed the trunk easily.

Lady Korinne resumed her reading, but after a few moments, she realized that Mirrel hadn't yet left the room. She looked up at her. "Yes?"

Mirrel felt her heart hammering against her chest like a smith's mallet upon an anvil. Her mouth seemed parched and she struggled to make a sound. "I, uh . . ."

Lady Korinne turned to face the maid and smiled. "Is there something on your mind, something you wanted to tell me?"

Mirrel nodded, thankful that Lady Korinne was so perceptive.

"Don't be nervous," said Korinne. "I'm the lady of the keep, not Mishakal." She gestured at the chair across from her. "Have a seat."

Mirrel moved slowly across the room and eased herself gently into the chair. It wasn't that she was nervous about telling Lady Korinne what she saw, for her eyes had not deceived her. No, the reason she was hesitant was that she was unsure about what Lady Korinne's reaction to it might be. For all Mirrel knew, she might refuse to believe her, banish her from the keep, maybe even from all of

Solamnia. Nevertheless, she'd seen what she had seen and she owed it to the lady of the keep to make her aware of it—just as any one of Lord Soth's knights would be bound to inform him of some curious occurrences within the keep.

"Now then, what is it?" asked Lady Korinne.

"Before delivering the linens here, I dropped off some others to the maids' chambers."

"Yes."

"In one of the rooms, the elf-maid looked as if she had been playing a harp that Istvan had lent her."

"I've heard she's quite a talented musician, especially on that instrument."

Mirrel took a deep breath.

"What is it?"

"Lord Soth was in the room with her."

The color drained from Lady Korinne's face and she suddenly looked quite pale. She placed a hand on the desk in front of her to steady herself.

"Are you all right, milady?"

"What happened?" asked Lady Korinne.

Mirrel shook her head. "Perhaps I shouldn't say. I don't want to dishonor milord."

Lady Korinne breathed deeply, composing herself. "Tell me," she said, her voice steady and surprisingly strong, perhaps even a little bit angry. "And I promise you your words will never leave this room."

Mirrel nodded, leaned forward and told her.

* * * * *

The night was cool, but Lady Korinne hardly felt its chill. She walked through the rows of the keep's small garden, her eyes open but seeing nothing through the emotional storm cloud that hung over her like a pall. It was made up of many different parts: rage, disappointment, sorrow, fear.

When the maid first told her what she had seen, Korinne's first reaction was to deny it. And in fact she'd tried to tell herself that it simply was not possible, that the great Lord Soth, Knight of the Rose, was bound by the Oath and the Measure and would surely never betray her in such a way. But as the maid continued to speak, Korinne knew in her heart that she was telling the truth. She had no proof, but evidence of Soth's waning love was always there, in the way he talked to her, in the way they kissed, in the way . . .

She was losing him . . . to an elf-maid.

But maybe it wasn't too late. Mirrel had seen the two kissing. Kissing, that was all. He was still her husband. Perhaps it wasn't too late to pull him back, catch him before he strayed too far.

It was worth a try. And one thing was for certain, she wasn't about to lose him without a fight. And she knew just what form the fight would take.

"You called for me, milady?"

Korinne turned and saw the young man named Engel Silversword. He had been sent to Dargaard Keep from Palanthas by Korinne's mother. He had high hopes of someday joining the Knights of Solamnia. Due to the fact that he had ties to Palanthas and the Gladria family, his loyalty to her would be assured, and since he had yet to become the squire of any knight, she could arrange to have him sponsored in a matter of days. If he served her well, she might even be persuaded to speak as a witness to his honor.

"Yes, I did," said Korinne. She sat down on a bench. The young man moved closer to her but remained standing at a distance of two paces. "I have a task for you."

"Anything, milady."

Korinne nodded.

"I wish you to travel to Vingaard Keep."

The squire immediately stood straighter as he realized this task was one of significant importance.

"When you arrive at Vingaard Keep, I wish you to contact my cousin, Lord Eward Irvine, Knight of the Sword. When you see him you will tell him that his cousin, Lady Korinne has asked that he call Lord Soth to Vingaard Keep on a matter of urgent business and that he keep him there for no less than two days. If he doubts you in any way, you may give him this as proof that I have sent you." She handed him a locket emblazoned with the Korinne family emblem.

Engel nodded. "Yes, milady."

Korinne rolled forward on the bench and spoke in a lower voice. "As you might have guessed, this is not something I wish others to know about."

"Of course not, milady."

"And if you speak of this to anyone I will deny everything. No one will believe your word against mine." Her words trailed off and she was silent for a long while, allowing the magnitude of what she'd said to settle in.

"I understand," Engel said. "I will not fail you."

"I know you won't."

Korinne's faith in the young man prompted him to stick out his chest with pride.

"You will leave tonight," she said. "Under cover of darkness. Now get out of the garden before someone sees you."

The young man was gone in seconds.

Korinne arched her neck and looked up into the sky. Solinari and Lunitari hung full in the sky like a pair of watchful eyes, one a bright and shimmering white, the other tinged with a slight crimson, the color of blood.

Chapter 14

Istvan sat hunched over his mixing table, dropping pinches of blue hyssop into a small pile of powdered comfrey. According to the journals he'd read, the hybrid mixture was supposed to do wonders for easing the pains in joints brought on by the passage of time. Old age.

He drew his mixing stick in circles through the reddish-blue powder until it was a deep-purple hue. Then he scooped it off the table with a flat stone and gently shook the mix into a small leather pouch. After closing one end of the pouch, he tied it around his waist so the mixture would always be close-at-hand.

He'd been taking the powder for several days now and couldn't yet decide whether it was working or not. He would continue the treatment for two more days. If his pain didn't lessen by then he'd end the experiment and dismiss the exercise as being nothing more than the wishful thinking of an old fool.

There was a knock at the door.

"Who is it?" asked Istvan.

"Parry Roslin," said a voice from the other side of the door.

Istvan's eyebrows arched. Roslin was the captain of the keep's guards. At this time of night, Roslin's visit could only have to deal with official business. "Come in."

"Beg your pardon, healer," said the large and stout, red-haired guard. "There are four elf-maids at the gate wanting entrance to the keep."

Istvan nodded thoughtfully. "So why are you telling me this?"

"Milord and milady have retired for the night."

"And what of knights Caradoc and Farold?"

"The women say they are here only to see Isolde and no other. They say they're here to bring her back to Silvanesti."

Istvan looked at the guard a moment. "I see."

"And because the elf-maid is in your charge I thought I'd bring the matter to your attention first."

Istvan was silent, considering the situation. He glanced down at the mixing table and saw the speckles of blue hyssop that had fallen in the cracks between the wood, blue hyssop on which Lord Soth had spent a tidy sum.

"You've done well," Istvan said at last.

Roslin smiled, as he'd probably had some doubts about whether he was doing the right thing coming to see Istvan first.

"Let them in, but take them directly to the elf-maid. Keep a guard posted throughout their visit, which is to be conducted in private. When they are done, escort them to the gatehouse. If Isolde is with them, call me. If not, send them on their way and deal with me no more."

Roslin nodded, and left the room.

Istvan got up from his chair, suddenly feeling much older and stiffer than when he'd first sat down.

* * * * *

"It's good to see you, Isolde," said one of the elf-maids.

"And you too," answered Isolde. "All of you."

"We missed you in Palanthas," said another of the maids. "It was unfortunate that you couldn't have been there with us. You would have liked it there."

Isolde made no comment.

The maids chatted for a while before the elderly elf-woman joined in. "So," she said. "Now that you have recovered from your injuries we can all return to Silvanesti the same as we left—as a party of five."

"I won't be returning to Silvanesti," said Isolde.

The other three maidens had been chatting between themselves while the elf-woman spoke, but now upon hearing the response from Isolde they grew quiet and the room had suddenly filled with tension.

"What did you say?" asked the elf-woman.

The silence in the room was complete.

"I said I won't be returning to Silvanesti. I have decided to remain here in the keep. For a little while longer at least."

The elf-woman rubbed a thin bony finger across her wrinkled forehead. Obviously, Isolde's decision didn't rest lightly on the woman's shoulders.

"Leave us alone for a moment," said the woman.

Without hesitation, the three elf-maids rose up and left the room leaving Isolde and the woman alone.

When the door was closed, the woman spoke. "You can't be serious."

"But I am."

"What possible place does an elf-maid have in the keep of a Knight of Solamnia?"

Isolde didn't have an answer to the question, or at least didn't have an answer she felt like relating to the elderly elf.

"Have they put you to work?"

"Not really. I help the healer in his herb garden, but it's not really work."

"Do you sing for milord?"

"No."

"Do you do any entertaining in the keep?"

"I play the healer's harp, but it's more for my own pleasure than anything else."

"Are you tutoring children?"

"No."

She looked at Isolde curiously. "Have you been made one of milady's maids?"

"No."

"Then why must you remain here when you belong in Silvanesti?"

"Milord needs me . . . to talk to."

The old elf-woman stared at Isolde with narrowed eyes for a long, long time. Finally she said, "Have you been *intimate* with the lord of the keep?"

All she had done was hold him in her arms and comfort him. At least that was all she had done in the beginning. Then she had kissed him, and then . . .

She felt in her heart that she had done nothing wrong. She had merely provided some comfort to a soul in pain, but she knew she couldn't tell that to the elf-woman with any amount of conviction. So, instead of answering the question, she merely lowered her head in silence.

The woman drew in a long breath. "May the great god Paladine take pity on your soul."

* * * * *

"This seems so sudden," said Korinne. "Must you go away again?"

"I'm afraid so, Korinne," said Soth. "Lord Irvine says my help is needed at Vingaard Keep on a matter of great urgency. Exactly what the problem is he did not say, but judging by the tone of his message, I think it's best that I depart as soon as possible."

"Very well, then," Korinne sighed, feigning disappointment. "If you must go, then Paladine be with you."

"Thank you, my love."

Korinne nodded and did her best to smile. "Give Lord Irvine my regards."

"I will."

* * * * *

The midday sun was high over the western plain as Lady Korinne stood at the window of her bedchamber waiting for her husband to leave the keep.

In the distance, four figures draped in robes were heading due south along the foot of the Dargaard Mountains after having left the keep some time ago. They were riding slowly, three of them high in the saddle, one hunched over from what was most likely old age.

It wasn't uncommon for people to come and go from the keep without her knowledge—it was impossible for Lady Korinne, and Lord Soth for that matter, to know about everything that went on within the keep's walls—but for some reason Korinne's curiosity was piqued by this party of four. They didn't seem to be merchants or mercenaries and Dargaard Keep was hardly ever visited by wizards, priests or rogues.

A curiosity to be sure.

Suddenly, the outside of the keep was alive with the sound of hoofbeats on the wooden drawbridge spanning the chasm. A second later Lord Soth rode out of the keep followed by six knights. They quickly headed east, the trail to Vingaard Keep taking them nowhere near the other four travelers.

Korinne watched Soth and the knights for a long time, not moving from the window until they were nearly out of sight. Before turning away, she glanced southward. The four riders heading that way were also gone.

She turned away from the window.

"They're gone, Mirrel," she said to her newest lady-in-waiting. "Begin making preparations for this evening."

"Yes, milady," said Mirrel.

"We'll set out after dark."

* * * * *

The moons had been hanging over the keep for several hours before Korinne heard the faint knock upon her door. "Who is it?" she asked.

"Mirrel."

Korinne hurried to the door and opened it. Mirrel stood there draped in a dark cloak, a garment which would make her all but invisible in the darkness. She had a second dark cloak for Korinne. "Put it on," she said, then added, "please, milady."

Korinne slipped into the robe and together the two women padded through the keep, taking the less-traveled routes on their way to the gatehouse.

To Korinne's surprise, the gate was unattended, the portcullis slightly raised. "Where are the guards?"

"I arranged for them to be away from their posts for several minutes. They should likewise be gone when we return."

"But how?"

"Don't underestimate the feminine charms of—"

"Never mind," said Korinne, cutting off Mirrel's whispers. "I've already decided I don't want to know."

"Perhaps it would be best that way, milady."

Korinne looked at the maid, amazed by her ingenuity, efficiency and her steadfast loyalty. Despite the fact that Mirrel had been the one to inform her of Lord Soth's indiscretions, Korinne was beginning to look upon their meeting as a blessing. Although she'd been lady of the keep, Korinne had sorely been missing a close and loyal friend. Now she had one.

They snuck through the gap left by the raised portcullis and crossed the drawbridge quickly, trying to stay out of the faint light of the moons. When they had reached some cover outside the keep, Korinne turned to Mirrel. "What now?"

"This way," said Mirrel. "There are horses waiting."

Again, Korinne was impressed by Mirrel's thoroughness, and for the first time since she'd thought of this wild scheme, she believed it might actually have a chance of succeeding.

They reached the horses, a pair of big and powerful black stallions.

They mounted the horses and without a word being spoken between them, rode off into the night.

Chapter 15

"The power to read the thoughts within the minds of men, women and children . . ." mused the Kingpriest as he sat upon his throne at one end of the main hall of the temple.

"And to put an end to those evil thoughts," he continued, "before they've even made a single step onto Evil's dark and twisted road. Is that not a power that had previously been reserved for the gods?"

A lone acolyte sat by the Kingpriest's side. The young man seemed unsure whether the question had been a rhetorical one or not. After a few seconds of silence, he spoke up. "Indeed it is, your worship."

The Kingpriest nodded.

The acolyte sighed, relieved he had answered the Kingpriest correctly.

"And to sit in sole judgment of people's evil thoughts, considering the severity of those thoughts and punishing them accordingly, even with death. Is that not the kind of power that had, up until now, been reserved for the Gods of Good such as Paladine, Mishakal, Majere, Kiri-Jolith, Habbakuk, Branchala and Solinari? Even the Gods of Evil: Takhisis, Sargonnas, Morgion, and the Gods of Neutrality: Gilean, Sirrion, and Reorx have been know to possess such powers."

A pause.

"Yes, your worship," said the acolyte.

"But now, it is not only the gods who have that power. I have it as well. And if I, the Kingpriest of Istar, have godlike powers, then am I still a mortal being or have I ascended to the next level? Beyond mortal and toward immortal?"

Another pause.

"Ascended to the next level, your worship," said the acolyte, the intonation making his words sound more like a question than a statement.

"Yes," hissed the Kingpriest. "If I have acquired the powers of the gods, then, by rights, I must be a god myself."

The hall was deathly silent.

The acolyte looked at the Kingpriest, nodded his head slightly and said in a trembling voice. "Yes, your worship."

"Then I will ascend to the heavens and take my place at the right hand of Paladine. The gods will greet me with open arms and thank me for spreading virtue and goodness across the four corners of Krynn."

The Kingpriest's eyes were looking upward, glinting with a sort of madness, as if he were looking through the stone ceiling of the temple and into the starry night sky above it.

The Kingpriest stood up. "If I have the power of a god, then I *will* become a god!"

The acolyte was silent, looking strangely at the Kingpriest.

"A god," he repeated breathily, as if considering the possibilities.

The acolyte lowered his head like one doomed. "Yes, your worship."

Chapter 16

Together, Mirrel and Lady Korinne rode south for over an hour before turning east and riding into the northern lip of a deep rift in the Dargaard Mountains called the Soul's Wound.

Korinne had heard stories about the inhabitants of these mountains ever since she was a child. Although she'd always felt it hard to believe the tales while living in the comfort of her parent's home in Palanthas, such was not the case after she'd moved into Dargaard Keep.

Everyone in the keep from the knights to the laundresses, from the squires to the cooks, could tell stories of the lost folk who supposedly lived in the most impenetrable valleys or on the most treacherous mountainsides of the Dargaard range. The lizardlike Bakali, the otherworldly Huldrefolk, the birdlike Kyrie, and the batlike Shadowpeople. All were reported to live deep within these mountains although none of these creatures had been reliably witnessed for hundreds of years. Still, that fact did little to alter people's beliefs in them and the interior of the mountain range slowly grew to be a darkly mystical place where those who were ill-suited to blend into Solamnic society found the perfect place in which to live out their lives in peace.

However, that didn't mean there was never any contact between the two worlds.

When Korinne first thought of making this trip she had only a vague idea of where she might find help. Mirrel had proved helpful in this regard, securing directions and ensuring they wouldn't be turned away once they arrived at their destination.

Their goal was a small stone cottage at the foot of a snow-capped mountain. The cottage was half-buried in earth and looked as if the mountainside had crept up to it over the past few centuries and would eventually engulf the structure with the passage of the next several hundred years.

There was a faint yellow light shining in one of the cottage's two exposed windows. Considering the time of night, the light was a good sign that whoever lived within was expecting company.

The two women slowed their mounts as they approached the tiny cottage, content to walk the last little bit after what had been an especially long and hard ride.

They secured their horses, the beasts seeming infinitely grateful for the rest, and approached the cottage's front door.

The wooden door was slightly ajar, but Mirrel stopped Lady Korinne from pushing it open and suggested that she knock first.

Korinne nodded at this, reminding herself that her status as lady of the keep would carry little weight in the home of a hedge witch. She pulled her robe back from her right wrist and knocked on the door with three sharp raps of her knuckles.

There was no answer.

"Maybe we should go," suggested Mirrel.

Korinne knocked again.

"Open is the door," said a gravel-throated voice. "Enter

if you wish."

Korinne looked at Mirrel and the younger woman nodded. Then Korinne pushed the door open and entered the cottage, Mirrel close behind her.

The ceiling of the cottage was low, and the two women had to stoop in order to move about without bumping their heads.

The hedge witch was sitting in an old wooden chair by a fire. The chair was oddly shaped and of a strange design that looked as if it could only be comfortable to the witch herself. Thankfully, there were two other chairs by the fire—chairs shaped for more normal postures. The witch extended a gnarled, bony hand, inviting the two women to take their seats. Korinne and Mirrel quickly sat down, grateful—like their horses—for the respite.

In the flickering light of the fire, Korinne tried to make out the witch's features. Other than her being human, Korinne could not discern any of the witch's finer features with any clarity.

As if the witch had read her mind, she waved a hand in the direction of the fire and the flames suddenly burned hotter. The inside of the cottage became brighter and Korinne could easily make out the craglike texture of the witch's skin, now brought out in high relief by the contrast of light and shadow on her face. There were also several moles under the witch's chin which seemed to be in a different position each time Korinne glanced at them—a trick of the light, she surmised. And finally, she looked at the witch's eyes. They were dark, almost black, even in the bright light of the fire.

Korinne was not repulsed. Compared to what she'd heard in tales of the lost folk, this witch was almost attractive.

"Have you seen enough?" said the witch, waving her hand at the fire once more. The flames suddenly died down and the inside of the cottage was once again dim. "Now, why is it that you've come? What is it that you want?"

Korinne's heart was racing. It felt wrong to be here, but

she'd come this far and she refused to give up now. "My name is Korinne Soth, Lady Korinne—"

"Who you are, I know," said the witch, cutting off Korinne's words. "What you want, I know." She smiled on one side of her mouth, showing the women several of her dirty brown teeth. "But I want to hear you tell me anyway."

Korinne paused. She'd spoken about her troubles only with her husband and Mirrel. No one else. But she was surprised to learn that she had no qualms about telling this hedge witch that she could not conceive. Somehow, she knew that what was spoken here tonight would never leave the stone walls of the cottage.

"I am barren," said Korinne, a hint of sadness in her voice. "Despite all my efforts, I have not been able to conceive."

"No?" the witch asked playfully. "How do you know that you are the one unable to conceive?"

Korinne was silent.

"How do you know that the problem does not lie with the great Lord Soth, Knight of the Rose?"

Korinne gasped. She'd never even considered such a thing.

"How do you know," continued the witch, "that Soth's seed is not to blame?"

Korinne felt compelled to answer. If she didn't the witch might continue to ask the same disturbing question. "I don't," she said, a slight tremor in her voice. "I don't."

"Then perhaps you should come back when you know."

"How could I find out?"

The witch let out a small, dry laugh. "Take a lover, or wait until your mighty lord produces a bastard."

"No," whispered Korinne. "I couldn't."

"I see. So what you want is not for me to make you fertile, but to *give* you a child."

Korinne was silent. She turned to Mirrel for some help, but the young maid seemed as befuddled as Korinne was. Finally Korinne simply said, "Yes."

"Well, I cannot," said the witch.

"Why not?"

"What you are asking me to do is very dangerous magic. Even if I did try and help, you wouldn't know if I was successful for many months. And by then it would be too late."

"Too late? For what?"

"To undo," whispered the witch. "If my magic works well, then everyone is happy. But if it does not, people might—"

"You must help me," Korinne said, getting out of her chair and moving closer to the witch until she was crouched at her feet.

Mirrel remained in her chair.

"And why *must* I help you?"

Korinne thought about it for a few moments, but couldn't think of much of an answer. She lowered her head and remained silent.

"Eh?" asked the witch. "What was that? Speak up dear, I cannot hear you."

Korinne felt her face getting flushed. There was no reason for the witch to talk to her in this way. No other reason than because she could talk to her this way under the circumstances. Korinne let out a sigh, finally conceding that she was in no position to make demands upon the witch.

When the silence became prolonged, the witch spoke again. "So, tell me again why I should help you."

Korinne thought about it again. Why should this witch, someone she barely knew existed until two days ago, help her, Lady Korinne Soth of Dargaard Keep?

"Because I love my husband dearly and want nothing more than to make him happy."

"Ah . . ." The witch's scraggly face brightened. "Sure of that, are you? Sure that a child would make Soth happy?"

Korinne considered it. Even though she couldn't be absolutely sure, she answered the question with as much conviction as she could muster. "Yes."

The witch nodded. "Then I might give you what you

ask for after all."

"Might?" asked Korinne harshly. She was about to say something else when she thought better of it.

"Yes, might." The witch paused. "There is still the little matter of a payment for my services."

"I can pay you any amount you desire," said Korinne confidently. "Anything you want, tell me what it is and it will be yours."

The witch's laugh sounded like boots sliding over a sand-sprinkled floor. "Look around you. Does it appear that I treasure material wealth?"

Korinne and Mirrel glanced around the cottage. It was obvious that the witch cared little for material things. Korinne's previously soaring heart fell into a deep dark chasm. If the witch wanted no material wealth, then what type of payment could she make? "What is it that you want?"

The witch smiled at the question. "I want," she said, "the one thing you value most."

Korinne thought about it. What was it that she valued most? It only took her a second to realize the answer was a simple one. She wanted a child more than anything else in the world. Soth wanted one as well. The value of a child in their lives was immeasurable. Priceless! But, how could she give up a child as payment when she couldn't have one in the first place? She decided to pose the question to the witch.

"How can I give you what I value most, when that thing is exactly what I've come here to ask you for?"

The witch suddenly smiled and for a moment it was almost as if there was a quality of beauty about her.

Korinne nervously smiled along with her.

"A very *wise* answer," said the witch. "The *right* answer."

Korinne let out a long sigh. So did Mirrel.

"If a child is the one thing you value most, then perhaps you deserve to have one." The witch got up from her chair.

For the first time Korinne saw the misshapen curve of her back, legs and arms. She wondered for a moment about what might have caused such a deformity, but quickly decided it was probably best she didn't know.

"I will give you a child," said the witch. "But I must tell you again that the magic you ask of me is very black and very, very dangerous."

Korinne chewed her bottom lip, afraid that if she spoke she might end up changing her mind.

"And I warn you," said the witch, "the success of the spell will depend entirely on the virtue of your husband, on the virtue of Lord Soth."

Lady Korinne thought about it. Mirrel had seen Soth and the elf-maid kiss, nothing more. How much harm could there be in that? And if she didn't do this, there was a chance they might do more than kiss the next time they met. And besides all of that, Soth was a Knight of Solamnia, a Knight of the Rose, a noble and honorable man whose life was dictated by the writings of Vinas Solamnus. The Oath and the Measure. This one small indiscretion with an elf-maid would hardly put a black mark on Soth's soul after years of living honorably in accordance with the strict knight's code. If such was the case, the witch's stipulation would be a blessing more than a curse. "He's a good man," Korinne said at last.

"Are you so sure?" asked the witch.

"Yes." There was a slight tremor in Korinne's voice, as if her conviction was losing some of its strength.

"You love him, don't you?"

"Y-yes."

The witch moved closer. "Perhaps you should fear him instead. There are dark branches in his family tree and it is only a matter of time before the darkness infects the entire trunk, all the way down to the roots."

Korinne's heart was pounding. She swallowed and reassured herself that the witch was merely playing games, trying to scare her.

"You still want the child, do you not?" asked the witch.

Korinne nodded.

"Then you shall have it."

The witch's eyes rolled back in their sockets as she placed a hand on Korinne's belly. The gnarled hand felt warm, almost hot, against her skin. The fire flared and the witch's lips mouthed an unfamiliar string of syllables and words.

Korinne felt a strange tingle inside her, the blossoming of something straining to make room for itself. Her eyes began to feel heavy with sleep. She tried to keep them open, but eventually was forced to give up the fight as all of her energy and strength was being drawn by the new thing inside her.

She could feel it.

Growing.

* * * * *

"Milady, wake up!"

Korinne felt a gentle pat against her cheek. "What? What is it?"

"We must be going. It will be light in a few hours."

Korinne's eyes fluttered open. Mirrel was there standing over her. She glanced around, and slowly recalled where she was. "Have I been asleep long?"

"Only a short while."

"Then we best be leaving." She tried to get up, but couldn't. Her limbs ached with exhaustion. Mirrel hooked an arm around her body and helped her to her feet.

As the two women made their way to the door, Korinne turned in the direction of the old witch and said, "Thank you."

And suddenly the cottage was filled with the sound of the witch's raspy laugh. "Don't thank me," she said. "You might want to curse me later."

The words made Korinne shiver.

Chapter 17

"How was your trip, my dear Loren?" Lady Korinne asked as both she and her husband retired to their chambers following his return from Vingaard Keep.

"Strange," said Lord Soth, a sour expression on his face.

"Oh, how so?" said Korinne, barely able to hold back a smile. She lay back on the bed and raised a closed hand over her mouth.

"Well, Eward Irvine is a fine and experienced knight. In fact he's been a Knight of Solamnia longer than I have." Soth paused to remove his boots. "Yet he called me with such haste to Vingaard Keep that I had thought there must be something happening there of grave importance, an insurrection or a rebellion of knights."

"But that wasn't the case?" Korinne prodded.

"No, far from it," said Soth. "When I got there he failed to greet me, then kept me waiting for hours. And then, once we finally met, he asked me to help him plan strategies for mock-battles between detachments of knights."

Korinne was silent, chewing her bottom lip to help keep her good news from spilling prematurely from her mouth.

"That's a task for pages and squires," said Soth. "Well, at least one thing is for certain. I'll be thinking twice before I answer the call of your cousin again."

He turned around to see Korinne lying on the bed, smiling gleefully.

"What?" asked Soth. "What is it?" He looked himself over to see if there was anything amiss with his clothing.

"Do you recall that you didn't want me to speak of children until I was sure I was with child?"

Soth thought about it. "Yes."

"Well, I am now sure."

Soth's mouth opened slightly and stayed that way for a long while. Then he swallowed and asked, "You are absolutely sure?"

Korinne couldn't blame him for asking. She had raised his hopes on the subject far too many times. In answer she simply nodded, then smiled.

"Paladine be praised!" Soth shouted, crawling onto the bed next to Korinne. He took her in his arms and hugged her.

Korinne felt tears welling up in her eyes.

"My wife is with child," he whispered. "This is wonderful news." Then he kissed her.

As her lips touched his, Korinne began to cry. And despite the joy of the moment, she couldn't help but taste the bitterness in the tears as they rolled down her face.

* * * * *

"A celebration!" said Lord Soth later that day. "In the grand hall. Everyone in the keep shall attend."

"What's the occasion, milord?" asked the keep's cook, an elderly yet still quite stout man named Pitte who had been preparing meals for three generations of Soths. He had been called into the grand hall along with several of the keep's other key stewards.

"I"—he paused and began again—"I am going to be a father."

The assembled men and women inhaled a collective gasp.

A broad grin broke across Soth's face as he finally had the long-awaited pleasure of telling someone—anyone—of his good fortune.

Lady Korinne stood by his side, holding his hand tightly and grinning from ear to ear.

A little distance away on Korinne's right stood Mirrel, who was also smiling broadly.

"Wonderful news, milord."

"A grand reason to celebrate."

"I'll prepare a grand feast, milord," said Pitte, obviously happy to soon be serving a fourth generation Soth. "It's a little early for the harvests to come in, but I can whip up a grand banquet with stews and soups, pastries and pies."

Soth nodded. "I'm sure it will be a fine meal, Pitte. You've never served us anything but."

Pitte smiled, revealing the few remaining teeth in his head. "Thank you, milord. When would you like this feast to occur?"

"As soon as possible, of course."

"Is two days soon enough?"

"Yes, wonderful," said Soth.

"Then excuse me, milord. I have many things to prepare." The stout old man bowed his head and turned, then scurried off to the kitchen.

"Now," said Soth. "As for the rest of you . . ."

* * * * *

Pitte had been good to his word and despite the short notice, he and his staff had done an exemplary job preparing the feast. In addition to the many varieties of meats and cheeses available, Pitte had also prepared many different colored dishes using vegetable dyes such as parsley for green, saffron for yellow and sandalwood for red. It was a small detail, but one that made the celebration all the more festive.

But best of all, was the celebratory cake that Pitte had baked in the shape of a cradle, frosted with white sugar and gilded with decorative roses.

Soth was grateful to the old man and couldn't help but think that even before his child was born, it was already being treated as something special by those within the keep. Whether it was a boy or a girl, its childhood would be filled with countless happy days.

The feast lasted for hours, the wine and ale flowing like water into the glasses of the gathered knights. One sign that they had drunk far more than was proper was their terrible renditions of songs praising the virtue of Vinas Solamnus. The songs droned on, one word sliding into the next until mercifully the sound would end with a raucous round of applause. Soth was grateful when Caradoc was persuaded to stand before the high table and offer the parents-to-be a token gift on behalf of the knights.

"My lord," said Caradoc, nodding first to Lord Soth, and then to his fellow knights. "I know it is perhaps too early for gifts for the unborn child, but the joy I and my fellow knights felt upon hearing the good news was far too great to let pass without even a token gesture."

He nodded at a pair of pages at the entrance to the hall.

"So, as a symbol of our heartfelt happiness over the news that a young Soth will soon be roaming the keep, the knights and I would like you to have these gifts"—he gestured to the items being carted in by the pages—"so that your offspring will grow up to be as great a knight as its father has already become."

The pages put down the gifts. Inside two crates were finely crafted wooden swords, shields and intricately tooled leather armor, all sized to fit the hands and body of a growing child through each of its stages of development.

Soth was speechless. Many of these items were family heirlooms, passed on from generation to generation. They would be just as at home on a mantle as in the hands of a child.

Soth rose from his seat, bowed concession to Caradoc and then to the rest of the knights. "I thank you, all. And a toast to the Knights of Solamnia, the greatest collection of *uncles* a child could ever wish for."

The knights erupted in a loud cheer, then the room was silent as everyone drank to the toast.

Soth leaned down, turned to Korinne and said, "I must thank them all individually."

"After such a gesture," Korinne said, shaking her head, "it's the least you can do."

Soth left the high table and immediately made his way to Caradoc.

"Korinne and I were touched by your gesture, Caradoc," Lord Soth said as he slapped a hand onto the shoulder of his seneschal.

"We've had them collected for months, milord," Caradoc answered. "We were simply waiting for the right time to present them."

"And waiting . . ."

"And waiting . . ." said a few of the other knights.

"Well, nevertheless, your thoughtfulness is greatly appreciated."

Caradoc waved his hand in a gesture that suggested that Soth should think nothing of it. Then the knight took a sip of wine.

Soth pulled away from the table of knights and was heading for an adjoining table when he ran into Isolde. She had been wandering the hall playing her harp for those attending the banquet. But from the look on her face, Soth knew she had something on her mind other than making good music.

"I wish to speak to you," she said.

Soth realized he was in an awkward position. To the rest of the people within the keep, Isolde was a special guest. And, because of her elven heritage, to some others she was a great curiosity. Either way, she hardly mingled without being noticed. If Soth spoke to her now, dozens of eyes would be watching.

"Very well," said Soth, stepping to one side of the hall where he could lean casually against a wall while the elfmaid talked to him.

"First of all, let me congratulate you and Lady Korinne on the good news."

Soth smiled politely. "Thank you."

Isolde glanced around the room, careful to make it look as if this was nothing but a simple meeting of two friends. "I wanted to tell you that since Korinne is with child and your problems seem to be over, perhaps it might be better if I returned to Silvanesti." She strummed her harp, tuning several of the strings after each pass of her hand.

Soth knew she was right. There was no place for her in the keep, especially now. But as he looked into her eyes and saw the overwhelming beauty of her face, he knew he wasn't ready to let her go, or perhaps he wasn't able. Whatever the reason, she had to remain close to him.

"No!" said Soth in something of a harsh whisper even though the noise within the hall was more than enough to drown out any part of their conversation. "You must stay. . . ." His voice trailed off, then suddenly gained strength. "Please."

Isolde shook her head. "What am I to do here? Istvan is wasting his own valuable time trying to find things for me to do."

"You can stay," Soth said, searching his mind for any reason at all for her to remain. "Perhaps you might be able to help Korinne with the child when it comes."

"Oh, I doubt that very much. Lady Korinne wouldn't want me anywhere near her child."

"She has no reason to dislike you."

"Perhaps not, but let us just say I have a feeling that I am not one of her favorite inhabitants of the keep."

Soth looked aside and accepted the congratulations of a woman who passed by; then he turned back to Isolde.

"I *want* you," he said, "to stay." He paused, considering his words. "As Korinne becomes heavy with child, I will be needing you more than ever." He looked at her for the longest time, letting his steel blue eyes pierce right through to her heart.

"All right," she said at last, her voice edged with a sort of doomed reluctance. "I will stay."

Soth's head arched back and he smiled as if Isolde had just said something tremendously funny. "Wonderful!" he said, shaking her hand. He raised the volume of his voice so those close-by could hear him. "Yes, indeed. I am a very happy man."

* * * * *

Korinne had watched as Soth moved through the hall, greeting people and gladly shaking hands. He seemed happier than she'd ever seen him before, and she was satisfied that she had made him that way.

But then Soth had turned away from Caradoc and found himself face-to-face with the elf-maid Isolde.

The sight had suddenly made Korinne feel sick to her stomach.

She had watched motionless and silent as her husband and the elf-maid talked to one another on the other side of the hall. There was nothing out of the ordinary in their mannerisms, nothing that might suggest they were anything more than friends. Of course, there *was* a bond between them. He had saved her life, after all.

Korinne had felt a little better when she saw the elf-maid idly tuning her harp and her husband intently greeting passersby in the middle of their little chat. When they were done, Soth had laughed politely at some joke the elf had made and they had parted as simply as any two friends would part.

There had been nothing to it.

Then why, even now as Soth happily moved about the room to chat with others, did this feeling of sickness continue to gnaw at her belly?

Chapter 18

The months passed like days for some, like years for others.

For those inside the keep, the months flew by as countless hours were spent preparing the nursery, making clothes or guessing what name the new Soth might be blessed with.

But for Lady Korinne the winter moved at a crawl. While some of her early months were spent performing such motherly duties as decorating the nursery, much of her time was spent resting in bed under the almost constant supervision of the healer, Istvan. His regular examinations always concluded with the same proclamation "Everything between mother and child is as well as could be expected."

But no matter how many times Korinne heard those words, they did little to ease the pain she felt inside. The child had become more than a simple burden upon her and at times she wondered why she had never heard other pregnant women complain of bouts of such constant, throbbing pain.

And as the months wore on, it was a surprise to no

one that an ever-increasing amount of Korinne's time was spent at rest. Throughout the night and much of the day she'd lie in bed, either asleep or in a half-awake sort of daze in which she was almost literally blinded by the pain.

As a result, the winter days and nights seemed to be at a standstill for Lord Soth, who in aching anticipation of the birth of his child, found he could spend little time with his wife. When she was up and about she tried to occupy herself with some pleasant detail concerning the child-to-be. Or, if she were free, he would be occupied by some tedious, but nevertheless important, matter of state. When she slept, the healer had ordered that she not be disturbed, and when she was lying in her bed neither awake nor asleep, she was too affected by her pain to be much of a companion, or even very receptive to Soth's awkward efforts at comforting her.

And so, on one of the coldest days of Deepkolt, Soth looked elsewhere in the keep for companionship. Weeks earlier, he had instructed the healer to provide Isolde with her own private quarters. The healer had done so gladly, putting the elf-maid in a room at the south end of the keep that had not one but two entrances, one leading in from the main hallway, and another leading in from a seldom-used storage room. Soth thanked the healer by promising to acquire more blue hyssop for him on his next trip to Palanthas, and never spoke of the matter again.

And now, Soth walked through the cold, damp storage room placing his hand against the inside of the moss-covered south wall to guide his way. When he came up against another wall, he patted his hands against it until he felt the rough grain of several wooden planks butted up against one another. Certain he'd found the door, he rapped his knuckles against the wood.

"Who is it?" came the sweet voice from inside.

"It is I," he said. "Lord Soth."

Seconds later, the door was being opened.

*　*　*　*　*

The months continued to pass.
Brookgreen . . .
Yurthgreen . . .
Fleurgreen . . .
At last spring was in the air.
New buds appeared on the branches.
Flowers began to bloom.
And Korinne's child was ready to come into the world.

*　*　*　*　*

Soth lay on the bed, his muscular naked body covered with a thin layer of sweat. At his side, the lithe form of Isolde, similarly damp with sweat, nestled into place within his arms. When she'd found a comfortable position she breathed out a deep sigh of satisfaction, then said, "The keep will soon have another mouth to feed."

Soth's smile was brief. Although he did not like to be reminded of his wife and unborn child when he was with Isolde, he'd never told the elf-maid not to mention Korinne, because the times she did were rare. "Yes," he said matter-of-factly. "Korinne is due to birth the child any day now."

Isolde looked at Soth with a coy sort of grin.

Soth noticed the look on the elf-maid's face. "What is it?" he asked.

"I'm not talking about Lady Korinne."

Soth was silent for a moment. "If not Korinne, who then?"

"Me," said Isolde. "I'm talking about me."

Soth's mouth opened, but he found himself unable to speak. He sat up in the bed and looked at the elf-maid grinning up at him like a kender who'd just borrowed a large cluster of priceless jewels.

"You mean . . ."

185

Isolde nodded.

At first, Soth was overjoyed, but slowly found himself becoming troubled by the news. All he could think of was the problems a bastard child would cause for him within the keep. The secrecy and lies, the problems his off-spring—both of them—would have when they would inevitably fight one another for the legacy of the Soth name. He thought of his own half-brother and half-sister, both killed due to his orders to ensure his own succession as sole heir to the Soth name and to the throne of Knightlund.

In a single horrible moment, Soth realized that although he had vowed to distance himself from his father he had actually become his father, producing a bastard child just as his father had done so many years ago—a half-elven child at that.

The words of his father echoed cruelly in his ears.

"Don't be so quick to condemn me, my son," Aynkell Soth had said. "You are of my flesh and of my blood. You always will be. There's too much of me in you for you to be so critical of my life."

Soth shivered at the recollection. Then he looked at Isolde, saw the joy in her eyes, and knew he couldn't bring himself to share with her the sense of dread that was claw-ing at his heart. "That's wonderful news," he stammered.

"It doesn't sound as if—"

Isolde's words were cut short by a knock upon the door that led out into the main hallway.

"Who is it?" asked Isolde, her voice calm.

"Beg your pardon, but is . . . milord with you?"

Isolde looked at Soth, her eyes wide with a mix of sur-prise and fear.

"Who dares to call for me here?" bellowed Lord Soth, letting the person outside know that he didn't look favor-ably upon such a blatant invasion of his privacy.

"It's Caradoc, milord."

Soth rose from the bed and moved toward the door.

"What is it?" he asked, the irritation gone from his voice.

"It's your wife, milord," said Caradoc. "She's birthing the child and is calling for you."

"I will be there at once."

He turned to face Isolde, unable to say anything.

Fortunately, he didn't have to. "Go," said Isolde. "Your wife needs you."

Soth dressed hurriedly and as he rushed down the hallway found that he could hear the agonizing screams of Lady Korinne even before he reached the healer's chambers. She was obviously in pain, a great deal of pain.

It is said that the pain of childbirth is the most easily forgotten, but Soth found this hard to believe.

When he reached the healer's quarters he knocked on the door even though, in this situation, he wasn't required to do so. After waiting a few moments, Soth realized no one had heard his knock over the loud cries of Lady Korinne. He opened the door and suddenly heard Korinne's screams at full volume.

At first Soth winced at the sound. Although he'd heard men in battle cry out in agony, he'd never heard such screams as he was hearing now.

He hurried over to Korinne's side. When she saw him, she relaxed somewhat and her wails lessened. He took her hand and held it as she panted to catch her breath.

She was drenched in sweat, her hair pasted down onto her forehead and across her face. Her lips were dry and cracked and her chest rose and fell at a frantic pace, as if she'd just completed a nonstop run from Palanthas.

"Loren," she said when she was able. "I've been calling for you. Where have you been?"

Soth found it hard to say anything. He saw the trusting look in her eyes, the relief on her face upon his arrival and felt sick that he'd betrayed her. "I was," he said. The next few words seemed to get stuck in his throat for a moment. "I was . . . reprimanding one of the knights."

"Really," she said, seemingly happy to have her mind

diverted by chatter. "Who was it? What did he do wrong?"

"That's not important now," said Soth. "What's important is how you are feeling."

"Can't you see, I'm doing wonderfully—" A sudden stab of pain sliced through Korinne's body and she arched her back. She let out a sharp cry, then lay back on the bed, her eyes closed and at rest.

Soth brushed a hand over Korinne's face and looked over at the healer.

Istvan had been busy off in the corner preparing herb mixtures while Soth and Korinne had spoken. Now he moved to Korinne's side, wiping her face with a damp cloth.

"What is happening?" asked Soth.

Istvan shook his head. "Everything appears to be progressing normally. I have delivered twenty-seven children in my time and all is as it should be. The pain she is feeling confounds me."

"Can't you prepare something to lessen it?"

"I've tried," Istvan answered with a shrug. "But nothing seems to be working." He looked Korinne over as he patted the damp cloth across her forehead. "Your presence seems to have calmed her. This is the first she's been able to rest for hours."

"Then I will stay until the child is born."

"Thank you," said Istvan. "It might help."

Soth looked at Istvan, wondering about the healer's choice of the word *might*. Something told Soth that the healer, as was his custom, knew more than he was letting on.

* * * * *

"I can see the head!" cried the healer, sweat dripping down off his nose. He'd wanted to call in an assistant hours ago, but Soth had forbidden it, not wanting any more people than were necessary to see Lady Korinne in such a compromised state.

Soth was out in the hall just on the other side of the door. He had been in the room for the longest time, but his constant concern over Korinne's agonized shrieks had prompted the healer to ask Soth to leave the room, allowing him to do his work without the interference and misguided concerns of an impassioned observer.

"You must push," said Istvan. "Push harder!"

"I can't," cried Korinne, at the point of exhaustion.

Istvan believed her. He had never in his years seen such a lengthy and painful birth. Everything about the delivery of this child was slow and complicated when in truth there were absolutely no signs warranting complications, or pain for that matter. But here was Korinne, in labor half the day.

"You must try," Istvan said, his voice showing far more compassion than normal. Usually he was very hard on women during birth, forcing them to work harder in order to end their ordeal more quickly. But Korinne had already suffered too much, for too long.

Korinne cut short a moan and pushed.

The child's head moved slightly, no more than the width of several hairs. "Yes, that's it! Very good! Again!"

"It moved?" exclaimed Korinne, her voice breathy and filled with relief.

"Yes, it's coming. Now, push again."

She grimaced and tightened her body, tensing her stomach muscles and trying to squeeze the child through the far-too-small birth canal.

"I see an ear!" cried Istvan. "Keep going!"

Korinne was almost laughing now. She probably felt the child beginning to move a little more each time. After so many hours, she was happy to see it finally out of her body.

She closed her eyes, pressed her lips together and grabbed at the wooden rails on either side of the bed.

Then she groaned sharply, and pushed.

Her fingernails cut deeply into the hard, polished wood of the rails.

The child's entire head appeared, followed quickly by its shoulders, neck.

And then . . .

The rest of its body slid out into the world, almost in a gush. Istvan caught the child, and gasped.

He held the child in his hands and for the longest time his mouth moved, but he was unable to speak.

Finally, he said in a whisper, "Mishakal have mercy."

* * * * *

Outside the room, Soth had been waiting for what seemed like hours. The screams of his wife had pained him and now that they had stopped, he feared the worst.

But as he continued to wait in silence, not knowing what had happened was far worse than hearing the constant cries of pain. At last he rose up from where he sat and opened the door to the healer's chambers.

The room seemed even quieter than the hall had been. Korinne was lying on the bed, her chest rising and falling in a deep and regular rhythm. Istvan sat at his desk with his head in his hands, no doubt exhausted by what had been a lengthy birth.

Soth looked around for the child, but did not see it.

When Soth closed the door behind him, Istvan jumped. The healer looked over at Soth, his face pale and his eyes wide in something very much like fear. As Soth moved closer, he noticed the old man looking even more aged and haggard than he remembered.

"Is she all right?" asked Soth in a whisper.

Istvan nodded. "Lady Korinne is resting. She will recover."

Soth nodded. "And what of the child?"

"It is resting as well, in the bassinet over there." He pointed to a small cradle made of dark wood, a simple but well-constructed piece Istvan had chosen from the numerous examples Soth and Korinne had received as wedding gifts.

Soth looked at Istvan for several long seconds. Something wasn't right. If the child was doing well, Istvan would be overjoyed, and Korinne would be holding the child to her breast even in her current state of exhaustion. And what had Istvan said? *It* was resting, he'd said. Not *he* or *she*, but *it*.

"Can I see . . ." Soth began.

"Perhaps it might be best if—"

"I said, can I see my child?" Soth asked, louder this time.

Korinne stirred. "Is that you, Loren?" she asked.

Istvan knew better than to defy Soth twice. "Of course." He got up from where he sat and walked over to the bassinet. Then he reached into the cradle and took out the bundled child, wrapped tightly in a scarlet blanket. He handed the bundle to Soth.

Soth found it awkward to hold the bundle properly, but he eventually managed to get a firm but gentle grasp. He hadn't held that many babies in his lifetime, but this child *felt* different. Its body seemed hard and bony.

Istvan turned away, taking up a position near Korinne.

Soth pulled aside the blanket and looked upon . . .

An abomination.

The child's eyes were open wide, shining black and glassy in the dim light from the candles. There were hard nubs of bones along the crown of its head, almost as if it were the offspring of a dragon.

Soth swallowed, his body shuddering in shock. He pulled the blanket further aside and saw . . .

That the child's two arms were on the right side of its body, a leg where the other arm should be. And the second leg was positioned in the center of the lower portion of the trunk, looking much like a tail.

Soth felt his knees go weak and his heart beginning to

creep up into his throat.

This was no child of his.

This was the spawn of Evil, the offspring of one of the dark and evil gods.

Soth took another glance at the child and grimaced.

It wasn't even a child.

It was a monster.

And even if there wasn't a dark god at work here, then it could have easily been the work of some other hideous beast; a centaur perhaps, or a satyr. What else could have caused such gross deformity of the human body?

The thought of Korinne with another man—with another *creature*—sent anger flaring through Soth's body.

He wrapped the thing back in the blanket and held it at arm's length.

"Have you seen him?" asked Korinne, her voice soft yet proud. "Is he beautiful?"

Madness roiled in the pit of Soth's belly, slowly making its way to his brain. "Take it!" Soth said to Istvan, holding the child out to the healer.

"What's wrong?" asked Korinne.

"So you think the beast beautiful, do you?" Soth shouted. "Have you been so blinded by love for the devouring dark that you can't even see the evil offspring you've created?"

"What?" cried Korinne, struggling to sit up. "Let me see him. Let me see my boy!"

"Boy?" said Soth, walking over to Istvan and snatching the blanket from his hands. He unwrapped the child and held it high above his head. "Is this your boy? Or is this the product of monstrous infidelity, evil faithlessness?"

Korinne simply looked at the child, blinking in disbelief. Her mind was reeling. Finally she shook her head. "No, I've always been faithful to you."

"Liar!" He shook the child as he spoke and Istvan quickly retrieved it.

"I have been, I swear to you!" repeated Korinne.

"Then how do you explain that . . . that monster?"

"My boy?" Korinne asked, looking to Istvan.

She paused in confusion and then suddenly her face became a mask of terror. She turned her wide eyes upon her husband. "It's your fault. You were the one who created it!"

"Has your lover made you mad as well?" shouted Soth.

"Your seed wouldn't give me a child, so I paid a visit to the hedge witch who *gave* me a child . . . the child you couldn't produce."

"So, it's born of the blackest sort of magic," Soth hissed.

"No, the blackest of souls," replied Korinne.

For a moment, Korinne's words sent a spike of fear through Soth's heart. "Istvan," he called. "Leave the room. Now."

Istvan made ready to leave, carrying the child.

"Leave it there!"

Dutifully, Istvan set the child in the bassinet and left the room, locking the door behind him.

Soth turned to face Korinne.

"What madness moves your tongue?"

Korinne was in tears. "The witch told me the health of the child would depend on the purity of *your* soul. I knew you'd been intimate with the elf, but I could never imagine you'd done so much evil in your life that you could produce such a . . . such a . . ." Her voice trailed off and she began to sob openly.

Soth looked at her, the words causing a sudden touch of fear to become mixed in with his rage. If it were true, if the child's health depended on his virtue, it was no wonder that it had been born a . . .

A sort of madness began to seep into his mind as he realized that, as much as he'd tried to avoid them, his father's sins had become his, had become his child's.

The sins of the father, passed on from generation to generation.

"What have you done?" Korinne shouted between sobs. "What black deed have you done?"

Soth's eyes narrowed as he glared at Korinne. The sudden shock he'd felt at her words had been erased by rage.

And now, utter madness was overtaking him. A potent mixture of rage, anger, jealousy, and self-hate. It consumed him like flame, controlled his actions.

Without answering her question, he drew a dagger from the belt around his waist and held it before him in his fisted right hand.

"What . . . what are you doing?" she screamed, her eyes wide with terror. "No, please—"

He was at one with the madness now.

As he moved toward Korinne, the sounds of her screams were suddenly mixed with the sickeningly hoarse grunts of the newborn child.

Minutes later there was only silence.

* * * * *

Caradoc and Istvan had been waiting outside the chamber while Soth was inside with his wife and newborn child.

Why Soth wanted to be alone in the room, particularly without the help of the healer, Caradoc didn't know. What he did know was that if Soth wanted to be alone in the room, then it was up to him to make sure he remain undisturbed.

When Korinne's screams began, Istvan abruptly got up from where he sat and desperately wanted to gain access to the chambers. It was his job, after all, to heal the sick and ease the suffering of those in pain. But rather than allow him entrance to the room, Caradoc had moved in front of the door, blocking Istvan's way.

"Perhaps it would be best to wait until milord calls you back inside."

Istvan had been troubled by this, and well he should, thought Caradoc, because there was something strange about the birth of this child. So much pain, it wasn't right.

Nevertheless, both Caradoc and Istvan's allegiance was sworn to the lord of the keep and it was their duty to follow his orders.

When Korinne's screams grew louder, Caradoc himself had wanted to break down the door to find out what was happening, but he steeled himself against the impulse and cast a cold eye toward Istvan to make sure the healer did not move.

And now they waited patiently for the appearance of Lord Soth, Caradoc cleaning his fingernails with the end of a stiletto, Istvan doing a variety of stretching exercises designed to ease the troublesome pain in his joints.

The door suddenly moved, then began to swing open on its hinges. Soth appeared in the doorway, his long black hair hanging down from his head like tattered threads, a touch of gray apparent around the temples and streaked throughout with wisps of white.

"Is everything all right, milord?" asked Caradoc.

Soth shook his head. "No, I'm afraid it isn't."

"What's happened?" said Istvan, getting to his feet.

"Unfortunately, both milady and the child . . . died during childbirth," said Soth, his voice surprisingly calm. He looked directly at Istvan. "Despite your best efforts."

"But I—" Istvan began to say.

Soth cut him off with a hard look, then turned to face Caradoc.

The seneschal shivered as Soth's cold eyes seem to cut right through him.

"I said, milady and the child died during childbirth." He said each word slowly and clearly. "Despite the heroic efforts of our most brave and gallant healer."

"Yes, milord," said Caradoc.

Soth waited for the healer to speak.

"Yes, milord," Istvan whispered.

Soth nodded, leaned forward to speak directly to Caradoc. "Get rid of the bodies," he said. "And make sure there's nothing left when you are done."

Caradoc swallowed. "Yes, milord."

"Good," said Soth. "Istvan. It's been a long night. Perhaps we should both get some rest." He put a hand on the healer's shoulder and led him away.

Caradoc entered the chamber. After two steps he realized his boots were sticking to blood that had pooled on the surface of the floor. Nevertheless he continued toward where the bed sat against the far wall of the room.

He stopped dead in his tracks long before he got there.

As he looked at the gore on the bed, his stomach spasmed and he swallowed in an attempt to keep from retching. He covered his mouth and tried to look away, but found he couldn't—his eyes were too firmly locked on the blood-soaked bed.

And while he did his best to block all thought from his mind so that he might be able to complete his assigned task, one thought kept coming back to him.

Even some of Soth's worst enemies—beings who championed the forces of evil and who were killed in the intense heat of battle—had never been so completely savaged.

Chapter 19

The silhouette of the pyre stood out in high relief against the red and orange streaks that colored the twilight sky. Atop the pyre on one side was a long, rectangular wooden box. On the other side was a much smaller box about the size of a traveler's trunk.

Lord Soth had specified that the bodies of Lady Korinne and the child be disposed of by fire in order to prevent the spread of disease. Although many who had been close to Korinne showed consternation over the matter, Soth insisted that it was necessary to protect the rest of those within the keep.

Protect them from what, he wouldn't say.

One of the most vocal opponents to such a ceremony was Korinne's mother, Leyla, who wanted the bodies of both her daughter and grandchild to be brought back to Palanthas so that they might rest alongside her husband Reynard in the Gladria family tomb. Soth said no to the request, and after that all others were reluctant to approach him on the subject.

As the last pieces of hardwood were being placed on the

pyre, the crowd slowly closed in around it, huddling together as if for warmth. Despite the rich warm colors painting the sky, the evening air was cooler than normal, a subtle reminder of the somber mood pervading the gathering.

Soth himself had been affected more than anyone by the deaths, as well he should. But more than simply grieving, he seemed to be pulling himself away from all but his closest friends and confidants. His knights were, of course, part of his shrinking inner circle, as was the healer and a few others who had always been close to him. But what raised more than a few eyebrows was his frequent contact with the elf-maid, Isolde Denissa.

While it was to be expected that there would be a bond between the two—he had saved her life, after all—they were seen together far more often than was appropriate for such casual acquaintances, particularly so soon after the death of Lady Korinne.

Then there were those who were thankful for Isolde's presence within the keep. Whenever Soth spoke to her or was in her company, he seemed less troubled and more easily able to deal with his pain. If she was helping the lord of the keep to better handle the sudden loss of Korinne and his child, then so be it.

As the last of the crowd moved in tightly around the pyre, Soth found himself standing next to Isolde. Then, as the torches were thrown against the kindling at the bottom of the pyre and the fire started to burn, Soth leaned to his right and spoke to her.

Many in attendance noticed the subtle movement, and thought it odd. Others took it as an ominous sign that things would be very different around the keep now that Lady Korinne was gone.

* * * * *

Isolde wept as she watched the flames begin creeping up toward the boxes containing Korinne and her child. To lose a wife and a child, a child so long-awaited and short-lived, was an event painful beyond imagining.

Soth was being strong through the tragedy, but the catastrophic nature of it had to have taken its toll on him. As heroic as his stature was, he was only a man.

She continued to weep as she watched the fire burn, the flames leaving bright orange coals in their wake. The flames rose higher, engulfing the boxes and obscuring them from view.

And then, as Isolde watched the fire burn, she felt the warm press of Soth's breath against her ear.

"Weep not, my love," he whispered. "After the required six months of mourning is observed, the keep will have another lady. And after that, there will be the arrival of another Soth child to be rejoiced."

Isolde continued to weep . . .

But slowly her tears turned into those of joy.

* * * * *

Six months later, in the middle of Darkember, Lord Soth and Isolde Denissa were wed in the grand hall in Dargaard Keep. The wedding ceremony was a far cry from the pomp and ceremony of Soth's first marriage to Lady Korinne, but no one in the keep thought it would be proper to have a wedding on such a grand scale so closely following the death of Korinne and her child.

Caradoc joined Soth at the altar, while Mirrel took her place by Isolde's side. Shortly after Soth had asked her to marry him, Isolde had asked Mirrel to be her lady-in-waiting. At first Mirrel had refused the offer, but Isolde eventually managed to convince the young girl that she needed her help in order to keep things running smoothly within the keep. It would be Mirrel's job to advise the new lady of the keep about rules of order and other matters of decorum. When it was put to her in that way, Mirrel quickly accepted the position in the hopes of somehow keeping Korinne's memory alive for years to come.

Other prominent guests at the wedding included Istvan, who seemed to have grown even closer to Lord Soth over the last few months. Soth was almost doting on the elderly healer. Soth's knights were also present, all thirteen of them in gleaming plate and mail armor, forming an honor guard for Soth and his bride. And finally, rounding out the wedding party, were the elf-maids who had been traveling with Isolde when they were unceremoniously attacked by ogres and subsequently rescued by Soth and his knights.

Sadly, the elf-woman who'd been escorting Isolde and her friends to Palanthas had been unable to attend. When Soth had asked why, one of the elf-maids had told him she was too sick to attend, while another had said she refused to attend because she considered the marriage to be a doomed one.

The only other person in attendance from outside Dargaard Keep was Lord Cyril Mordren, High Clerist of the Knights of Solamnia. He had been summoned from Palanthas to conduct the ceremony, but responded with surprise because he hadn't been called to the keep to perform any burial rights following the death of Lady Korinne. Nevertheless, he performed the wedding ceremony adequately enough, although he did glance several times at Isolde's belly which—although difficult to be certain—seemed to be heavy with child.

"You are now wed, husband and wife," said Lord Mordren, concluding the ceremony. "You may kiss her, if you wish."

Soth took Isolde in his arms and kissed her full on the mouth.

The hall was filled with the sound of clapping hands. A polite amount of applause. Nothing more.

* * * * *

"Did you see her?" asked one of the serving girls as she set the plates upon the high table for the wedding feast. "Out to here."

"Maybe she's getting fat," said another girl, putting the cups into place. "You know, living too well in the keep and all of that."

"Have you ever seen a fat elf?"

"No, but . . ."

"I say milord sure didn't waste any time."

"Nooo!"

"Oh yes, and there's others that say worse."

The second woman stopped placing cups on the tables. "What do they say?"

The first girl looked left and right before speaking. "They say that Lady Korinne didn't die birthing the child. They say she died after."

"Who's they?"

"Them that knows."

"Who?" the second girl demanded.

"Mirrel," the first whispered. "The elf's lady-in-waiting herself."

The second girl just shook her head. "No. I can't believe it. Not milord."

The first serving girl looked at the other, glaring. "You believe what you want. My guess is that the whole truth might never be known. All I know is that it's been six months since milady died and if I didn't know any better I'd say the elf is about that far along. Maybe more."

"It can't be."

"Well, we'll see. But I'll bet a month's wages there'll be a little Soth running around the keep sooner than you'd expect."

After a few moments of silence, the second girl said. "I don't think I want to take that bet."

"Hmmph!" said the first, satisfied she was in the right.

The two girls continued working in silence.

* * * * *

Darkember passed, followed by Frostkelt and Newkelt.

Over the course of the three months, Isolde's belly swelled ever larger until one night early in the new year, she went into labor.

Istvan, the keep's healer, wasn't looking forward to bringing another child into the world, especially into the increasingly mysterious world of Dargaard Keep. Since the death of Lady Korinne the keep had become a shadow of its former self. It was no longer a place of life and vitality, but rather a place shrouded by darkness and permeated by a sense of foreboding.

But despite his personal apprehension over the matter, Istvan was bound to Lord Soth and dutifully worked to bring the new Soth offspring into being. Unlike that of Lady Korinne, Isolde's delivery was almost effortless and without pain. Still, Istvan couldn't bring himself to look at the child at first, afraid it might be another grotesque monstrosity. When he finally did look at it, however, he was relieved to find it was a boy, a large and healthy boy with all of his little parts in the right places, including a thick head of coal black hair just like that of his father.

So, with mother and child resting comfortably, Istvan called on Lord Soth, inviting him to join his wife and newborn child.

"Is everything all right?" asked Soth, his usually strong voice sounding somewhat unsure of itself.

"Yes," said Istvan.

"Everything?"

"The mother and the boy are both doing well."

"The boy?"

"Yes. A strong and healthy boy. Congratulations." Istvan paused a moment to give Soth the chance to express his appreciation for a successful birth.

But instead of expressing his gratitude to the healer,

Soth pushed by Istvan and rushed into the room to join his wife and newborn son.

Istvan sighed and closed the door to his chambers, allowing the new family a few moments alone.

* * * * *

"You're a handsome young devil, aren't you," cooed Mirrel as she tended to the newborn Soth. The child, a half-elf, had been named Peradur in honor of Soth's great-great-grandfather who had been the first of the Soth clan to become a Knight of Solamnia under the command of Vinas Solamnus himself.

The child made soft, gurgling sounds. It was a happy, content baby, and Mirrel was proud that the child was doing so well. While she knew of Soth's unfaithfulness to Korinne and it was clear the child had been conceived while Soth was still wed to Lady Korinne—indeed while she was heavy with a child of her own—Mirrel still loved the child. It was an innocent bystander faultlessly caught up in a web of deceit. And besides that, Lady Korinne had wanted so much to have a child that she would have wanted this child to grow up as if it were her own.

If anyone were to blame in this whole mess it was the hallowed Lord Loren Soth of Dargaard Keep, Knight of the Rose and philanderer of the highest order.

She'd been making her opinions known to anyone in the keep who would listen and those people numbered more and more each day. She knew it was dangerous to speak such words so freely, knew she could lose her position in the keep—perhaps even her life, judging by some of Lord Soth's past deeds—but she couldn't stop herself. Lady Korinne had risked everything to give her husband a child, and he had repaid her by bedding the elf while she had been bed-ridden. Then he had brutally murdered her when the child turned out to be somewhat less than healthy.

She couldn't prove the last point, but she knew it almost

intuitively. Once the healer had told her that Lady Korinne had lived through the birth, then quickly recanted, saying he had become confused with the birth of another child that same day.

It wasn't like the healer to make such mistakes. He was old, but his mind was still as sharp as many of his instruments. If he had been mistaken about such a subject, then there had been a reason for it. After hours of long thought over the matter, she surmised that he had told Mirrel the truth in order to circumvent his oath of loyalty to Lord Soth.

As a result she'd been busy spreading the word.

Not many had believed her at first, but over time more and more people began wondering if it might be true, and that was enough.

For now.

Eventually, she would make Soth pay for murdering Lady Korinne, but for now she was content merely to tarnish the image of the great and heroic knight. The rest would come later.

The baby swung his arms in wide arcs and laughed. "You're going to be a good knight when you grow up, a better knight than your father is, which shouldn't be all that hard to do."

"Mirrel!"

Mirrel gasped at the sound of Isolde's voice and slowly turned around. The elf was standing in the doorway. How long she'd been there Mirrel couldn't tell, but she was fairly certain that she'd been there long enough to hear her speak poorly of milord. "Yes, milady."

Isolde stepped into the room. She was a beautiful being, even for an elf, and many said her beauty far outshone that of Lady Korinne's. Mirrel didn't see it that way. In her mind, no one could match the beauty of Lady Korinne, especially inside where she had been most beautiful of all.

"I've heard some distressing things during my walk through the keep this morning."

"Distressing things," said Mirrel. "Like what?"

Isolde stepped into the room and sat down near Mirrel and the baby. "People are saying that Lady Korinne didn't die during childbirth, but was killed after the fact."

Obviously Isolde had paused to give Mirrel the chance to condemn such accusations, but Mirrel simply sat in silence with her hands folded on her lap.

"I've tried to quell the rumor, but it's strong and still it persists."

Mirrel knew she was treading on unsteady ground, but she decided to venture forth. After all, this could be her best chance to convince the elf of the truth. "Perhaps it's true, then."

"It is not!"

"What if it is?"

Isolde looked at Mirrel for a very long time. Finally, her eyes narrowed and she said, "It's you, isn't it? You're the one spreading the rumors, telling lies."

"No lies, milady," said Mirrel, realizing that if she'd gone this far, she might as well go all the way. "The truth."

"Liar!" shouted Isolde.

Mirrel refused to be shouted down into silence. She defiantly thrust her chin forward and began to tell Isolde of her and Korinne's midnight journey to the home of the hedge witch and the warning the old witch had made about the child's well-being—that it depended solely on the purity of the Lord Soth's soul.

"Enough!" cried Isolde, her hands over her ears and her head turning from side to side. "Lies, they're all lies!"

"What possible benefit would I gain by lying?" asked Mirrel. "What reason do I have for lying, other than undying loyalty to Lady Korinne?"

"Out!" screamed Isolde.

The child had begun to cry.

"Out of my chambers! Out of this tower! Out of Dargaard Keep!"

"You can send me away," said Mirrel getting up to

leave. "But ridding yourself of the truth won't be as easy!"

Isolde thrust out her hand, pointing at the open door.

Mirrel left without another word.

* * * * *

The portcullis was raised long before Mirrel was ready to leave. Along with the guards manning the gatehouse and drawbridge, there were several of her friends waiting to say good-bye. None of them looked happy to see her go. After all, Mirrel had been one of their own, elevated in status through the sheer good graces of Lady Korinne.

"Don't worry," said a laundress. "You'll be back in the keep someday soon."

Mirrel just stared at the woman, a look of pity on her face. "What makes you think I'd want to return to such a damned and cursed keep as this?"

The women were shocked by the words, unable to say anything in reply.

"With the way things are going," added Mirrel, "I'm lucky to be leaving while I'm still able."

This was far truer than Mirrel liked to let on. It had been fortunate for her that Lady Isolde had had the arrogance to handle her banishment by herself. For if Isolde had gone to Lord Soth with the problem, Mirrel might have suddenly disappeared under curious circumstances, or have simply been murdered by Caradoc or one of the other knights.

"Then may Mishakal light your way," said one of women as Mirrel headed toward the bridge.

Mirrel stopped, turned and looked at the woman. She nodded thanks and said, "And yours as well."

Then she turned away and exited the keep.

Outside, it was late afternoon and the light of day was slowly being shrouded by the gathering darkness.

Chapter 20

The night sky was clear of clouds and the stars twinkled against their black backdrop like diamonds under a midday sun.

The Kingpriest of Istar stood alone on the balcony of the highest tower of the temple. He was dressed in one of his finest silken robes. It was yellow and white, and bejeweled with all manner of rare gemstones, including diamonds.

He had come to address the gods.

His brethren.

He stepped up onto a platform so that he was standing above the balcony's rail and unencumbered by such mundane man-made concerns as walls and rails and floors. He stood, almost on the air, with nothing before him but the cool night air, and nothing above him but the black star-studded night sky.

"My fellows," he began, raising his arms over his shoulders. "I have labored for many years to bring peace to the races and tribes of Krynn; indeed it had been my life's work. Once peace was achieved I made sure that it would last for hundreds of years, something even you as gods could not do for the people consigned to your ever-watchful care. Further to that, I made the Proclamation of Manifest Virtue, declaring that Evil in the world was an affront to both mortals as well as we gods."

Clouds slowly began to move in from the north and west.

"I single-handedly vanquished Evil from the face of Krynn, and further enabled Good to spread across the land by leading the Siege on Sorcery, exiling the evil mages and ensuring their wicked brand of magic would never again be used for the purposes of evil."

The clouds continued to roll in. Many of the stars, including the brighter ones, began to wink out.

"And now, with the Edict of Thought Control, I have acquired the power to read the thoughts of the people of Istar, stopping evil deeds before they can be enacted, and thereby defeating Evil before it has a chance to make its presence known. I have put an end to Evil as we know it!"

The cloud cover was complete now.

Thunder rolled within.

"So friends and colleagues, I implore you, since I have proven that I have powers comparable to yours, I ask that you allow me to ascend to the heavens and take my rightful place between Paladine and Mishakal as one of the greater gods of Krynn. Together, you will help me rule over Krynn so that Evil will never again dare to make its presence felt."

The thunder grew louder.

"Take me now!" cried the Kingpriest. "Elevate me to my rightful place in the heavens and I will show you how to—"

A bone-jarring clap of thunder seemed to explode inside the clouds over the temple. The shock waves of the blast shook the temple to its foundations.

The Kingpriest struggled to keep his balance on the platform, managing to remain upright until the rumbling sound of the thunderclap had finally run its course.

"I demand that you make me one of you!" cried the Kingpriest.

The clouds began to roil angrily and the wind picked up, making his robes billow like flags in a storm.

"I command you!"

A bolt of lightning shot out from the clouds, hitting the Kingpriest's platform and shattering it into a thousand splinters.

The Kingpriest toppled from his lofty perch, landing on his back and falling unconscious.

It began to rain, hard and cold.

The drops falling on the Kingpriest's face stung his flesh like bitterly cold needles. He blinked his eyes open, saw the storm overhead and raised a clenched fist toward the heavens.

"You will come to regret this," he cried.

Thunder boomed.

Jagged lightning pierced the blackness of the night.

"You might control the heavens, but I"—he placed a hand over his chest—"control the world."

Another bolt of lightning shot out from the clouds, this time slamming into the slim standard-bearing tower above and behind him.

The tower began to topple.

The Kingpriest scrambled to get out of the way, and just managed to get inside before the tower crashed down onto the balcony, causing it to break away from the temple.

Chapter 21

Mirrel spent several uneventful days riding across the Solamnic Plains on her way to Palanthas. She was a capable rider and a strong young woman who could handle herself on the sometimes harsh trail to the capital of Solamnia.

She had family in Palanthas, distant relatives who would take her in for a time until she got settled in the city and began a new life for herself. That was one of the reasons she was traveling to Palanthas, but not the most important one.

The thing that drove her so swiftly across the plains was the faint hope that she would be granted a private audience with the High Justice of the Knights of Solamnia, Lord Adam Caladen. If she were somehow granted that audience, she would be able to tell Lord Caladen what she had been telling those in Dargaard Keep these past few months. Only she wouldn't tread as lightly as she had in the keep. If she were able to speak to the high justice, she would tell him of Lord Soth's deeds as plainly and as graphically as she could.

If nothing came of it afterward, then at least she would be content in the knowledge that she had done her best to bring the truth to light. If people were still unwilling to look upon that light, then she would turn her back on it and let the matter rest once and for all.

When she told her relatives of her plans they thought her insane. The high justice was an important and busy man, they said, who had no time for a simple maid—a simple *former* maid—from an outlying keep.

But she remained undaunted. She was not just a simple chamber maid. She had been at one time, but she had been elevated in status and had been Lady Korinne's lady-in-waiting. Surely the high justice would be happy to meet with her.

But her first visit to the Hall of High Justice on the shores of the Bay of Branchala in the west end of Palanthas was anything but successful. She was made to wait for hours in a cold and damp room, only to be forgotten by the knight who had told her to wait there.

That night, she traveled the darkened streets of Palanthas to the home of Leyla Gladria where she was immediately taken in. There she told her story to the elderly woman who was keen to hear anything having to do with the all-too-brief life of her beloved daughter and even briefer life of her long-awaited grandchild.

Finally, Mirrel had found a sympathetic ear, and more.

"I knew that man would be bad for my daughter, knight or no!" she said. "I always felt there was another side to Soth, a darker side. But he was so charming from the first, much too charming if you ask me."

Mirrel listened attentively and patiently to the elderly woman as she talked for what seemed like hours. She didn't mind, even when Leyla Gladria began repeating herself or crying out loud. Mirrel realized that the old woman still needed to come to terms with the loss of her daughter, and understood that if she could help ease some of the elderly woman's pain, then she would be fulfilling her oath of loyalty to the former Lady Korinne.

When Leyla Gladria's bitter words came to an end and she had composed herself somewhat, she looked at Mirrel and nodded. "If it's an audience with the high justice you want, then that's just what you'll get."

* * * * *

"According to what I remember of these mountains, the hedge witch's cabin should be somewhere near the foot of that mountain there." Soth pointed at a great snow-capped mountain, one of the tallest peaks in all of the Dargaard Mountains.

"Lead the way," said Caradoc. Soth's seneschal was unsure of the purpose of their journey to this nearly uninhabited part of the Dargaard Range. He had mentioned something about killing a witch to preserve the truth, but none of it made much sense. Eventually, Caradoc had merely shrugged it off as yet another mysterious aftereffect of the tragedy that had befallen Lord Soth.

The two knights headed south into the deep dark rift in the mountain range called the Soul's Wound. After an hour's ride they came upon the small stone cottage, an odd structure partially obscured by the encroaching mountains which loomed over it like a tidal wave ready to crash down upon it at any moment.

"There it is!" cried Caradoc.

Soth kicked at the ribs of his mount and hurried toward the small stone cottage. Caradoc followed.

The windows of the cottage were dark and lifeless.

Soth dismounted and walked up to the front door. After a moment of hesitation he drew his broadsword, then reared back and kicked down the door. He crouched down to fit through the doorway and entered the cottage with his sword held out in front of him.

Slowly he moved through the room, searching the dark corners.

For what? Caradoc wondered.

At last he turned back toward the entrance, an angry scowl on his face. "The hag is gone!" he said.

And then suddenly his broadsword was slicing through the air in a fit of rage, smashing chairs and tables and anything else the blade could find and destroy.

Caradoc first covered his face to protect it from flying debris, then stepped outside and waited patiently for Soth's fury to run its course.

* * * * *

The next morning a trio of knights arrived at the home of Mirrel's relatives and a most handsome man with long red hair and an equally long scarlet mustache knocked on the door.

Mirrel answered the door, still dressed in her nightdress.

"Are you Mirrel?" asked the knight. "The former lady-in-waiting of Lady Korinne of Dargaard Keep?"

"Yes," said Mirrel, at a loss as to what was going on.

"Lord Caladen has asked us to escort you to the Hall of High Justice. Please make ready to leave immediately."

Mirrel hurriedly changed her clothes, then rode with the knights to the Hall of High Justice. Upon their arrival they were sent immediately into the inner hall. Then Mirrel alone was led up to a heavy wooden door bearing the symbol of the Knights of Solamnia—the majestic kingfisher with its wings half extended, grasping a sword with its sharp claws. There was a rose beneath the bird, and a crown above it.

She knocked on the door.

"Come in," said a voice.

She opened the door. Sitting in the middle of the room was Lord Caladen. Across from him was another chair, presumably for her to be seated upon. There were no other windows or doorways to the room; what was said within it never went beyond its four walls.

She entered the room and sat down, her heart pounding hard inside her chest and her throat uncomfortably dry.

Lord Caladen smiled.

At once, Mirrel felt more relaxed.

"Leyla Gladria has told me that I might be interested in hearing what you have to say."

"Very interested," said Mirrel, breathing a deep sigh of relief.

"All right, then. Tell me."

And she did.

* * * * *

Murder, thought Lord Caladen. It was a serious charge. And the murder of a man's own wife and child, well, there was no more serious matter on the face of Krynn.

But could someone as vaunted as Lord Loren Soth, Knight of the Rose, be capable of such a crime? He was an excellent leader, a fearless warrior and from all accounts a kind and just man.

From all accounts, except for the very vivid and detailed one told by Lady Korinne's former lady-in-waiting. If the woman was to be believed, Soth had been unfaithful to his wife with an elf-maid, even when his wife had been carrying his child. This charge was not all that hard to believe considering the reputation of the knight's father, Aynkell Soth.

But while being a philanderer was against the Oath and the Measure, Lord Caladen was inclined to look the other way on such matters. He wanted to disbelieve the accusation of murder, dismiss the charges as the misguided vengeance of a dismissed lady, but too many things she'd said had made too much sense.

There were rumors regarding the matter, rumors which had traveled to Palanthas well before the arrival of the former maid named Mirrel. People in the keep had heard the sounds of a child's cries, suggesting there had been a live birth. The same people had heard Lady Korinne's screams, suggesting she had survived the birth as well. And there was the matter of the cremation to consider. Even if Soth had been devastated by the deaths of his wife and child, a lightning quick cremation was not in keeping with Solamnic customs. There should have been a period in which Korinne lay in state so that people could have paid their respects, and then she should have received a proper burial within the Soth family crypt. Such a ceremony was automatic for someone of Lady Korinne's standing.

Like everyone else, Lord Caladen had heard the rumors that the cremation was performed to prevent the spread of disease, but like everyone else he had a hard time believing it. For what manner of disease causes a woman to die while giving birth?

So, if not to prevent the spread of disease, why then, would the ceremony have been conducted so quickly?

To hide evidence of foul play. It was the only reason Lord Caladen could think of. It was the only explanation that made any sense. Obviously, something was amiss.

And when he thought of how quickly Soth had remarried, and how soon after Korinne's death a second child had been born.

Clearly, an investigation was in order.

"Fenton!" called Lord Caladen, summoning his assistant Garnett Fenton, Knight of the Sword.

"Yes, Lord Caladen," said Fenton as he entered the lord's office.

"Send a message to Dargaard Keep . . ."

Chapter 22

It was several weeks before Lord Soth was able to make the trip to Palanthas and by that time the rumors were circulating among the Solamnic Knights of Palanthas like snowflakes in a blizzard. The many knights stationed in the great port city were split as to the reason why Soth had been summoned to the Hall of High Justice. Some believed that he had been negligent in his duties as a Knight of the Rose or had otherwise broken the code of the Oath and the Measure. Others believed he had done something worse, breaking not only the laws of the Knights of Solamnia, but the laws of good conduct by which all in Solamnia—indeed most of Krynn—aspired to live. Still, others emphatically believed him to be completely innocent of everything and anything. To them, this summons was simply a ruse to discredit the good Soth family name.

The lengthy wait for Soth's arrival provided Lord Caladen ample opportunity to make inquiries about what Mirrel had told him. Much to his dismay, many of the most crucial points had been corroborated by others, some of whom had absolutely no other motive than to speak the truth.

His findings left him no alternative other than to make sure that justice prevailed, no matter what it might do to the reputation of the Knights of Solamnia. In his mind, the knighthood would be better served by the quick and severe condemnation of a guilty knight than by any attempt to ignore or hide the truth. Truth was an unstoppable force and would eventually win out over lies. When that happened, it would bring down more than just a single knight; it would cripple the entire knighthood. No, this was something that had to be dealt with swiftly. And the more swiftly the better.

Soth was greeted by a party of six knights—two from each of the orders—at the base of the High Clerist's Tower, the stronghold of the Knights of Solamnia that guarded the mountain pass leading into the city.

"Beg your pardon, Lord Soth," said Sword Knight Garrett Fenton, leader of the escort party. "But the high justice requests that you enter the city alone."

While this was somewhat irregular, it wasn't totally unheard of. Still, Soth didn't understand why he couldn't remain in the company of his own knights for the rest of the journey. He had been summoned to the city on a matter of routine business, after all. Nevertheless, he respected the wishes of the high justice and parted company with his loyal knights, saying, "Wait for me. I won't be long."

"We'll be here, milord," said Caradoc. "Or more precisely, we'll be waiting for you in The Drookit Duck."

Soth laughed. The Drookit Duck was a popular tavern on the southeastern rim of Palanthas. Visitors to the city who stopped there quite often never made it further into the capital. "Save a tankard for me."

"I make no promises," said Caradoc.

All of Soth's knights laughed.

His six escorts did not.

* * * * *

Soth was taken along a route that led directly to the Hall of High Justice. As they rode the streets, Soth noticed that there were a lot more knights out and about than usual.

Suddenly, he began to have a bad feeling about what was going on. Not only were there knights lining the route, but many of them sat atop their mounts with their swords drawn and at the ready.

Soth took firm hold of the reins and tried to break ranks, but found himself blocked in on all sides by his escorts.

Then he reached for his broadsword, only to see it pulled from its sheath by the knight who had been riding to his left.

In mere seconds Soth had gone from being Lord Soth, Knight of the Rose to Lord Soth, prisoner of High Justice Lord Adam Caladen.

"What is the meaning of this?" he growled at his fellow knights.

None answered.

"Have you all gone mad?"

Again silence.

He struggled to dismount but found it too difficult to move in the tight space left for him by the other knights. Nevertheless, he continued to struggle.

"Lord Caladen will explain it all to you when we arrive at the Hall of High Justice," said Garrett Fenton. "Until then, Lord Soth, I ask that you conduct yourself with the utmost dignity and honor."

Soth bit his bottom lip and inhaled an angry breath, but made no more attempts to escape. As they arrived in the courtyard in front of the hall, there were a dozen knights there to receive him, all clad in armor, all with their broadswords drawn.

And at the edge of the large crowd that had gathered, he recognized a familiar face that did not belong to any knight.

It was a woman's face.

He looked closely at her, realizing it was Isolde's former lady-in-waiting, the same lady-in-waiting who had served his first wife Korinne so faithfully in the year leading up to her death.

What was her name? Miriam? Miranda? Mir. . . Mirrel, that was it. She'd been banished from the keep by Isolde. Everyone had thought she would travel to Istar, but apparently she had gone straight to Palanthas instead. Straight to High Justice Caladen.

"You may dismount now," said Fenton.

Soth got off his horse and the knights moved in around him.

Mirrel moved in closer too, no doubt to get a better look at him in a state of disgrace.

Soth saw her standing there, just a few feet away, separated by a ring of Knights of Solamnia.

Lucky for her, thought Soth.

If not for the knights, she might have already been dead by his hand.

* * * * *

The mood inside the Hall of High Justice was somber. Despite there being many windows along the walls of the hall, little light would shine in until much later in the day. For now the hall was a shadowy place and that cast a pall over the proceedings.

Lord Caladen sat on a great chair that looked almost like a throne. To his left was a young Crown knight, or perhaps just a squire, whose job it would be to make records of the proceedings. To his right was Rose Knight Drey Hallack, who served as an advisor to Lord Caladen on matters of the Oath and the Measure—a subject he had spent most of his life studying.

Farther to the right sat Lord Cyril Mordren, the High Clerist and Olthar Uth Wistan, High Warrior of the Knights of Solamnia. They would not be participating in the inquiry, but were present to show their solidarity with and support for Lord Caladen. An empty chair sat at the far right in honor of Solamnic Grand Master Leopold Gwyn Davis, who had recently died after a long illness. A Grand Circle of Knights was being organized to elect Davis's successor, but the gathering, which required at least three quarters of the established circles of knights to send two knights representatives to vote, was still many months away.

Over to the left of Lord Caladen sat seven Knights of Solamnia—two Crown, two Sword and three from the order of the Rose—whose simple majority vote would decide the fate of the accused.

Seeing the Hall of High Justice set up for a hearing told Soth that things were far more grave than he had imagined. If he had been called to Palanthas on a simple matter of a breach of the knight's code, an audience with the high justice alone would have sufficed. The presence of the seven-knight jury told him the charges were much more severe. The only other time Soth had seen a juried hearing had been when one knight had been charged with the murder of another.

Obviously Soth had been accused of murder. Luckily, although he'd been taken prisoner by his escorts, he was still considered innocent until his peers had cause to find him guilty.

Lord Caladen raised his right hand and the murmur that had been a constant background noise in the hall slowly died down.

Soth remained standing in front of the high justice, his shoulders squared and his chest thrust proudly forward. He would concede nothing to his accusers.

"Lord Loren Soth of Dargaard Keep," said Lord Caladen. "You have been called to the Hall of High Justice to answer questions in an official inquiry into the death, and circumstances surrounding the death, of your wife, Lady Korinne Soth and her newborn child."

A collective gasp swept through the hall as the rumors were finally laid to rest and the reason for Soth's summons was made known to all.

Soth felt his face grow hot as his blood began to roil in anger within him. It was only an inquiry, but he could still be found guilty as a result of the information that came to light. And even if he was cleared of any wrongdoing, his good name would be tarnished for all time by the mere accusation. When this was over, he vowed, those responsible would be made to pay.

A heavy, heavy price.

"A great tragedy," said Soth, his voice even and noncommittal. "One that has wounded me deeply." He paused. "I had wanted nothing more than to forget the catastrophe, and had begun the journey down that path." He paused again. "But of course, in the interest of justice I will answer any questions you may have. Then this matter will be put to rest in my mind, heart and soul."

Lord Caladen nodded.

The sound of voices rose in volume until the high justice leaned over to the recording secretary and asked for silence.

"Silence!" cried the recording secretary.

Once again, the hall grew quiet.

"Lord Soth," began Lord Caladen. "There seem to be those who believe that Lady Korinne did not die while in the process of birthing her child."

"People are entitled to their opinions, however vile," said Soth.

"They say that instead of dying naturally during the birth, she was murdered by a blade after the fact."

There was another collective gasp. This time it was peppered with whispers of, "No."

"An opinion entirely without merit."

Lord Caladen brought his hands up in front of his chest and brought them together as if in prayer. "Perhaps," he said. "Perhaps not."

Soth was silent.

"Most interesting of all is that those who believe Korinne and the child to have been murdered have also made known their beliefs about who it was that wielded the deadly broadsword."

"And who might that be?"

Lord Caladen drew in a breath. "You, Lord Soth."

* * * * *

The doors of The Drookit Duck burst open and a young man ran into the tavern, frantic and out of breath.

"You're liable to bust a button running like that," laughed Caradoc.

"Are you the knights who arrived with Lord Soth?" asked the young man when he was able to speak the words.

Caradoc put down his tankard. "We are. What of it?"

"Lord Caladen has just accused your lord of murder in the death of Lady Korinne and the child."

"What?"

"Lies!"

"A joke, surely?" cried the other knights, incredulous at the news.

All except for Caradoc.

Upon hearing the inevitable news, he simply lifted his tankard and took another sip of ale.

* * * * *

"I did no such thing!" shouted Soth, his voice strong and unwavering. "I loved my wife dearly and would never have done anything to hurt her." He glanced around the hall. "What gypsy would make such a wild and unfounded accusation? Who dares make such an outrageously damaging claim?"

"Lady Korinne's former lady-in-waiting for one,"

answered Lord Caladen.

Soth laughed contemptuously while shaking his head. "Would you take the word of a simple maid over a Knight of the Rose, a man sworn to live his life by the strict code of the Oath and the Measure?"

"No," replied Lord Caladen. "Young Mirrel's words were not enough to convince me to begin these proceedings. There were others."

The high justice gestured to a knight standing guard at the back of the hall. The knight left the hall and a moment later he returned, leading an elderly elf-woman through the crowd toward the high justice.

Soth recognized the old woman and felt a brush of relief. He had saved the woman's life and rescued her party from a band of ogres. Surely, she would be moved to speak well of him.

"What is your name?" asked the recording secretary.

"Olsla," said the old woman. "Olsla Stirling."

"And would you please tell me what you know about Lord Soth and his relationship with his former wife Lady Korinne?"

The elf-woman looked at Soth, her eyes narrowing slightly. A clear sign of derision.

Soth realized that the woman was likely upset that he had stolen Isolde out from under her nose. He wasn't aware that she had come looking for Isolde, but that is what he guessed must have happened.

"Many months ago," the elderly woman began. "I journeyed to Dargaard Keep to reunite Isolde Denissa with her fellow elf-maids."

"Why had she been taken there?" asked Lord Caladen.

"She had been whisked to the keep by Lord Soth in order to receive attention from the healer of Dargaard Keep."

"So Lord Soth saved her life?"

"I cannot say. He might have. Then again, she might have lived even without his help. What I can say for certain is that when I tried to bring Isolde back home to Silvanesti, she refused to rejoin our party."

"Why was that?"

"She told me she had decided to remain in the keep. She said that Lord Soth needed her there."

Lord Caladen nodded. "Why was that?"

"Apparently, he found comfort with her"—the elf-woman's voice cracked slightly—"because his wife could not bear him a child."

The hall suddenly became very noisy.

"Ridiculous!" bellowed Soth. "If I am to be charged with such a serious crime, I expect such charges to be backed up by more credible witnesses than a former laundress and a senile old elf-woman." He turned to face the crowd. "It is their word against the word of a Knight of Solamnia, a knight of the highest order possible."

"Hear, hear!" shouted several in the hall who were obviously pro-Soth.

"Agreed," said Lord Caladen, who waited for the noise to die down before continuing. "Agreed. Would you then accept the word of Istvan the healer, the only man who was present when Lady Korinne gave birth to the child?"

Soth was at first surprised by the mention of the healer's name as he was unaware that Istvan had made the trip to Palanthas. But knowing that Istvan would soon be speaking on his behalf allowed him to breathe a heavy sigh of relief. Istvan was loyal to him alone, had been loyal to the Soth family for decades. He would surely corroborate Soth's claim of innocence.

"Absolutely, Lord Caladen. The word of Istvan should be the final word on this matter so it may be settled without doubt, once and for all."

"Agreed," Lord Caladen said. "Bring in the healer."

Again Lord Caladen gestured to the knight standing guard at the rear of the hall. Moments later, the hunched figure of Istvan was led through the crowd of people.

Soth nodded toward Istvan as he passed, but the healer

did not return the gesture as his frightened eyes were focussed on the high justice.

"What is your name?" asked Lord Caladen.

"Istvan," he said. "Istvan, the healer."

"Do you go by any other names?"

"No."

"You are the healer of Dargaard Keep?"

"Yes?"

"Did you treat the elf-maid Isolde Denissa when she was brought to the keep?"

"Yes."

"And what did you make of her injuries?"

"Well," said Istvan, hesitating. "Well, she was quite severely injured and, I might add, if Lord Soth hadn't brought her to me when he had, she might not be alive today."

Soth cracked a slight smile. Istvan was part of Soth's inner circle. If the high justice thought he could persuade Istvan to speak afoul of him, the man was grossly mistaken.

Lord Caladen's face remained impassive as he continued questioning Istvan. "You also were present when Lady Korinne gave birth to her child in the keep?"

"Yes."

Lord Caladen inhaled a breath. "Did she and the child survive the birth, or did she die while in the process of giving birth?"

Again Istvan hesitated a moment. "It was a difficult pregnancy and Lady Korinne was in pain almost daily as the child came to term. Unfortunately, the pain became too much for her and she died while giving birth to the child. Sadly, as a result of further complications, the child died as well."

Voices grew louder at the back of the room.

Soth smiled broadly. If the only eyewitness to the birth said Korinne had died birthing the child, then the high justice would have no option but to issue a full and public apology for this travesty. Soth would be dismissed at once.

But Lord Caladen did not look to be satisfied with Istvan's statements. It was as if he didn't believe what the healer was saying. Then he looked over at Soth and saw the wide smile on the knight's face.

"I warn you, Istvan. As healer of Dargaard Keep, you are bound to live by the code of ethics outlined in the Oath and the Measure."

"Of course, milord."

"Then you understand that it is a grave breech of honor to tell a falsehood, especially in such a place as the Hall of High Justice."

"Yes, of course."

"Good. Then you would be more than happy to take part in a little test that will settle once and for all the fact that you are indeed telling the truth."

Istvan had been backed into a corner. He had no other choice but to agree. "As you wish," he said.

Soth glanced around, wondering what in the name of Paladine was going on.

Lord Caladen raised his right hand and beckoned someone in the crowd to come forward. A short, thin figure wearing dirty white and yellow robes moved away from the crowd.

"A mage?" said Soth. "What sort of game is this?"

"No game, Lord Soth. Only a search for the truth."

"But if I'm not mistaken, this"—he gestured to the man in the white and yellow robes—"is a mage. Surely you are aware of the fact that magic has been outlawed by the Kingpriest of Istar. What purpose can this mage serve in the Hall of High Justice?"

Lord Caladen waited for silence, then spoke. "Not all magic has been banned by the Kingpriest. Some magic, that which has as its purpose the promotion of Good, the quest for truth and knowledge, is still sanctioned."

"But I don't—" stammered Soth.

"If Istvan is telling the truth, then he won't be troubled by having this good mage cast a spell of truth over him, since it will only serve to prove that his words are truthful."

Soth too had been caught by his own words, just as Istvan had been before. If he argued the matter it would seem as if he had something to hide. But, if he readily agreed to the test and the spell proved successful, the truth would become known to all.

He couldn't risk it.

"I protest Lord Caladen, Istvan has already spoken—"

"And you have said that you would accept what the healer said as being the final word on this matter. Now remain quiet and let the healer speak." He nodded in the direction of the mage.

The mage pulled back his right sleeve to reveal a glassy blue stone in his hand. It was connected to a leather thong that was wrapped tightly about his fingers. He moved the stone closer to Istvan and it suddenly began to glow with a strange incandescent light. The mage began mumbling a series of words and guttural tones. After several minutes the mage nodded to Lord Caladen, then stepped back, leaving Istvan standing absolutely rigid, his eyes staring blankly at the far end of the hall.

"Istvan is now under the power of a truth spell and is unable to tell a lie, even if he so wishes," Lord Caladen said to the people within the hall. It was obvious he wanted to show that no trickery was being used and that the spell hadn't been cast simply in order to make Istvan say what the high justice wanted to hear. "Istvan, I'm going to ask you a question and I want you to answer by saying the word *green*."

Istvan nodded.

"What color is the sky?"

"Blue."

"Very good."

"Now, Istvan, when Lord Soth brought Isolde Denissa to Dargaard Keep, were her injuries life-threatening?"

"No."

"How so?"

"Her injuries would have healed simply with the passage of time."

The hall was silent.

"When you assisted Lady Korinne in the birth of her child, did she survive that birth?"

"Yes. She was in fine health. In fact, the child's birth eased her pain considerably."

Dead silence.

"And what of the child? Did it survive the birth?"

"Yes. It survived. Only it was hideously deformed."

"If mother and child survived the birth, then how did they both come to die a short time later?"

"Soth entered my chambers and sent me from the room. When I saw him again he reported to me that they had both died during the birth."

The silence continued.

"Did anyone else enter the room after you allowed Lord Soth into the chamber?"

"No."

"What did the bodies look like when you saw them next?"

"Hacked to bits. It was hard to recognize any of the pieces as being human."

Lord Caladen took a breath and nodded to the mage.

The wizard stepped forward and released Istvan from the spell.

Istvan looked about the room as if he were unsure of what had happened.

Soth had watched the proceedings with his mouth agape, unable to say a word. Now he simply stood defiantly, shoulders straight, lips tight, chin thrust forward—a classic portrait of the noble and gallant Knight of Solamnia.

However, the image of the great knight, of strength and gallantry, did little to mask the truth.

Soth was a murderer.

"Knights of Solamnia," said Lord Caladen, addressing

the seven knights in the jury. "You've heard the words of Istvan the healer, words spoken under the power of a spell of truth. How do you judge the accused?"

The seven knights spoke quietly between themselves for several moments before Lord Walter Dukane, a Knight of the Rose, stood up and addressed the high justice.

"Guilty on all counts," said Lord Dukane. "By a unanimous vote."

Lord Caladen nodded solemnly, then turned slowly to face Soth. "Loren Soth," he said, stripping Soth of the title of Lord Soth. "I hereby find you to be in gross defiance of the Oath and the Measure and guilty of the murders of your wife and child, crimes punishable by death. You are to be immediately held in custody and will be duly executed at a public beheading in the center of Palanthas at precisely noon tomorrow."

Soth, his face a rigid mask devoid of any emotion, was led from the hall by way of a side door.

At the rear of the hall, people shook their heads in disbelief.

Several others wept.

Chapter 23

A kender father stood on the front steps of his cottage on the outskirts of the village of Mid-O-Hylo, watching the foglike clouds descend from the high mountains in the west and the low mountains in the east.

The light gray mist was covering the land in a shroud that, unlike other fogs he had seen, seemed very dark and gloomy.

"What's happening father?" asked the kender's young son as he ran up the path toward the cottage, his ponytail bobbing and swishing behind him.

"Something."

"What something?" asked the boy.

"Something," repeated the kender. "But what something, I do not know."

"Something strange, I bet," said the boy, watching the mist continue to invade the lands surrounding the village, further blotting out the light from the sun.

"Yes," said the kender.

"Something weird, I'd say."

"Yes."

"It reminds me a lot of the snowy crystal glass I found in the hand of that sleeping knight on our last trip to Thelgaard."

The elder kender said nothing, his eyes fixed on the mist. The swirling tendrils of smokelike fog seemed to have taken hold of him, quashing his usually carefree attitude. It was an attitude that had served him well for all of his years, even when things had looked most grim.

For the first time in his life, the kender knew fear.

"Get inside the cottage," the kender told his son.

"But this is creepy, father," said the young one. "Can't we stay out and watch the fog some more?"

The kender began to step backward in the direction of his home. His son, however, remained where he stood, waving his hand through the mist as if trying to catch it between his fingers.

"All right," said the father. "You can stay outside and watch it if you like, but I'm going inside to watch it through the windows. It looks even spookier that way."

"Spookier?" said the youngster. "I want to see. Let me in."

The young kender gleefully ran into the house, followed closely by his somber father.

When they were both inside, the father shut the door and locked it tight for the first time since he'd installed the shiny brass lock that he'd found improperly appreciated in the door of a tavern in Caergoth.

He knew he was insulting the door's purpose by locking it, but he was much too afraid of the overspreading doom-filled pall to care.

Chapter 24

"Obviously there has been some grave error in justice," said Caradoc, standing before the knights in The Drookit Duck, one foot on his chair and another atop the table.

"Injustice indeed," cried one of the knights. He couldn't tell which one of the knights had spoken, and therefore couldn't tell if the words were said in support or condemnation of Lord Soth.

Most of the knights were still in shock over what had transpired. They had journeyed to Palanthas on a matter of routine business, only to have their leader sentenced to death.

It seemed like madness.

After all, Lord Soth was the epitome of everything the Knights of Solamnia stood for, a shining example of everything that was good and honorable about the knighthood.

But there were those among the knights who were beginning to question their lord. And with good reason. They had seen the elf-maid Isolde Denissa after the ogre attack and although none had said so at the time, many thought it odd that Soth insisted he bring her back to the keep. And then there was the sentencing itself. Soth had been questioned in the Hall of High Justice and found guilty by seven fellow Knights of Solamnia. Unanimous decisions in such matters were rare, so the outcome of the proceedings had to be respected. And what of the high justice? Would he sentence a Knight of Solamnia, a Knight of the Rose, to death, if such action wasn't warranted?

Caradoc considered the death sentence against Lord Soth. If Soth were gone, it might clear the way for Caradoc himself to take control of the keep. An intriguing possibility, but unlikely. As a base of operations for the Knights of the Rose, Dargaard Keep would likely be taken over by another Rose knight and Caradoc would quickly fade into the background as an anonymous Knight of the Crown. No, his status was tied indelibly to the fate of Lord Soth and, even if Soth were disgraced, it would be better to be his seneschal than just another Knight of Solamnia.

In the interim, the gathered knights had begun to mutter and grumble, and Caradoc sensed an insurgence gaining momentum. He could not let such thoughts take up root in the minds of his fellow knights. If he did, all hope of Soth returning to Dargaard Keep would be lost.

"There isn't one of us who doesn't owe his life to Lord Soth," he said. "I know he's saved mine several times and I suspect the same holds true for all of us."

The majority of knights were leaning toward supporting Caradoc, but there were still a few who remained unconvinced.

"You, Knight Krejlgaard," continued Caradoc. "Did he not pull you from the darkest depths of the Vingaard River after you fell from your mount during a crossing?"

The Crown knight lowered his head and was silent.

"Meyer Seril, didn't Lord Soth provide food for your family when their entire crop was destroyed by locusts?"

"Aye," said Seril. "That he did."

"And you, Derik Grimscribe, didn't our lord sponsor your petition to the knighthood when all the others felt you too weak for the order?"

"I'm ashamed to admit I had forgotten," said Grimscribe.

"Seems many of us have!" shouted Caradoc. "And we should all be ashamed for doubting—even for a second—the innocence of our lord. For I know, with a certainty and a strength of conviction I have never felt before on any matter"—Caradoc paused and lowered the volume of his voice—"if one of us had been found guilty of such a crime and sentenced to death, Lord Soth wouldn't be wasting time debating our guilt or innocence."

The knights spoke among themselves and it appeared to Caradoc that he had managed to persuade the last few dissenters to see the other side of the sword.

"What have you got in mind, Knight Caradoc?" asked Colm Farold.

Caradoc looked right and left even though the tavern had been cleared and no one was in the room except for his fellow knights. Still, he spoke in a hushed voice. "I propose we rescue him."

"But he's being guarded by knights such as ourselves," said Farold.

"Tonight, he is. Yes," said Caradoc. "But perhaps not so tomorrow morning."

Farold nodded. "I'm with you."

The confidence and conviction exhibited by Farold seemed to inspire the others.

"I'm with you as well," said Meyer Seril.

"And I," nodded Derik Grimscribe.

Until one by one, all of Soth's knights were in agreement.

* * * * *

The morning sun was nowhere to be seen. It remained hidden behind a layer of dark and heavy clouds that caused the night's darkness to linger far longer than usual.

To add to the chill in the air, a cold wind was blowing in over the Bay of Branchala, something more than a few residents of Palanthas interpreted as an omen, convincing them to spend the day indoors. Others simply refused to watch, not wanting their memory of the gallant knight to be tainted by the humiliating spectacle of a public execution.

Still, the majority of people had braved the wet and cold and ventured out to watch the beheading. Already, the streets were lined with citizens from all classes, from clerics and merchants, to tradesmen and laborers. Fruit vendors were doing an especially brisk business, suddenly finding eager customers for all their wares, even the most rotten of fruits, vegetables and eggs.

Soth was awakened at dawn and offered a final meal of bread and water, which he refused. Then he was led onto the back of a cart, stripped down to the waist and chained by the wrists to a heavy timber post that rose up from the center of the cart's wooden floor.

The knights entrusted with the task of preparing Soth for transport seemed to be unenthusiastic about their work. Indeed they almost treated the job with disdain, saying nothing to the disgraced knight and avoiding looking directly into his eyes. Here was one of their own, one of the greatest Knights of Solamnia, reduced to the level of a common criminal.

In their hearts, the question as to whether Soth was guilty or not was of little consequence. He was a Knight of the Rose and he deserved a better fate. But in their minds, the knights knew that the Oath and the Measure had little sympathy for knights who strayed from the path. And to that end, it is even written in the Measure that knights must be more severely punished for their crimes than the common man because anything less would hurt the collective reputation of all knights.

For that reason, the Solamnic Knights tending to Soth on

the morning of his execution wanted nothing more than to complete their task quickly and be done with it.

Soth understood this and made it easier on them by saying nothing as they secured him to the post.

At last it was done and his wrists were securely bound and fixed to the top of the post. Soth made a token effort to pull himself free, but knew that any decent squire could have done a proper job of securing him.

As the knights collected their things, one lingered behind. He was a young Crown knight by the look of his clothes, but nothing else about the man was familiar to Soth, most likely because he was recently petitioned to the knighthood.

He looked at Soth, a hint of sorrow in his eyes. "Paladine have mercy on your soul," he said.

Soth looked at the young man and realized that he had probably been suckling at his mother's breast when Soth first became a Solamnic Knight. The thought of this *boy* taking pity on him, angered Soth to no end.

He laughed at the young knight, then said, "No, boy. May Paladine have mercy on *yours!*"

The knight looked shaken by Soth's words, stumbling as he got off the cart.

Soth continued to laugh.

*　*　*　*　*

Soth's loyal knights had been up for hours, making plans by lamplight until the sun's rays were bright enough to properly illuminate the secluded livery stable they'd moved their meeting to in order to avoid being watched or overheard by spies of the high justice.

What they planned to do would not be easy. Had Soth been taken prisoner by a band of ogres, or barbarians, or been placed under some spell by a pack of goblins, his rescue would have likely been a simple matter.

But instead, he was the prisoner of the Knights of

Solamnia. His followers would have virtually no advantage because the knights they would be pitting themselves against were just as skilled as they were. And to make matters worse, there would be more guards than rescuers, making the chances of freeing Soth unharmed very slim indeed.

They had discussed tactics long into the night and it was Caradoc who finally came up with something that might tip the scales in their favor. "We are Knights of Solamnia, are we not?"

"Yes, of course," the knights agreed.

"And it is assumed that we will accept Soth's fate and conduct ourselves according to the Oath and the Measure."

The knights were silent, awaiting Caradoc's next words.

"Well then, any attempt to free our lord would come as a surprise since none would expect us to reject the decision of the high justice."

The knights remained silent, considering it.

Finally, Wersten Kern spoke. "But what you're saying is that such a rescue wouldn't be expected because what it amounts to is treason, something that will likely mark us as outlaws and get us banished from the Knights of Solamnia."

Caradoc sighed. If Kern was having second thoughts, then some of the others were as well. That meant that Caradoc had one last chance to convince the knights of their task. If he failed now Soth would be doomed. "No, not treason," said Caradoc. "Our rescue will be an act of tremendous loyalty toward our lord. And in regard to becoming outlaws, how do you know that our reputations haven't already been damaged through our association with Lord Soth? We can't even be sure that we'll be allowed to leave the city without being put on trial ourselves."

Kern pondered Caradoc's words, then finally nodded. "Caradoc is right. We're probably already damned in the eyes of the other knights." A pause. "If that's the case, then

I think using the element of surprise is the best chance we have of rescuing Lord Soth and leaving Palanthas alive."

The knights muttered agreement.

"All right then," said Caradoc. "Perhaps we should begin working out the details."

* * * * *

The horse cart started with a sudden lurch, then rolled smoothly—if not noisily—out into the courtyard of the Hall of High Justice. There the driver stopped to pick up his escort of four mounted knights in highly polished plate armor, one positioned at each of the cart's corners. With the knights in place, the cart left the courtyard and began its journey through the streets of Palanthas.

The layout of the city was like that of a gigantic wheel, with each road being a spoke leading directly to the hub. They were currently in Old City, which was made up of the Hall of High Justice, the ancient library of Astinus, the palace, homes for the Knights of Solamnia and other structures important to the city's defense, politics and finances.

In a few minutes the procession passed through the wall that separated Old City from the newer parts of Palanthas. On the other side of the wall, the streets were wider and less crowded and the air seemed fresher, cleaner and infinitely more breathable.

Soth took a deep breath . . .

And was hit hard on the side of the head by a rotten egg. It was the first of many.

* * * * *

The wheel-like layout of Palanthas proved to be of benefit to Soth's knights. Because all of the city's roads led to its center, each of the knights could take a different route to the execution site and therefore inconspicuously arrive as a group and remain unnoticed until it was time to free

Soth and make good their escape.

Meyer Seril had volunteered to follow the route that Lord Soth would be taking. He joined the procession as it emerged from the wall separating the old and new cities, then fell into line with the others following.

Despite the fact that Seril had been wearing his helm and looked like most of the other Knights of Solamnia in the procession, Soth had recognized the three white stockings on his mount and nodded to Seril as he passed.

Seril had given a slight nod, acknowledging Soth.

After that, Soth held his head even higher, despite the fact that he was continuously being pelted with rotten eggs and tomatoes, even several hardened cakes of dried horse dung.

It broke Seril's heart to see his lord being treated in such a way. When he saw a commoner to his right throwing an egg—an egg which hit Soth squarely in the back—Seril moved his horse forward until it was in front of the offending peasant. Then he pulled hard on his reins, forcing the horse to miss a step and kick with his hind legs in order to regain its balance.

The horse's right rear hoof shot up from the ground, catching the man in the chest, knocking the wind out of him and sending him flying backward through the air.

Seril looked back and saw him lying flat on his back, struggling to regain his feet, but unable to do so.

"Beg your pardon," said Seril apologetically. "Are you all right?"

The commoner was too busy trying to catch his breath to answer.

* * * * *

Colm Farold was the first of Soth's knights to arrive at the city's center square—the execution site. He had traveled in from the southeast corner of the city and therefore had the shortest distance to cover. Shortly after Farold, Caradoc appeared from the road leading in from due south. Then Wersten Kern came in from the north, leading a second horse by its reins. It was a large horse, and appeared to be strong enough for the task that would be asked of it. But despite the horse's obvious size and strength, it lacked the same lineage as the mounts belonging to the Knights of Solamnia. When they set out across the Solamnic Plains the horse would inevitably fall behind. The question was, how long would it be before that happened?

As more of his loyal knights began to appear in the square, Soth seemed to become more defiant. Indeed, he was standing straighter now and did not flinch when struck by the rotten projectiles thrown by the angrier members of the crowd.

His long black hair was tangled and matted, pasted against his dirty flesh in some spots, but standing up on end and looking as ragged as wildfire in others. His hard, muscled body was mottled by splotches of red, green and yellow, giving him the appearance of a barbarian in war paint rather than a disgraced Knight of the Rose.

The cart Soth was standing on slowly moved into place next to the execution platform. On the platform, the black-helmeted executioner patiently waited for his victim to be brought into position. Although the sky was still overcast, the executioner's huge double-sided axe still glinted menacingly in the sunlight that managed to break through the clouds.

As the cart came to a stop, Caradoc clenched the reins of his mount more tightly in his fist. It was up to him to give the signal to the rest of the knights.

Caradoc checked the position of the sun, then made a final survey of the scene. Off to the right, the higher officials had yet to take the places that had been set aside for them. There were knights along the fringes of the crowd, but none seemed to be paying too much attention at present because nothing much was happening and the thought of Soth attempting to escape was probably the furthest thing from their minds.

Caradoc looked at each of Soth's knights in turn. Each one nodded slightly, signifying they were ready. Then he glanced at Lord Soth; he looked anxious to make good his escape. Caradoc raised his hands, gesturing at Soth to be patient.

A commotion erupted at one edge of the square as the high justice, high clerist, and high warrior appeared. Caradoc waited for them to near their places, then gestured with a slightly upraised finger to a woman standing on the opposite side of the square.

"My baby!" she cried. "Someone's taken my baby!"

Attention suddenly swung from one end of the square to the other as everyone began looking around them in search of the woman's lost child.

Caradoc lifted his hand high in the air, signaling to the other loyal knights that it was time to make their move.

In seconds Wersten Kern rode up to the execution platform and leaped onto it. Without hesitation he gripped the executioner's huge double-sided axe in his left hand and brought his armored right hand around for a hard blow directly to the executioner's exposed chin.

The man dressed in black stumbled backward, then fell off the platform onto the people below.

Before the executioner had landed on a single spectator, Kern had swung the axe around and was chopping at the chains connecting Soth to the post. After several blows it was obvious it would take too long to cut through the heavy forged steel.

"Cut the post," urged Soth. "At the bottom."

Seril quickly began directing his efforts on the post itself. Two . . . three . . . four blows and the post came free, leaving the bottom of it splintered with several jagged edges.

Soth immediately grabbed hold of the post and began to swing it like a club, knocking down the first two Solamnic knights who had climbed onto the cart in an attempt to stop the escape.

"This way, milord!" shouted Kern, leaping off the platform and onto his horse.

Soth was still shackled to the post and couldn't hold it anywhere but at the one end to which he was chained. He did his best to hold it high in front of him as he leaped from the cart to the platform.

Another knight scrambled up from below the platform. Soth blocked the knight's sword with the heavy post, but could not move it quickly enough to use it like a sword. He blocked another blow from the sword, then swung the post in a long circular motion, knocking the knight off the platform as if using an arm to sweep earthenware from the top of a dinner table.

Soth then leaped onto his horse, kicking at the beast's ribs even before he was settled onto its back. As the horse lunged forward into the crowd, Soth rested the post on his shoulder, giving his exhausted arms the chance to recover, but still keeping the makeshift weapon at the ready.

Colm Farold and the other knights were busy keeping back the Solamnic Knights of Palanthas. If any broke through their ranks they might be able to block off Soth's escape route.

Surprise had definitely worked to their advantage. Several of the Palanthas knights were unprepared for fighting and hesitant to engage Soth's knights given that they were fully armored and fighting more fiercely than any opponents the knights of Palanthas had ever come up against.

As Soth raced through the crowd with Wersten Kern leading the way, a Palanthas knight rode up alongside Soth.

Soth looked over at the knight and recognized him as Sword knight Eiwon van Sickle.

"What are you doing?" van Sickle shouted. "You are making a mockery of the Oath and the Measure."

"According to the high justice, I did that long ago. What more damage can I possibly do?"

Knight van Sickle raised his sword. "Stop at once and

face your destiny like a true knight!"

Soth laughed at that, his eyes opening wide and filling with a new bright and fiery madness. "My destiny lies far beyond the walls of this dying city," he said as he rode through the streets of Palanthas. "One day my name will be known from Palanthas to Istar, from Ergoth to Balifor."

"Your destiny lies in Palanthas," said van Sickle. "Prepare to meet it." The young knight swung his sword with both hands.

Soth held the post up high by his chains, the jagged end pointing to the ground. The thick wooden post blocked the blow, forcing van Sickle to raise his sword for another strike.

At the same time, Soth brought the post back and swung it in a great circle, catching van Sickle squarely in the back. The blow knocked him forward, over the head of his horse. He hit the ground heavily, was trampled by the horse, and was lost in a cloud of dust.

Soth hefted the post back onto his shoulder and hurried to catch up with Kern and the others.

They had cleared the city streets and were now in the open area between Palanthas and the High Clerist's Tower. Hopefully the knights stationed there were unaware of what was happening.

Unfortunately, the knights guarding the tower looked to be out and about. Up ahead, several of them were already looking in Soth's direction to see what all the commotion was about. No doubt they had heard the sound of the charging horses. There were also lookouts positioned in the tower.

If the knights weren't ready for them now, they would be by the time they reached the tower.

Soth took a moment to look behind him.

There was a party of knights there too, charging hard and appearing to be gaining ground.

Up ahead, Caradoc rode in the lead of the escaping knights. Colm Farold struggled to catch up with him.

"There are too many ahead," said Farold breathlessly as he came alongside Caradoc. "Surely they'll cut us down as we try to break through their ranks."

Caradoc said nothing, and continued to ride hard because there were just as many knights behind them as ahead. It was obvious something had to be done, but what? He was Soth's seneschal and had become accustomed to taking orders in Soth's presence, not giving them.

"The mountains!"

The voice came from somewhere behind.

Caradoc looked back and realized the words had come from Lord Soth himself.

"The mountains!" Soth shouted.

Caradoc slowed slightly in order to let Soth catch up.

"Head for the mountains. There are too many of them for us to fight."

Caradoc thought about it. It was a good plan. The knights could survive for months in the mountains, where there were an infinite number of places to hide. And, the longer they stayed in the mountains, the better they could prepare for their ride across the plains. Caradoc nodded and sped back up to the front of the line of knights, then suddenly broke left.

Heading north.

The rest of the knights followed.

* * * * *

"We're gaining on them!" cried Garrett Fenton, the first Solamnic Knight to pick up the chase out of Palanthas.

Behind Fenton, seven other knights were on horseback. More would follow. Up ahead he could see the knights stationed at the High Clerist's Tower were also mounting up.

Soth and his knights were insane if they thought they could get away.

"We'll have them in another minute!"

But suddenly the fleeing group diverged from the trail, turning left and heading into the mountains.

Fenton jabbed his horse in the ribs, hoping to coax the beast into running just a little bit faster. But his horse was already up to top speed. It continued at the exhausting pace for another few minutes until Fenton and the other knights had reached the spot where Soth and his Knights had turned.

They turned as well, riding into the rough terrain and forests at the foot of the mountains.

But after a few minutes they slowed, unsure which pass their adversaries had taken. Finally they stopped.

The escaping knights had vanished into the mountains.

Fenton turned to face the other knights. "Post lookouts in the tower. They'll try and head to Dargaard Keep before long. When they do, we'll have a party of knights ready to ride."

* * * * *

"It's true milady," said Knight Valcic. "We've heard the news now from several sources."

Soth and his knights had been gone for over a week, but only now was Isolde hearing of her husband's fate in the Hall of High Justice.

"There's a good chance he's still alive," said Valcic, obviously trying to look on the brighter side of things. "They say he's hiding out in the mountains."

"Thank you, Knight Valcic," said Isolde, dismissing the young man with a wave of her hand. Then she walked over toward her bed and fell down on top of it.

Lord Soth, Knight of the Rose, she thought.

Outlaw!

It was hard to believe that one so respected and revered could fall so hard, so far, so fast.

And for what? The murder of Korinne and the child.

Ridiculous! She was sure of it.

Lord Soth had saved her life, had spent all of his life fighting for the cause of Good.

Something was wrong about all of this. When he returned to Dargaard Keep, she would ask him about it. And then they would begin the process of clearing his good name.

Yes, that was it. That's what she would do.

She brought her hands together, intertwined her fingers, and prayed to Mishakal for guidance.

Somehow, she knew, the Healing Hand would provide it.

Chapter 25

Brin Scoville rubbed his full belly after eating his fill of yet another satisfying dinner prepared by his wife. While he had toiled the entire day in the fields, she had labored within their modest kitchen making not only that evening's supper, but dozens of jars full of jams and other preserves.

It was hard work, but necessary to get them through the coming harsh winter on the plains.

And for some unknown reason, this winter seemed to have the makings of one of the worst yet. Scoville wasn't sure how he knew this. Perhaps it was his aching corns, or the stiff soreness down the length of his back, or the wintry sniffles that had come a few weeks early this year. Whatever the reason, Scoville knew it was going to be a long, cold winter. Best to be prepared.

He watched his son and daughter play with a set of wooden blocks on the rug in front of the fireplace. They were darling children, quiet and well-mannered with a bright and happy future ahead of them. Sometimes, Scoville would watch them play for hours, just for the simple pleasure of it.

Just then his wife brought his pipe and some tobacco to the table. He looked at the pipe, then at his wife, and smiled. "Thank you, dear."

She simply nodded and continued clearing the dishes.

With a practiced hand, Scoville filled up the bowl of his pipe—not too tightly—and went to the stove. He searched for some glowing embers with which to light his pipe.

To his surprise the fire had gone out and the coals were cold. "Wasn't there just a fire in the hearth?" he asked.

His wife turned around and looked strangely at the dead black coals. "I just finished cooking; they should be red hot."

Scoville put his hand over the ashes, then poked at them with his finger.

Cold as ice.

In fact the entire house seemed to be chilled.

"Papa," said his son. "The floor is getting cold. Could you light a fire for us?"

It was still too early to begin lighting fires in the main fireplace, but without a fire in the kitchen there was nothing else to keep them warm.

"I can do without a fire in here," said the wife. "Light the fire for the children and we'll all go to bed warm tonight."

"Right," said Scoville, moving into the main room to be with his children. "Well now, who wants to help?"

"Me," said the boy.

"I do," said the girl.

Together the children piled leaves and kindling onto the hearth while Scoville worked a piece of flint.

But the flint did not spark. No matter how hard he tried, no matter what he used against the flint, it simply would not spark.

He continued to try, without success.

The sun began to set.

Darkness and cold descended upon the house.

"Come now, Brin, children," said the wife. "We'll be warm enough in bed."

The two children, chilled by the long wait, were more than eager to retire to the warmth of their clean flannel sheets and heavy woolen blankets.

Scoville continued to try to light the fire long into the night.

He went to bed tired, cold and at an utter loss as to the cause of the lack of spark or flame.

Something wasn't right, he concluded.

Chapter 26

Under the cover of a jutting rock face and shaded by a thick stand of fir trees, Meyer Seril examined the broad blades of the axe he'd taken from the executioner. One side had been pitted by his attempts to cut the chains in the central square of Palanthas. The other side, however, was still finely honed. He turned this side of the axe around to use it as the cutting edge.

"Swing the axe as hard as you can," said Lord Soth, kneeling on the ground, his shackled wrists resting on the sides of the post so that the chain lay squarely across the wood. "I trust you, Knight Seril."

Seril nodded to Soth, thankful for the vote of confidence. The chain was made of heavy steel and would require a tremendous blow from the axe to cut it. The axe was designed to cut through flesh and bone, not steel. The first blow would likely ruin the blade, so he might as well make it a good one.

He raised the axe over his head. It wavered there for a brief moment, then came streaking down. There was a sharp clink of metal striking metal.

Seril lifted the axe away.

Soth lifted his arms off the log.

The chain was still whole, but one of the links had nearly been severed.

Seril looked at the axe. The blade's edge was severely dented. There was still enough cutting area, but only enough for another blow. He raised the axe once more and brought it down with as much force as he could muster.

There was another clink of metal on metal, then the satisfying bite of metal into wood. The axe blade was embedded in the post.

Soth's arms were free.

They buried the post under a pile of leaves and humus and moved on. While it might be possible for them to hide indefinitely in the mountains, none of the knights wanted that. The longer they remained in the mountains, the more time the pursuing Solamnic Knights would have to organize search patrols.

The problem was that the Knights of Solamnia from Palanthas knew that Soth and his knights would be attempting to return to Dargaard Keep and would therefore be on the lookout for them. In addition, there might be knights sent northward from Vingaard Keep to search the plains. They considered splitting up in order to divide the forces pursuing them. But inasmuch as they were *all* outlaws now, splitting up might only mean that there would be a greater chance some of them might be caught attempting to return to Dargaard Keep. And besides that, they were a loyal band. If they succeeded or failed, they would do so together. Dargaard Keep would be the only place where they would be truly safe, so it made the most sense that they all try to get there as quickly as possible.

To that end, they decided to strip themselves of their armor and leave it behind. Giving their mounts lighter loads to carry would allow them to run faster and farther than those of their adversaries. Also, if they were caught by their pursuers there would likely be so many of them that no amount of armor would be enough to protect them from harm.

So, their plan was a simple one. They would hide out in the mountains while they rested and gathered food and supplies for the mad dash across the plains.

In the meantime, they would head north toward the end of the mountain range—a point aptly named Destiny's Hand.

* * * * *

After two nights in the mountains, the knights and their mounts were suitably rested and prepared for the ride back to Dargaard Keep. Early on the third morning, long before the sun came up over the horizon to light their way, Soth and his knights headed east, riding down from the mountains as swiftly as they could. They quickened their pace to a full gallop as they rode out onto the naked plain.

Their horses couldn't continue the pace indefinitely, but they hoped they would be able to put enough distance between themselves and the knights in the High Clerist's Tower to see them safely to Dargaard Keep.

The sun wouldn't be rising for several hours.

Soth hoped it would be enough time.

* * * * *

Bram Springdale, a young Sword knight who less than three months ago had been a squire, was the first to see the plume of dust rising up off the plain.

Springdale had been stationed in the upper battlement of the High Clerist's Tower since dawn but hadn't spotted anything suspicious. As he continued his precise scan of the horizon—a quarter turn every few minutes—he noticed something out of the corner of his eye: a sort of haze rising up from the ground many, many miles to the northeast, roughly halfway between the High Clerist's Tower and the town of Bright Hart.

He squinted and concentrated on the leading edge of the dust storm. Whoever was creating it was in an awful hurry, and heading almost due east away from the mountains. He tried to count the black dots of the horses and made out five, perhaps six individual dots—Soth and his knights.

Springdale picked up the large steel bell by his side, stepped to the edge of the battlement and swung the bell over his head.

The bell clanged loudly.

Moments later there was much commotion below.

"Soth and his men," shouted Springdale to the knights gathered at the base of the tower. "Northeast of here, midway to Bright Hart, riding hard."

The chase was on.

Within minutes of Springdale's sounding of the alarm, twelve knights left the High Clerist's Tower. A few minutes later another six were away, these riding in a wider arc in the hopes of intersecting with Soth's men in the middle of the plain.

The first group of knights rode at a full gallop for as long as they could, but dressed in full armor, they soon had to slow their pace in order to let their horses catch their breath. By midafternoon, they still hadn't been able to clearly see the plume of dust on the horizon and were forced to make camp on the banks of one of the many tributaries running into the Vingaard River.

The horses were grateful for the respite.

The knights were not.

* * * * *

"Wake your sleepy heads," said Soth, giving the feet of his knights a gentle push with the toe of his boot.

It was still the middle of the night and the darkness was total. To the southwest a faint glow could be seen where the lights of Palanthas reflected against the clouds. Due east was Dargaard Keep, but they were too far away to see any sign of it—perhaps in another day or two.

The knights grumbled and moaned, but Soth ignored their complaints. It was far more important that they continue moving. When they reached Dargaard Keep there would be more than enough time to rest.

After they munched on nuts and berries from their packs, the knights set out on foot with their horses in tow. It was still too dark to travel any faster and a constant gallop would run the horses into the ground.

When the sun rose they would mount up.

But for now any extra distance they could put between themselves could prove crucial in the end.

* * * * *

"A rider!" came the call from above. "No, a group of riders, approaching the keep."

The knights sitting idly in the great hall of Dargaard Keep seemed to come alive at the news.

Darin Valcic was the first one to hurry up the tower to have a look for himself. "Where?" he asked when he joined the lookout stationed on the uppermost level of the keep.

Arnol Kraas, a squire, pointed east to a bit of haze rising up off the plain. "There!"

Valcic's eyes weren't as sharp as Kraas's but he could still make out the telltale cloud of dust. "How many riders do you think there are?"

"Five or six," said the squire.

Other knights began to arrive, each scanning the horizon.

"It's them," said Valcic.

"It's who?" asked Kraas.

"Lord Soth and our fellow knights, of course. Prepare a proper reception and a feast for their arrival." Valcic turned away.

"What's that?" asked one of the knights.

"What?" Valcic asked, turning back around.

"There's another plume of dust further away on the plain," said the knight, pointing.

Valcic squinted and concentrated on the direction the other knight had pointed. It was difficult to make out because the dust had blended into the sky and had looked like nothing more than a rain cloud. But now that it was pointed out to him, Valcic realized it was another group of riders.

A much larger group.

Soth was being chased.

"Never mind the reception for Lord Soth," said Valcic. "Ready the horses, bring out the armor." A pause. "And prepare for battle."

Usually such a call was answered by a loud and enthusiastic cheer.

This time, however, there was only silence.

* * * * *

"We're gaining on them!" cried Garrett Fenton.

It was true. Despite the fact that Soth's knights held the advantages of fewer riders, faster horses and greater motivation to reach their destination, the Solamnic Knights from Palanthas were edging ever closer. At this rate they would be on top of them in another day, perhaps even sooner.

"Yes," agreed Eiwon van Sickle. "But will we catch them before they reach the keep?"

Fenton didn't answer.

Instead, he kicked at his mount and shot off at a gallop.

* * * * *

When Soth first saw the knights approaching he was sure they had been sent northward from Vingaard Keep to intercept them. But as they came closer, he recognized the familiar shades of reds worn by the knights of Dargaard Keep and realized that, with their help, they just might make it after all.

When they finally came together, both parties stopped.

"Good to see you Lord Soth," said Darin Valcic. "Alive and well."

"Aye, and it's good to see all of you. A fine sight for my tired and sore eyes."

"Not to break up this fine reunion," said Caradoc, "but perhaps we should ride now and greet each other later." He turned around. "Our pursuers are nearly upon us."

Soth looked behind him and was surprised to find that the knights from Palanthas had indeed closed the gap. If they were able to keep up their pace, they'd be upon them in a few short hours.

"Right!" said Soth. He urged his horse forward. It protested slightly, but then was off . . .

On the final dash to the keep.

* * * * *

They were minutes away from Dargaard Keep. Although still at a gallop, Soth's horse was slowing, holding up the mounts of the others which still had some wind left in their lungs.

He kicked at the horse's ribs. Foam was already forming at the mouth of the beast, but it valiantly tried to pick up the pace. After a few more steps it stumbled and fell forward, sending Soth hurtling hard onto the ground.

Several of the knights ahead of Soth kept riding, unaware of what was going on behind them. Those trailing stopped to help Soth to his feet.

"You can ride with me," offered Colm Farold.

"No," said Soth, looking at Farold's horse. "You'll be

lucky if the creature takes you the rest of the way to the keep."

"You can have my mount, milord," said Darin Valcic. "It's as fresh as any horse in the keep and I would be honored to have it carry you to safety."

Soth was touched by the gesture, but could not accept it because it likely meant Valcic would be giving up his life in exchange for his own. "Thank you, Knight Valcic, but I can not accept."

"I insist."

"I suggest you settle the matter soon," said Caradoc. "Or neither of you will make it to the keep alive."

Soth looked at Valcic.

Valcic nodded.

Soth mounted the knight's horse.

And was gone.

* * * * *

Darin Valcic turned west to face the oncoming knights.

There were ten knights abreast at the front of the pack maybe more. Judging by the plume of dust rising up behind them they might have been six or seven deep, perhaps more than fifty knights in all.

It would be a short battle, but Valcic was determined to put up a fight worthy of a true Knight of Solamnia.

He drew his sword, held it before him with both hands.

A moment later the knights were upon him.

He held his breath . . .

And suddenly, the knights parted, riding around him and leaving him alone on the plains to choke on their dust.

* * * * *

Now on a fresh horse, Soth led his knights in the final charge toward the keep.

He looked very little like the knight who had left

Dargaard Keep little more than a week ago.

He had the appearance of a dirty and disheveled wild-man whose clothes were little more than rags. His muscular upper body was bruised and stained by the remains of rotten fruit, eggs and dirt that had been hurled at him in Palanthas. And his long black hair flowed back from his head like wildfire, putting an air of madness about him.

But despite it all, he still rode erect and proud on his mount, and his eyes . . .

His eyes were still as alive and piercing as ever.

Soon the knights clattered across the drawbridge and into the keep. Two of the horses who had made the trip from Palanthas stumbled their last few agonizing steps before falling in utter exhaustion.

A moment later the portcullis came crashing down and the drawbridge slowly began to rise up.

Outside, the pursuing knights brought their horses to a halt at the edge of the chasm surrounding the keep, then quickly retreated out of the range of any archers who might be waiting for them on the battlements.

* * * * *

"Are we going to lay siege to the keep?" asked Eiwon van Sickle, regarding the formidable structure before them.

Garrett Fenton looked to Dargaard Keep and then shook his head. "No, I'm afraid it would take far too long and require too many knights. And to what purpose?"

"So what are we going to do? Surely, High Justice Caladen isn't going to allow Soth to get away with his crimes."

"I've received instructions from the high justice. I assure you, he won't be getting away with anything," Fenton said.

"But how—"

"Think about it for a moment," Fenton interrupted. "Soth has lived his life as a revered and respected knight.

Now, news of his crimes will be all over Ansalon in a matter of weeks. Anywhere he goes he will be called a murderer and mocked as a fallen knight. For a Knight of Solamnia, especially one of Soth's stature, such a fate is worse than death itself."

"Yes," said van Sickle. "I can see that." His body seemed to shiver at the thought. Still, he persisted. "But we can't just let him go."

"No," Fenton said. "There will be conditions that must be met."

Hours later, he rode slowly toward the keep under the protection of a white standard. When Fenton reached the bridge, it did not come down.

He remained seated on his mount and laid forth his conditions.

"Loren Soth," he said loudly enough for all those on the west side of the keep to hear. "You are hereby dishonorably dismissed from the Knights of Solamnia. Furthermore, if you should ever venture outside the boundaries of Knightlund it will be the duty of every Knight of Solamnia to hunt you down like a common criminal and carry out the execution order of the high justice."

Fenton paused a few moments. "If you understand these terms you may indicate so in an appropriate manner."

Several minutes passed before a column of pale white smoke rose up from the uppermost battlement of the keep.

Seeing the smoke, Fenton nodded. "Very well, then. It is done."

The Solamnic Knights turned their horses around and headed back to Palanthas.

BOOK THREE

DEAD OF KNIGHT

Chapter 27

"Tell me it's not true!" cried Isolde. "Tell me Korinne died during the birth and not by your hand!"

She had asked the question many times before, but never in as many words. Now, as he'd done so many times before, Soth remained silent, unwilling to face her.

"Tell me, please," repeated Isolde, this time on the verge of tears. At least if he denied it, if he adamantly claimed that some grievous mistake had been made, there might still be a chance for redemption, a chance to clear his good name.

His name and hers.

But if it were indeed true, if he had in fact killed his former wife and child, people would know that she had been carrying his child while he was still married to Korinne. Then they would assume that because Isolde had been with child it had been that much easier for Soth to turn his back on Korinne. Nay, more than turn his back.

To . . .

She had trouble with the word.

To *kill* his wife and newborn child.

If that were true, she would be an accomplice to the murders. She would be as guilty of the killings as Soth himself.

If it were true.

If Soth was indeed guilty of the crime, he would never regain his status as one of the greatest Solamnic Knights of all time. Instead he would be a disgraced knight who would be killed on sight if he ever left the keep. And she would be similarly disgraced—a subject of ridicule should she ever venture beyond Dargaard Keep's cold blood-stone walls.

After all, who could pardon such a heinous act? Even the Healing Hand, Mishakal, would be hard-pressed to forgive such an atrocity.

If it were true.

"Tell me they made a mistake," she pleaded. "Tell me you did not kill Korinne and the child!"

Soth drew in a long breath, looked Isolde in the eye and spoke to her directly. "Lady Korinne died as a result of the severely deformed child that she bore."

Isolde listened intently to the words. They didn't sound like much of a denial, but Soth's voice was unwavering and it was edged with just a hint of conviction.

She desperately wanted to believe him. For a moment she thought to ask him again in order to cull more reassuring words from him, but decided against it. Those few words would be as much as she would get out of her husband. They would have to do.

Especially now.

He had changed so much these past few weeks. His face used to be bright and quick to smile. He had laughed every so often and had looked content. Now his face was masked by a shroud of darkness. His eyes, once alight with passion, now smoldered with loathing for everyone and everything around him. He constantly grumbled about everything and even shunned the company of his knights, the same brave men who had literally snatched him from the brink of death.

They'd saved his life, but they hadn't been able to save his honor. That had been crushed and with it so too had the man.

If only there was a way to regain his honor, their honor, the honor of the Soth family name.

Isolde prayed to Mishakal for guidance.

* * * * *

The summer months passed and the keep grew cold and damp. It was as if the sun never shone on its walls, as if the fires in its hearths were more smoke than heat.

Soth tried to attend to his duties as he had before, but now there seemed to be very little for him to do. The people of Knightlund had turned west to Vingaard Keep for protection from marauders, and for advice in land and financial disputes.

Soth wasn't surprised. Who would seek the advice of a murderer? Certainly no one of sound mind. It was something he never thought he would say, but he longed for the days when he sat in judgment, settling trivial land claims and disputes over money. At one time he would have done anything *not* to have to listen to commoners' petty arguments, but now he would give *everything* just to listen to them once more.

He sat in his throne chair in the middle of a large empty room. For some reason the chair was comfortable now and he could sit in it for hours without moving, his eyes closed as he relived the past.

"Why don't you go out for a ride?" asked a voice from somewhere in the shadows.

Soth didn't need to look up. He knew it was Isolde. He did not answer her.

"Loren?" she called, stepping into the hall.

"What is it?" snapped Soth, his eyes narrowed in anger.

"Why don't you get out of the keep for a while?"

"And why don't you tend to the child and leave me to my own affairs?"

Isolde was visibly hurt by the sharp words of her husband, but continued moving forward, undaunted.

"It pains me to see you lingering within the keep like a shadow. I look at you and I see a ghost from your former life."

"Enough!" shouted Soth, rising from his throne.

But Isolde would not stop. "The knights seem lost, too. They've looked to you for direction for so long, and suddenly it's not—"

"I said enough!"

"You are still a Knight of Solamnia," she continued. "You all are. No matter what has happened, you must continue living your life in accordance with the Oath and the Measure. Anything else for a knight is the same as death—"

Soth had heard enough. He placed his large hands on Isolde's tiny elven shoulders and pushed her roughly to the floor.

She hit the cold hard stones with a loud thump, but did not cry out.

Soth looked at her for the longest time, ashamed at what he'd done, and hating himself for what he had become.

Isolde slowly picked herself up off the floor.

Soth left the hall without saying a word.

Isolde stood up and brushed off her clothes. As she did, a single tear fell from the corner of her eye. The tear was not for what had happened, for clearly Soth was not himself these days. Gone was the brave and valiant warrior, the Soth she'd come to know and love. And in his place was this dark and brooding man who had forgotten everything for which he had once stood.

She left the hall and headed for the chapel.

She had been praying to Mishakal for guidance and in a way she had been guided. She was beginning to feel more certain that she knew what was required for the benefit of herself, her son Peradur, and for all those living inside the keep.

Soth needed to find a way in which to redeem himself.

She entered the chapel and knelt down in her familiar place, her legs covering the darker spots her knees had rubbed into the wood these past few weeks, and prayed.

She prayed to Mishakal to show her a way in which Soth might find redemption.

* * * * *

The room had been the healer's chambers for years, but because Istvan did not return from Palanthas following Soth's hearing, Isolde had decided the room could be converted to a nursery. Soth had wanted the room left abandoned, but Isolde had insisted. Further protests on Soth's part would have required some sort of explanation, so in the end he reluctantly yielded to her request.

In spite of the memories he tried to bury, Soth found himself coming here more and more often to spend time with his son, Peradur. One reason was that he had the time to spend, another was that he felt if he spent time with the child now, he might be able to prevent his sins from being passed on as his father's sins had been passed onto him.

He wasn't sure how being with the child might prevent this, but because Soth's father Aynkell had spent very little time with him as a child, Soth felt that doing the opposite might produce the opposite result—a young man whose soul was free of the black marks incurred by the previous generations.

Whatever the outcome, it was worth the effort given that Soth felt he couldn't make things any *worse* for the boy if he tried.

"There's a good boy," he said, the soft tone of his voice sounding strange coming from such a big man. "A good boy who will one day grow to be a good knight."

The child smiled.

"A great knight."

The child giggled.

Soth took a small wooden sword from a chest full of toys and noisemakers. The sword was made of soft fir wood and rounded at each on all sides in order to prevent the child from accidentally hurting himself. Soth placed the hilt of the sword in the child's tiny hand and instinctively his fingers curled around it, holding the sword tightly.

Soth smiled approvingly, his quiet, hissing laughter sounding like steam from a cauldron. He let go of the sword, allowing Peradur to hold it by himself. For several seconds he held it aloft as proudly as any champion knight, but then the blade began to waver until it fell back against the child's chest. Then, taking hold of it with both hands, Peradur brought the soft wooden sword to his mouth and began chewing on it.

Again Soth laughed, but his joy was short-lived.

He wanted nothing more than for his son to follow in his footsteps and become a Knight of Solamnia, keeping the Soth legacy alive for yet another generation. But now it seemed that dream would never be realized.

And he had no one to blame but himself.

First of all, the Knights of Solamnia had never accepted a half-elf into the knighthood. To the best of his knowledge, Soth couldn't even remember a half-elf serving as a squire. Secondly, while at one time the Solamnic Knights might have accepted a half-elf whose name was Soth, those days were over. Because of his deeds and heinous violation of the Oath and the Measure, it was highly unlikely that any young man carrying the taint of the Soth name would ever be allowed to join the knighthood.

The boy was barely a few months old and he'd already been judged because of his father's deed.

Because of the sins of his father.

Soth watched Peradur chew on the sword, his pink gums gnashing against the wood. As he did so, Soth wondered how could it be that something as innocent as a child, something that was supposed to bring him such joy, had only brought him more remorse, greater shame, and above all, such heartfelt pain.

No sword had ever hurt him like this.

And worst of all, it would be a pain that would never fade with the passage of time. For what might the child feel toward him when he finally came of age?

Anger?

Resentment?

Disgust?

Shame?

The thought of it made Soth shiver.

"Excuse me, milord," said a soft voice.

Soth turned and saw the young maid, Jenfer Clinyc, who had been entrusted with Peradur's care ever since the dismissal of Mirrel. She stood in the doorway in a way that suggested she knew she was intruding. Soth liked the girl; she was good with the child, unassuming and unpretentious around others, and most importantly, was absolutely devoted to both Isolde and Peradur.

"It's time for the young knight's bath," she said with a smile.

Soth nodded, touched his son's head gently, then rose to his feet. He took one last look at the child, then turned and left the room.

He walked down the hall and through the keep, heading toward the chapel. When he arrived, he eased the door open.

He was surprised to find Isolde there, but let none of it show. Instead he quietly stepped into the chapel and knelt down by her side.

Whispering under his breath, he began to pray to Paladine, patron of the Knights of the Rose and spiritual father of the Knights of Solamnia, to bring some light and hope into his life.

Chapter 28

The roar of the flames was deafening.

Every stick of wood in the keep seemed to be alight, crawling with orange flames that licked at the walls like the tongue of some great serpent.

And then, in the midst of the fire, a voice.

"Father!" came the cry.

The call of his son, Peradur.

Soth ran through the burning keep, his eyes stinging from the smoke, his clothes clinging to his damp skin.

"Peradur!" he called into the midst of the flames.

"Father, over here!"

Soth moved forward.

Suddenly he felt an intense heat burning his back. He spun around and saw his cloak trailing behind him, burning as brightly as a tallow-soaked torch. He tore the clasp from his neck and threw the cloak to the ground where it was immediately engulfed in flames.

"Father! Where are you father?"

"I'm here!" he answered. "I'm coming!"

He drew his broadsword and used it to cut a swath through the flames and burning timbers that had fallen from the ceiling.

Finally he reached the nursery. It billowed with smoke as the flames chewed their way across the rafters supporting the room's ceiling.

"Father, save me!"

Soth was in tears from the smoke and could barely see more than the few feet in front of him.

"Father, help me! Please!"

He moved forward, being drawn by the sound of his son's voice.

Suddenly, there it was—the cradle. He had made it. He took a final few steps and looked inside the cradle.

The haglike face of the witch smiled up at him.

"Father, help me!" the witch cried out, the young boy's voice suddenly sounding hideous coming from such an ugly, gap-toothed mouth. She laughed wickedly, the cackle cutting through the roar of the fire like a sword through the leg of an ogre.

Soth recoiled in horror and screamed from the utter depths of his soul.

"No!"

* * * * *

She was floating.

Light shone all around her, a soft glow warming her from the inside out.

And a voice.

A beautiful voice was speaking to her.

Isolde heard it not with her ears, but with her mind.

It was telling her softly, so softly, what must be done.

And she understood.

And then there came a sound so loud and sharp that the dream shattered around her like glass. Isolde looked sleepily around the room, certain that the ground had shook and that the walls were about to topple.

"No . . ."

The shout contained a measure of sorrow along with terror. Isolde rolled over and realized the cries had come from her husband.

"Loren, wake up!" she said, placing her hands on his shoulders and shaking him.

No effect.

She shook him harder. "Wake up!"

Soth's eyes blinked open and he gasped for air. His face was a pale shade of white and damp with sweat. His wide eyes darted around the room as if he were familiarizing himself with his surroundings.

"It's all right," said Isolde. "It was just a dream, a bad, bad dream. Like before."

"No," whispered Soth. "No. This was worse. This was terrible, horrible."

"What was it about? What happened?"

"No." He shook his head. "It was too horrible. I'd rather forget it than have to go through it again."

"Perhaps that might be best," Isolde nodded. She looked at him for the longest time, drying his face with a bedsheet as she gathered the strength to say the words. Finally she took a deep breath and said, "I had a dream as well."

"I hope to Paladine it was less disturbing than mine."

"It was," said Isolde. "In fact, it was a revelation."

"Really?" Soth rolled onto his side to face her. "Tell me."

Isolde smiled. "You know I have been praying to Mishakal to show me a way in which you can redeem yourself," she said.

"Yes," said Soth. "You have told me of your prayers."

"Well, tonight I believe they were finally answered."

Soth looked at her for several seconds. She smiled at him again, but remained silent. At last he prodded her, "Please, tell me more."

"It wasn't a nightmare at all," Isolde began. "It felt warm and comfortable and wonderful. And a voice spoke to me, a female voice. I'm sure it was Mishakal herself."

Soth was skeptical. As benevolent as Mishakal was—she was called the Healing Hand, after all—he doubted that she would trouble herself to speak directly to a mere mortal. But as he studied the countenance of Isolde, the absolute conviction in her expression was too strong to be so easily dismissed. He decided to open up his mind and listen carefully to her account. "What did the voice say?"

"I didn't understand it all." She shook her head. "Some parts didn't make any sense to me."

"If you could repeat exactly what the voice said, then perhaps I might be able to make sense of it."

"I suppose I could try." She closed her eyes and concentrated. Her eyelids fluttered and her thin lips trembled as they parted slightly. Suddenly her eyes opened and she began speaking as if someone or something was speaking through her.

"The former Knight of Solamnia named Soth," the voice said, "can redeem himself and his followers by journeying to the Temple of the Kingpriest in Istar."

Shocked but nevertheless intrigued, Soth leaned closer to Isolde so he might hear her better.

"Once there, he must confront the Kingpriest and order him to abdicate from the position or suffer the wrath of the gods."

Isolde's mouth closed and for several seconds she was still and quiet. But then after a deep breath she—or whoever was using Isolde as a messenger—began speaking again.

"The Kingpriest will refuse and will strike down Soth with a bolt of lightning. But that will not be the end of Soth's quest. By the grace of the gods Paladine and Mishakal, he will rise again in order to continue the fight. Each time the Kingpriest dispatches him to the netherworld, Soth will rise up again, more powerful than the last time until his strength and power are sufficient to finally lay the Kingpriest to rest."

Isolde seemed to grow tired, but Soth knew enough not to disturb her until she was done.

"When that is accomplished, when the Kingpriest is gone from the face of Krynn, only then will Soth be allowed to pass in peace from this world to the next."

Soth drew in a long breath.

"If he fails, all of Krynn will suffer for the arrogance of the Kingpriest. The skies will burn, the land will heave . . . Life as we know it will be changed forever. This event will come to be known as the Cataclysm."

Isolde's eyes closed again, but this time she fell back onto the bed, exhausted.

Soth gathered her in his arms and held her tight, stroking her hair and face until she awakened.

"Are you all right?" he asked.

"I think so," said Isolde, putting a hand to her head. "I remember hearing a strange voice, something about the Kingpriest and forces of great destruction . . ."

Soth nodded.

"Then it's true," Isolde said, suddenly gaining strength. "Mishakal has shown us a way to redemption. After you've completed the quest you can rejoin the knighthood and everything will be the way it was before." She shook her head as her eyes grew wide. "No, even better than it was before."

Her smile slowly faded as she realized that Soth wasn't sharing her excitement.

"What's wrong?" she asked. "What is it?"

"It's the nature of the quest."

"What about it?"

Soth sighed. Obviously Isolde had simply acted as a messenger of the gods and was unaware of what was contained in the message.

"I must battle the Kingpriest of Istar," said Soth in a tone that suggested he was doomed.

"What is the problem? You are a Knight of the Rose, a great warrior."

"Perhaps, but I am no match for the likes of the Kingpriest."

"Then you can prepare yourself for the battle, undergo special training."

Soth shook his head. "You don't understand." He still didn't want to say it, but he was finding it more and more difficult to avoid the inevitable. "If I accept this quest, the only time my soul will ever be allowed to rest in peace is when I finally rid Krynn of the Kingpriest."

"I still don't understand," said Isolde. "What are you saying?"

"I'm saying that the only way I can successfully complete this quest and save the world from destruction is to sacrifice my own life in the process."

Isolde's lips moved, but she was unable to make a sound.

Chapter 29

On Sancrist Island . . .

The gnomes and humans watched in awe as the normally blue skies above the island roiled and blackened while the long-dormant volcano beneath Mount Nevermind began to rumble uneasily.

In Qualinesti . . .

Unstoppable brushfires burned through Wayreth Forest, eating up vast tracts of healthy oaks, maples, ash and vallenwood trees, as well as the fruit-laden orchards of apple, peach and pear trees.

In Silvanesti . . .

Fires raged through the fabled Silvanesti Woods, the intense flames and black smoke blocking out all evidence of the sun.

In Ergoth . . .

Water flowed through the lands in and around the city

of Daltigoth, flooding farms and forests alike, but also washing away homes and buildings, many of which had stood for centuries.

In Istar . . .

People scurried to find a safe place to hide from the flooding red tides that began to wash through the city's streets like blood after a hard and long-fought battle.

In Solamnia . . .

The wind began to pick up over the plains, churning the waters of the Vingaard River and blowing sand and dust across the sun-dried earth as if in an attempt to scour it clean.

Chapter 30

"It is a heavy price to pay," said Soth.

"I know," said Isolde calmly. "But think of the change it could bring, if not for all the people of Krynn, then for your son."

Soth wasn't as disappointed by Isolde's words as he was surprised. Since she'd had the vision, she had been steadfast in her conviction. She desperately wanted him to travel to Istar and give up his life in order to prevent the coming Cataclysm. Soth wasn't afraid of sacrificing his life for others because his current life wasn't worth all that much to him. What surprised him was Isolde's seeming lack of concern about what her life would be like without him.

"And what of you and our son? Will you have the strength to go on without me in your life?"

Isolde moved forward and hugged him long and hard. "It will be so very hard, and I don't know if I'll be able to live without you, but I must try to be strong." She paused. "For I do know that when you succeed, you will forever be a part of both of our lives because we will have you to thank for them."

Tears streamed from Isolde's eyes as she held him tight.

Soth thought about her words. It was true what Isolde had said. If he succeeded, all the people of Krynn would have him to thank for their lives.

But what of Isolde and the boy? She seemed heartbroken that he would never be coming back, yet was still brave enough to admit that it was for the best.

At last the scales had been tipped.

Soth would travel to Istar.

* * * * *

"But to give his life—" said Derik Grimscribe, chewing on a piece of day-old bread.

"To do so in order to save all of Krynn from death and destruction," interjected Colm Farold between sips of tea. "Certainly that is a worthy enough reason to make such a sacrifice."

The knights sat around a rectangular table discussing the latest news. Apparently their lord had been shown a way to redeem himself, restore his good family name and become a hero equal in stature to the great Huma himself.

But while most of the knights were eager to have the honor of their lord restored to its full and even greater glory, there were those who were skeptical about the vision and the quest it proposed.

Perhaps it was the messenger of whom they were wary. Not all of the knights were as taken by Isolde Denissa as Soth was.

Perhaps it was the price Soth had to pay in order to complete the quest. Why did Soth have to die at the hands of the Kingpriest? Couldn't the Cataclysm be avoided in a way that wouldn't cost Soth his life? Questions had arisen that caused some of the knights to doubt the validity of the vision, and suggested to them that it was all an elaborate ruse concocted by the high justice to carry out the death sentence imposed upon Soth. Others felt it was a vision sent by the Kingpriest himself because Soth was probably the only knight who was strong enough and brave enough to stop the priest's bid to take his place among the gods.

"He's being used as a pawn in a power struggle that doesn't concern him," said Grimscribe.

"No," countered Farold. "He's being given a chance to save himself and the knighthood."

"Save himself," laughed Grimscribe. "How can you say that if he must give up his life in order to succeed?"

"Because if he is successful and saves Krynn from the Cataclysm, he will not have died in vain. He will live forever, a hero to all."

* * * * *

Soth knocked on the door of the knights' chambers for Wersten Kern and Meyer Seril. It was a big room with the space needed to store their armor, swords, shields and other personal belongings. There was a bed at each end of the room and a desk in the center for reading and writing. There was also a table and two chairs in between the beds.

Kern and Seril were both seated at the table, passing the time by playing a board game called Briscopa that had apparently become quite popular in Palanthas.

The two knights looked up at Soth and he bowed slightly, realizing that he was intruding upon their leisure time. "Please excuse the intrusion."

"No intrusion at all," said Seril.

"Please come in, milord," said Kern.

"Thank you." He stepped into the room and sat on the bed between them. He looked at Meyer Seril. "Excuse me, Knight Seril, but the reason I'm here is to ask something of Knight Kern."

"Of course," said Seril, getting up from his seat. "We can finish the game anytime."

Soth waited until Seril had left the room before speaking. "I've decided to take on the quest," he said, his voice still somewhat unsteady, as if he were still trying to accept his own decision. "I will be setting out for Istar in the morning"—he paused for a heartbeat—"and I'd like you to join me."

Kern was speechless.

"Understand that while I am asking this, the decision to accompany me is completely voluntary. If you wish to remain in the keep, no one will ever know of your decision and I will not look upon you with any disfavor."

Kern still said nothing.

"The only others I have asked to join me are Caradoc and Colm Farold. And now you. My three most loyal knights."

At last Kern swallowed and was able to speak. "I'd be honored, milord," he said in a rush of breath.

Soth nodded and placed a hand on Kern's shoulder. "Thank you."

* * * * *

The sun shone brightly over the jagged peaks of the Dargaard Mountains as if Mishakal herself, the Healing Hand, was showing Soth the way.

Unlike his departures in the past, there were few people present to see him off. The knights were there, of course, some wishing they could accompany Soth, others no doubt happy to be left behind.

Isolde was present, dressed in a dark rose-colored gown which she wore as a show of support for her husband's quest. If she was saddened by the prospect of Soth's departure, her faith in Mishakal and her own strength of character were helping her to hide it well.

Soth hoped some of that strength would be passed on to

his son. It would serve him well in his later years as a Knight of Solamnia. Soth realized that such a thought was something of a wild fantasy, given that the Knights of Solamnia would never accept the half-breed son of a disgraced knight. But, if his quest were successful, if he saved Krynn from the ravages of the Cataclysm, there might be a chance for his son.

He approached Isolde, took her hand in his. "Speak well of me to the boy."

"I will."

"And make sure you tell him that I gave my life as much for him as for the all people of Krynn."

"I won't have to tell him," said Isolde. "Minstrels and storytellers will sing it to him wherever he may go."

Soth nodded, and leaned forward to kiss her.

As the kiss ended, Isolde lowered her head, covered her face with her hands and wept softly.

Soth resisted the urge to try and comfort her—it was too late for that now—and moved on to the maid who held Peradur in her arms. He took the bundled child from her, held him close to his face and whispered, "When you grow older, don't curse me for abandoning you. I am doing this for you because I know your world will be a better place without me in it."

The child made a gurgling sound, as if in understanding.

Soth kissed his son's forehead and returned him to the arms of the maid. After a final look at the child, he turned away and joined the three waiting knights—Caradoc, Farold and Kern.

Then he rode out of the keep without looking back.

* * * * *

Normally it would take Soth and his knights at least ten days to reach Istar, but at the rate they were traveling it would likely take them closer to twenty.

For Soth, there seemed little point in rushing headlong toward his death. Traveling at a relaxed pace allowed him to enjoy what would be his last few weeks of life. It also gave him the chance to reflect on his life, the mistakes he'd made, the errors in judgment, the sins he'd committed.

By the end of the third day, Soth was convinced that sacrificing his life was the best thing he could do. After all, he was a Knight of Solamnia and the only thing he'd ever wanted in his life was to be one of the greatest men the knighthood had ever seen. For a time he had achieved that goal and had basked in the glory of being one of the best.

But now, he was no longer best. He was least. He was worst. He wasn't even a knight anymore, but a man sentenced to death. Soth was a fugitive from justice and a source of shame to his beloved Knights of Solamnia.

He had made a mockery of the knighthood.

Succeeding on this quest would return them to their former glory.

He would give up his life.

It was for the best.

* * * * *

The knights headed east after leaving Dargaard Keep, then traveled south along the eastern foot of the Dargaard Mountains.

On the morning of the third day, they changed their direction, and began heading southeast through Estwilde, along a seldom used trail that would take them across the broad, hilly basin between the Dargaard Mountains and the northeastern tip of the Khalkist Mountains.

Unlike the smooth grasslands of the plains of Solamnia, Estwilde was covered by rugged foothills, pine forests and high mountains.

And while Estwilde was famous all over Krynn for its dangerous inhabitants—everything from evil humans to goblins, from ogres to hill dwarves—Soth and his men saw not a soul on their journey.

"Do you think they recognize us as Knights of Solamnia and are keeping a respectful distance?" pondered Colm Farold after they'd been riding the trail through Estwilde for almost a day without seeing any sign of life.

"Since when do ugly beasts such as goblins and ogres respect anything about the knighthood?" asked Caradoc.

The knights laughed.

Soth did not.

"It is Paladine," he said.

"What?" asked Farold.

"It is Paladine," Soth repeated. "He is guiding our way, assuring safe passage so I may complete the quest unhindered by such distractions as ogres and goblins."

The knights fell silent. They had never heard Soth speak so solemnly about his quest before. The jovial camaraderie they had been experiencing was gone.

Caradoc tried to get it back. "Well as long as Paladine is watching out for us, maybe he could see to it that a goat crossed our path. I'm half starved."

Something appeared up ahead along the trail.

"What's that?" asked Wersten Kern, pointing.

"Caradoc asked for a goat," said Soth. "What else would it be?"

Caradoc and Kern drew their swords and kicked at their mounts.

Indeed it was a goat.

And a delicious one at that.

* * * * *

The air in the northern tip of the Khalkist Mountains was cold and dry. The knights had been riding for more than ten days and were growing weary in the thin mountain air. Still, they continued on undaunted but looked forward to getting past the hilly, barren mountainsides and onto the much warmer plains of Istar.

At least as they neared Istar they would come into contact with others. The journey so far had been rather dull because Soth had few words for them and they'd exhausted most topics of discussion days ago. And, truth be told, with Soth doomed to an inevitable and horrifying death, no one felt much like talking. Crossing paths with someone else, be they human, elf, dwarf, ogre or some manner of beast, would be a blessing.

They passed the northern coastal settlement of Thoradin, a sprawling village referred to as a "kingdom" by the mountain dwarves who lived there. The knights kept themselves a half-day's journey to the south of the village lest they be spotted by wandering dwarfs and asked to pay a visit to the king.

And now they entered an area of the Khalkist Mountains rumored to be crawling with Zakhar, a reclusive and mysterious race of dwarves horribly disfigured by an ancient mold plague and ostracized from the rest of dwarven culture. According to the tales, the Zakhar—a word meaning "cursed ones"—killed any non-Zakhar who trespassed on their land.

The knights looked forward to meeting up with the Zakhar. In addition to giving their swords a workout, the ugly beasts would provide them with something to talk about the rest of the way to Istar.

"Did you see that?" asked Caradoc.

"See what?" said Farold.

"There, up ahead on the trail. Movement in the brush."

"I didn't see anything," said Kern.

"There was something," said Caradoc. "I swear."

"Perhaps the cold has numbed your brain," said Kern. "There is nothing there."

"Quiet!" commanded Soth. "There *is* something there."

The knights all looked ahead to see what it was. There, standing on the trail were three elf-maids.

"Well, well," said Caradoc. "Of all the things to come

across in these godforsaken mountains, the last thing I expected to see was a trio of elves." He smiled. "And pretty ones at that."

"Silence!" shouted Soth.

Caradoc pursed his lips. Farold and Kern dared not speak.

Soth rode up ahead, stopping in front of the elf-maids who seemed to be in no hurry to give Soth room to pass.

"Step aside, good elf-woman," Soth said firmly. "We have business with the Kingpriest in Istar that cannot be delayed."

The elf-maids laughed.

Soth's horse took one step forward. "I said step aside!"

The tallest of the three maids, a svelte, black-haired beauty with similarly dark eyes stepped forward and smiled at Soth. "What makes you think the Kingpriest, one who is a god on Krynn, would want to speak with the likes of you . . . Soth?" She said his name in a long hiss, and when she was done, she looked as if the word had left a bad taste in her mouth.

Soth was surprised that the elf-maid knew his name, but made sure not to let it show on his face.

"I am Lord Loren Soth of Dargaard Keep, Knight of the Rose."

The elf-maids laughed. "You are nothing, Soth. You are the son of a clerk, a mock-knight. You tried to deny your ancestry, tried to hide it behind the great deeds of your uncles and cousins. But now all of Krynn knows you were never meant to be a knight because you've proven it, being too cowardly to accept your fate like a true Knight of Solamnia."

Again Soth was shocked that these maids knew so much of his personal history. It angered him that such matters had become common knowledge across the continent of Ansalon.

The other knights came up from behind to join Soth, taking up a position on either side of him.

"My past is certainly of no concern of yours. And neither is it of any concern to the Kingpriest."

"Oh, but you're wrong, Soth. So wrong. If a mere mortal is sent to dispose of the Kingpriest, then at the very least that mortal should be a knight of the highest honor. Not a common criminal. Not a murderer of women and children. Not the killer of his own half-brother and sister."

Caradoc inhaled a gasp at the mention of this. Like Soth, he had done his best to bury the despicable deed deep in his past.

"How easily we forget such trivialities as the murder of our siblings, eh Soth?"

Soth said nothing. Outwardly, he could only seethe in anger at the elf-maid's words, but inside, being so casually reminded of those earlier killings had left him thoroughly shaken.

"Pay no attention to them, milord," said Farold. "They have obviously been sent by the Kingpriest to stop you. The Kingpriest knows of your quest, knows you can stop him and he is afraid of you. That much is obvious by this feeble attempt at trickery."

"Ah, the loyal Knight Farold," said the elf-maid to the left of the dark-haired woman. She was slightly shorter than the dark-haired elf and had a full head of long red hair that was the color of blood. "Another disgraced knight. A traitor to the knighthood who could not abide by the decision of the high justice, who could not allow his beloved Lord Soth the chance to die with what little dignity remained."

"Enough!" cried Soth. "I will not have my knights spoken to in this way!"

The red-headed maid continued on as if she hadn't heard Soth's warning. "The same is true for Knight Caradoc and Knight Kern. The Oath and the Measure suited all of you until it sought justice against the vile Soth. Then you forgot your years of training and devotion. And for what? To save a butcherer of women, a slaughterer of innocent children?"

"Enough, I said!" repeated Soth, his anger barely contained.

"The truth is a powerful weapon isn't it, Soth?" said the third maid, shorter and heavier than the others with bright blonde hair that hung down over her shoulders. She was easily the least attractive of the three and spoke in a harsh voice that grated against Soth's already fatigued nerves.

"I do not fear the truth!" said Soth. But even as he spoke the words, he remembered the trial and how he feared the news of his deeds would devastate Isolde when she learned of them. But even though that was behind him now, the thought of it compelled him to add, "At least not any more."

Indeed, what truths did he have to fear now?

"Perhaps you *should* fear the truth," said the blonde maid. "For the truth I know would be enough to drive any man insane."

"Step aside and let us pass," Caradoc interjected. "We are wasting too much of Lord Soth's precious time."

"Let her speak," ordered Soth.

"Milord," pleaded Farold, "these maids have been sent by the Kingpriest with the sole purpose of preventing you from reaching Istar and completing your quest. Remember the Cataclysm mentioned in the vision. Remember what will happen to the people of Krynn. Remember your son."

"Ah, Soth's son, Peradur," said the fair-haired maid. "How sure are you that he is actually your son?"

"What?"

"Milord, we have no time for—"

"Silence!" shouted Soth. "What of my son?"

"Your son?" she said mockingly. "Or the son of every able-bodied man in Dargaard Keep?"

Soth gritted his teeth.

The fair-haired maid simply laughed again. "You couldn't

give Lady Korinne a child. What makes you think you were able to give one to Isolde?"

Soth considered the question. "Korinne was barren. She could not conceive."

Again a laugh. "Foolish Soth. Korinne had no difficulty conceiving after she paid a visit to the hedge witch. And even a horribly painful birth didn't stop her from producing a child." She shook her head and pointed an accusing finger at Soth. "You were the one unable to give her a child."

Soth's mind was reeling. He felt dizzy with rage and heartbreak.

"But I did produce a child. Peradur is my son!"

"No, Soth. Not yours. Whose exactly, none can say. But not yours."

"You lie," spat Soth. "I saved Isolde's life. She adores me. She would never be unfaithful to me. She would not dare."

All three of the elf-maids cackled at this.

"Foolish man," said the dark-haired elf-maid.

"Soth, the unwise," said the redhead.

"Did it never strike you as odd that Isolde was the one to receive the vision which sent you on your quest?"

"I prayed to Paladine," Soth said between clenched teeth. "He showed me the destruction that would be brought on by the Cataclysm. Isolde prayed to Mishakal. The goddess showed her how it could be prevented."

"So gullible," said the dark elf.

"Soth, the naive," said the redhead.

"And did you not think it suspicious that Isolde, a woman who swore her love to you, and supposedly bore your child, would so readily be willing to send you off on a journey that could only end with your death?"

Soth had wondered about this, but was able to dismiss his concerns because of the strength of Isolde's faith. Now, suddenly, he wasn't so sure anymore.

"While you and your knights have been riding clear

across Ansalon on a fool's quest, Isolde has been bedding all the knights and squires you've left behind. She's even been intimate with a few of the footmen, as well as a few others you might not want to know about." The elf-maid's eyes grew wide as she took obvious delight in striking a blow deep into Soth's heart. "But perhaps it's best this way," the maid continued. "At least now Isolde will be reunited with the father of her child—whomever he might be."

"Silence!" Soth cried.

He wanted to shut the words from his mind but he could not. The elf-maids had known so much about him, known the truth about Lady Korinne's death, known the truth about the murders of his half-siblings. If they knew the truth about those matters, then why wouldn't what they said about Isolde also be true?

That meant that . . .

Peradur was not his child, but a bastard.

And Isolde was not a loving wife and devoted mother, but a harlot seductress who cared not whom she slept with.

The more Soth thought about it, the more sense it made. Isolde had been so forward with him, seducing him while he'd still been wed to Korinne, even while Korinne was in pain and heavy with child. She was an ambitious social climber willing to bed her way into the position of lady of the keep.

If she'd been capable of that, what was to stop her from being unfaithful to Soth while he was away? What was to stop her from simply finding another knight in a position of power now that Soth was an outlaw? And finally, what better way was there to bed whomever she pleased than to send him away on a quest from which he would never return?

The more sense it made, the more he raged.

The elf-maids continued to babble on, but Soth could no longer hear their individual words. It just seemed to be a wall of black noise designed to drive him mad.

"Silence!" he cried.

The elf-maids continued.

"She sees every man as her lover . . ."

"Enough!" he shouted.

"And she loves every man she sees . . ."

"Si-lence!" he screamed.

The elf-maids would not stop.

Soth drew his broadsword.

"Milord, no," gasped Farold.

But it was far too little, too late.

Soth's blood ran hot, heated by flames of jealousy and betrayal, even hatred. Rage clouded his thoughts, took control of his mind and body, governing his actions. He dismounted his horse in seconds.

The elf-maids were still speaking, almost in chants of torment now, not caring that Soth was fast approaching them with his sword raised high above his head.

"Her desire burns hot . . ."

Soth was upon them.

"Her bed is alight with flames of passion . . ."

With a single, swift motion Soth struck down the lovely dark-haired elf, cutting her in two from her left shoulder to her right hip. The pieces of her fell to the ground, but her large dark eyes still watched him and her mouth still moved, her words could still be heard.

"With you out of the way . . ."

Soth struck her again.

"She will be free to indulge herself . . ."

Again and again he struck her, until the maid was silenced.

Breathing hard, he moved on to the elf-maid with red hair, swinging his sword from left to right in a powerful arc that cut her down like a small sapling.

"When she's done with the men of the keep . . ."

Soth raised his sword, hilt high, point to the ground.

"More will come from miles around . . ."

And brought it down through the maid's throat, choking off her next word, replacing it with a muted gurgle.

That left just the blonde.

Soth lunged forward and ran his sword through her.

She seemed to laugh as the blade pierced her body. And when she spoke it sounded as if she felt no pain at all.

"Lord Loren Soth," she cackled. "Lord Cuckold of Dargaard Keep."

Soth pulled the sword from the maiden and began hacking with powerful two-handed blows. The maid fell to the ground, dead, but Soth still would not stop. He just kept striking the body until it was little more than a spot of gore strewn across the rocky ground.

And still he would not stop. He continued to hack and stab at the maids like a madman.

"Milord!" cried Farold.

The knights moved forward, grabbing at his arms to make him stop. Soth finally let the tip of his sword rest against the ground as he stopped to look at the carnage.

Then, as they watched, the remains of the three elf-maids slowly began to fade into the rocky slope of the mountainside.

"Phantoms," gasped Kern.

"Sent by the Kingpriest to stop us from reaching Istar," added Farold.

Soth, however, remained silent.

To him, it mattered not what the messengers had been. Flesh and blood or phantom, their message had still been true.

"Now we can continue on our way," said Caradoc, pausing a moment so that Soth could agree.

But Soth said nothing.

Instead he turned for his horse, mounted it and began riding west in the direction from which they had come.

Farold, Caradoc and Kern watched Soth ride away.

"Where in the name of Paladine is he going?" asked Kern.

"Dargaard Keep, most likely," said Caradoc.

"And what of us?" asked Farold.

"Do we have a choice?" asked Caradoc.

"We could continue on to Istar," said Farold. "We could confront the Kingpriest ourselves."

"Which would accomplish nothing," said Caradoc. "Soth had the knowledge that he would continue to rise from the dead until the Kingpriest was vanquished. We have no such guarantee. We would simply die and the Kingpriest would carry on." He looked at Farold, then at Kern. "I, for one, refuse to give up my life so foolishly."

"Agreed," said Farold.

Kern simply nodded. "If Soth is headed back to the keep," he asked, "what will he do when he gets there?"

The three knights were silent as they considered the question. They looked at the barren ground where the elf-maids had died and subsequently vanished.

Finally, Farold raised his head and looked with a stricken expression at his fellow knights.

"For the love of Paladine," whispered Kern, "no!"

Caradoc didn't bother to respond. Instead, he turned for his horse and mounted it. Then he kicked at its ribs, sending the beast surging forward.

Farold and Kern followed.

* * * * *

Traitorous, cheating, conniving, lying, evil, wicked elf-wench.

Soth continued to ride west, his mind locked in a continuous and destructive cycle of anger, hate and rage.

She sent me in search of my death.

He was pushing himself and his mount to the limits of endurance. He should have fallen to exhaustion long ago, but both he and his horse seemed to scarcely feel the strain.

Now it is her death toward which I ride.

He kicked at his horse, forcing it to run faster and it responded with a longer stride.

Deceptive, scheming, corrupt, deceitful, disloyal, wanton trollop.

* * * * *

Caradoc's horse staggered after catching its hoof on a rock. The beast snorted and righted itself, but after a few steps it began to stagger.

The knights had been riding for what seemed like days.

But for all their efforts they had been unable to make up any distance. Soth and his horse seemed to be creatures possessed of an otherworldly sort of power that would not forsake them until they reached their destination.

Suddenly, Caradoc's horse faltered, this time plowing into the ground with all its weight.

Dead weight.

Caradoc gathered himself up.

Kern and Farold noticed Caradoc had fallen behind and circled back toward him.

"Ride with me," offered Farold, patting his horse's sweat-soaked haunches.

Caradoc shook his head. "Thank you, but"—his voice broke as he struggled to catch his breath—"even if I had a fresh horse, it would matter not. We are pursuing a demon we will never catch. Soth is utterly possessed by a jealous rage. Even if we could catch him, I seriously doubt we could ever stop him."

Farold's horse snorted, as if in agreement.

"I believe you are correct," said Farold, his voice followed by a long sigh of defeat.

"This is a matter that is out of our hands," agreed Kern.

The two knights dismounted, took their horses by the reins and, along with Caradoc, took up the chase again, this time on foot.

* * * * *

Night was falling, but Soth continued to ride.

As Farold, Caradoc and Kern struggled to make their way through the Khalkist Mountains, they could just make him out in the distance—a faint silhouette against the pale red and white light of the moons.

Chapter 31

The tremors shook the ground for hours.

All through the city of Istar, screams could be heard.

Men, women and children cried out in agony and terror as cracks opened beneath their feet, swallowing them where they stood.

No one was safe.

Nowhere was safe.

The land itself was opening up, devouring entire families, entire homes, whole rows of houses, like some angry maw that was as insatiable as it was terrifying.

The sky had gone from blue to black, and was now tinged with red as it rained fire and destruction onto what was left of one of the greatest cities on the face of Krynn.

In the temple, the Kingpriest refused to concede defeat, refused to admit that his own righteous pride had brought on the wrath of the gods.

Like a madman, he still held out hope that the gods would come to their senses and plead for him to ascend to the heavens and take his rightful place alongside them.

"Is this the sign?" he shouted over the noise and rumble of the absolute chaos going on around him. "Is this the prelude to my ascension?"

He had hardly finished uttering the words when a ball of flame as big as a mountain streaked across the sky.

Chapter 32

The keep's guards had been warned of Soth's approach long in advance of his arrival. When he rode over the drawbridge, the portcullis was raised and waiting for him to enter.

Soth looked around, surprised at the expressions on the faces of those who had come to greet him. They all looked as if they were seeing a ghost.

Of course, such a reaction was understandable because Soth was to have never returned from his quest, but he saw it somewhat differently.

To his mind, they were all looking at him in this way because he had come back early and caught Isolde in the middle of an infidelity. The thought renewed the anger within him, making his blood run even hotter.

Soth dismounted. The people around him said nothing. The inside of the keep was filled only with the sound of his horse, which was snorting harshly while doing its best to remain standing after the long, hard ride. Soth walked among the people gathered in the entrance area, his boots and armor clanking with each step.

"Where is my wife?" he bellowed.

"Sh-she is in her chambers, milord," said Parry Roslin, captain of the guards.

"With whom?" he said, placing a strong right hand around Roslin's throat.

"She is with your son, I believe."

Soth pushed Roslin roughly aside. Some of the guards moved hesitantly to Roslin's aid.

"Here I am, here I am," came a voice from somewhere on the upper levels of the keep.

Soth heard that voice and the madness swirling within his mind intensified twofold.

"My lord, what brings you back so soon?" she said, coming into the entrance area with Peradur in her arms.

"Glad that I have returned, I see," Soth said, his voice dripping with sarcasm.

Isolde seemed confused by this. "Of course I am glad to see you, but what of the quest?"

"The quest," he smiled. "You mean, what of my death?"

"I do not understand," she said, shaking her head.

"Of course you don't. You don't understand how I've come to see the light. But now I know how you've been unfaithful to me . . . since the beginning."

"What are you talking about?" Isolde's voice was broken and disjointed with fear. Her eyes were glassy, on the verge of tears.

"Oh, how well you play the innocent," Soth said mockingly, his voice sounding hollow and chilling, as if it had already been touched by death. "Even now as I confront your unfaithfulness."

"What?" she said, truly surprised. "I've never been unfaithful to you."

Soth said nothing, his mind too clouded by rage to hear anything other than the taunting words of the elf-maids that had been echoing in his ears ever since he had returned to the keep:

She sees every man as her lover . . .
And she loves every man she sees . . .
Lord Loren Soth, Knight of the Rose,
Lord Cuckold of Dargaard Keep.

"I've never been unfaithful to you," Isolde repeated, her voice begging him to believe her. She began to move away from him, stepping backward into one of the keep's larger halls.

Soth rushed forward. "Liar!" he cried, placing a hand on her shoulder and pushing her heavily to the floor.

Isolde fell backward, clutching Peradur close to her breast. When she came to a stop, she looked up at Soth with wide eyes that were filled with terror and disbelief.

A loud roar could be heard outside the keep, shaking it roughly as it thundered past. In seconds the tremendous sound faded, replaced by the pungent smell of burnt wood and leaves, and other things that could not be named. The sky dimmed as the light from the sun was blocked by a layer of smoke.

Soth and Isolde paid little attention to the event as they were too involved in what was happening within the keep to care.

"What is the matter with you?" she asked, her voice edged with as much anger as terror. "I am your wife! I bore you a son!"

"A son, you say. Not my son! How are you so sure the child is mine?" asked Soth, towering over the fallen woman, forcing her to crawl awkwardly backward with a single hand just to keep her distance.

Soth's words struck her heart like a dagger. The tears she had been holding back streamed from the corners of her eyes. "How dare you accuse me," she said. "I loved you always. You saved my life. How could I ever do anything to hurt you?"

"You lay with me while I was still wed to Korinne. If you ignored one oath of matrimony, why should I believe you would honor the one you swore to me?"

"After Korinne was with child I wanted to leave the keep. But *you*, you were the one who wanted me to remain. You asked me to stay here so that you could be unfaithful to Korinne."

Peradur had begun to cry, wailing loudly after listening to his parents argue for so long. The child's cry reverberated through the keep, which had quickly emptied after the extent of Soth's anger had become apparent. It was possible that there still might be people in the hall peeking around corners, but if they were there, they were keeping themselves well hidden.

"So, you accuse me," said Soth, "when it is you who make a mockery of our marriage, bedding any man you please."

"By the hand of Mishakal," Isolde whispered. "What demon possesses you?"

"Do you even know who the child's father is?"

"You are his father," Isolde said softly between sobs. "You are."

"Treacherous, deceitful, lying witch!"

Isolde said nothing. Instinctively she crouched onto the floor to protect her child, and wept.

Soth stepped forward, drew his sword.

Isolde looked up.

"In the name of Paladine," she whispered. "No, please—"

At that moment the keep was rocked by the shock waves created by the impact of the fiery mountain-sized ball as it slammed into the unsuspecting city of Istar.

Like everywhere else on Krynn, Solamnia heaved from the impact. The keep began to crumble. Jagged cracks began to appear along mortar lines between the bloodstones. Items throughout the keep toppled from their places. The keep was filled with the sounds of clattering steel, smashing pots and the cries of people caught by falling debris.

The floor of the hall in which they stood began to split apart. The shaking of the ground caused Isolde to stumble backward onto the floor with the baby cradled in her arms.

"Help me," she cried, trying to rise up.

Soth shook his head. "Help you who have betrayed me so completely?"

She raised a hand toward him, but instead of assisting her, he turned his back on her.

The ground rumbled once more, shaking the keep to its very foundations.

Isolde screamed.

Soth turned around just in time to see the great chandelier hanging above the hall come loose from its mount. As if in another dimension, or shrouded in some spell, the chandelier fell slowly, seeming to fall inches at a time, taking forever to reach the floor.

Instinctively, Soth was compelled to do something to save her. He began moving toward Isolde, but like the chandelier itself, he could hardly move fast enough.

In the end Soth was left helpless and could only watch as the chandelier's ornate silver and gold swords, crowns and roses, impaled Isolde, nailing her to the jagged floor of the hall, unable to move.

In an instant, all Soth's maddening rage was gone.

He looked at his wife, saw the blood flowing freely from her wounds and open mouth, and could only think of how he had failed her utterly.

"Take him," came the ragged, garbled voice of Isolde.

Soth looked over at her and saw that despite her injuries, she had been able to protect the child from harm. She extended her arms, and held the blanket-wrapped child up to him.

"Take him," she said again.

Soth knew he should take the child and care for him, protect him from the ravages of the Cataclysm, and shelter him from all the hardships of life that would surely follow such devastation. But as he moved forward to take hold of the child, he heard a voice whisper in his ear.

It was a male voice, strong and powerful and unlike anything he'd ever heard on the face of Krynn. Hearing it now, he knew it could only be the voice of a god.

Our children shall bleed for our sins.

Soth stopped in his tracks.

It all made sense to him now. He had suffered for the sins of his father, and instead of accepting his fate and rising above it, he had only compounded his father's sins by committing even more ghastly ones of his own. His sins were far worse than anything his father had ever done. If he saved Peradur now from the flames, it would only be to give him a life of misery and shame as he would be destined to suffer for the sins of his father, and those of his father's father. And as he suffered, he would commit sins of his own, worse than Soth's.

It was a never ending cycle.

But not if Soth chose to break it. He could end the cycle.

He took a step back.

The chandelier's candles toppled and rolled across the floor. The flames licked at Isolde's robes and in seconds set them alight.

"Save him," Isolde begged as the flames began to obscure her face.

Soth remained still, impassive.

"Save your son!" Isolde's voice came out of the flames as if it had already become disembodied, an ethereal thing in the midst of so much destruction.

Soth did not answer, nor move to save the boy.

The fire continued to work its way over her body, chewing at her arms and finally engulfing the shrouded child in flames.

Then the fire began to spread outward from the center of the hall, flowing like water through the keep, up the walls and across the ceiling.

Finally, the voice, Isolde's voice, shouted a curse upon

Soth, the words seeming to come from somewhere above the flames.

"You will die this night in fire," she said. "Even as your son and I die. You will live one life for every life your folly has brought to an end!"

There were more words, but Soth didn't hear them.

All he could hear were the screams of incredible agony and pain coming from all corners of the keep.

He tried to block out the horrifying sound.

But could not.

* * * * *

Farold, Kern and Caradoc felt the ground shake and stopped their horses in their tracks.

They could see Dargaard Keep in the distance, its rose-like towers a welcome sight after such a hard and eventful journey.

But as they stood there looking at the keep in all its glory, they felt the ground give way beneath their mounts and a rush of hot air push against their faces.

"Look there!" shouted Kern, pointing to the sky.

A huge fiery mass, one as big as a mountain, streaked across the darkened sky, leaving a trail of bright yellow-orange fire in its wake.

The trail of fire burned white hot, then turned to smoke, blocking out the sun and leaving the land eerily dimmed.

"Is this it?" asked Farold.

"Is this *what*?" asked Kern.

"The Cataclysm," answered Caradoc.

Indeed, these were cataclysmic events. The land itself seemed to be trembling as if in fear that the end might be near.

"I'm afraid so," said Farold. "Only the gods can produce fire where it cannot be. Surely the burning sky can be nothing but the powerful manifestation of the gods' wrath."

"Wrath?" asked Kern, aghast. "Against Lord Soth?"

Farold nodded. "Against Soth, against the Kingpriest, against all of the people of Krynn."

"Soth could have stopped this," Caradoc said in disbelief, almost as if he were asking a question.

"The Kingpriest's powers of persuasion proved stronger than Soth's strength of will."

Just then, the keep itself burst into flames.

"Merciful gods, no!" cried Farold.

Caradoc and Kern leaped onto their horses. Caradoc waited, then lifted a stunned Farold behind him onto the horse's haunches. All three knights rode hard toward the keep.

In minutes they were close enough to see the devastation that the flames were inflicting upon the keep. It seemed that every inch of it was on fire. Even places where flames simply were not possible burned brightly.

The stones themselves were ablaze.

The knights tried to get nearer to the keep, but the intense heat and flames continued to push them back until they were forced to move away and helplessly watch it burn.

But even as they watched the fires slowly die, gouts of flame began shooting up from the ground behind them, forcing the knights forward in the direction of the keep.

"What's happening?" shouted Kern.

"We are part of the keep, part of Soth's world. We belong inside."

"What are you saying?"

"The gods won't allow us to be spared," answered Caradoc, his voice surprisingly calm, as if he knew his deeds would eventually catch up with him and he would be made to suffer as his lord had. "Our destiny is too closely linked with Soth's. We cannot escape the flames."

The fire was all around them now, pushing them ever closer to the keep.

With flames behind them and a burnt but clear path

ahead of them, they were pushed across the bridge and into the smoldering keep.

Once inside, the fire suddenly began to burn anew as rivers of flames streamed down the bleeding stone walls.

And then, like the rest of the knights in the keep, they gave themselves up to the flames . . .

Joining Lord Soth.

* * * * *

The fire continued to burn.

All around him flames shot up from the floor, ringing him in fire. But no matter how hot and intense the flames were, Soth remained untouched by their flickering tongues.

Like a doomed man on his way to his own execution, Soth exited the hall, leaving the burning mass of his wife and son behind.

He walked through the flaming keep, ignoring the dying people around him.

"Help me, milord!" cried a laundress.

"You could have stopped th—" said a guard, his words cut off by the flames eating away at his throat.

Soth continued on, seemingly unaffected by the magnitude of the tragedy, toward his throne room.

The place where he would die.

When he arrived, he found the entire room engulfed with flames and filled with thick black smoke. But as he walked toward his throne, a path opened up for him across the floor. When he reached the throne he turned around, took one last look at the devastation—the devastation that he could have prevented—and sat wearily down on his throne.

He breathed a final smoke-filled sigh, and waited for death to claim him.

The flames were upon him in seconds.

He did not scream.

Epilogue

When at last, after days of burning, the flames died down, Dargaard Keep—once the pride of all Solamnia and one of the wonders of Krynn—was little more than a black and charred husk retaining its roselike shape, but none of its former glory.

There had been some who escaped the flames. They had managed to leap from the burning keep and across the yawning chasm surrounding it. But those survivors were few, as most of the inhabitants had succumbed to the flames, dying horrifically only to be reborn as wraithlike beings who haunted the keep in the service of its lord.

Lord Loren Soth.

The Death Knight.

* * * * *

Weeks later, some signs of life returned to the grounds around Dargaard Keep. While the land surrounding the keep, once green and lush, had been blackened by ash and become almost devoid of life, some flowers had begun to bloom.

In the charred garden within the keep and on the grounds around it, black roses bloomed, their thorns long and sharp and quite painful to the touch.

Travelers sometimes picked the odd, gloomy flowers, but never more than one or two at a time. And most important of all, never did they linger afterward for fear of attracting the attention of the lord of the keep and incurring his wrath.

Lord Loren Soth.

Knight of the Black Rose.

* * * * *

As the sun set on the gray plains of Solamnia, the flame-blackened drawbridge leading into the keep rumbled and was slowly lowered across the chasm.

In silence, Soth's thirteen retainers, former Sword, Crown and Rose knights, appeared through the archway under the raised portcullis. They were skeletal warriors now, still loyal to their lord, even in death. They exited the keep mounted upon their horses, which had also been transformed by the flames, for yet another nocturnal patrol of Nightlund.

* * * * *

Soth sat on his throne. The walls of the keep that surrounded him were black and charred by the fire. Soth's armor had also been blackened by the flames.

His flesh had burned too, but he had not died.

With each agonizing movement, his burnt and charred flesh cracked and broke off in pieces. The pain had been less these past few days as most of his skin had slowly fallen off of his body. In another week it would be gone completely, leaving only a cold, hard skeleton.

If anything remained alive in his new undead form, it was his eyes. They burned the color of the same bright orange flames which had consumed him. But they burned also with anguish, regret, and the pain of never ending torment, as he knew he would remain in this form for an eternity so that he might be properly punished for his sins.

The pain of it all was sometimes too much for him to bear. Orange tears fell from his eyes and sizzled like water on a hot iron as they hit the ground below.

To compound his torment, around him circled the banshee spirits, spirits he had brought to life when he so brutally killed the elf-maidens who had confronted him on the way to Istar.

In life they had tormented him with their words. In death they did the same, their words transforming into song.

They would never let him forget.

And now, as he sat on his throne pondering his former life and current unlife, the banshees' keening wails continued to rip into his mind and tear relentlessly at his soul.

And though his heart did not beat, it was nevertheless shattered and racked by the agonizing pain of regret.

He tried to close his eyes.

But as death would not come to relieve him of this world . . .

Neither would sleep.

SONG OF THE BANSHEES

And in the climate of dreams
when you recall her, when the world of the dream
expands, wavers in light,
when you stand at the edge of blessedness and sun,

   Then we shall make you remember,
shall make you live again
through the long denial of body.

For you were first dark in the light's hollow,
   expanding like a stain, a cancer

For you were the shark in the slowed water
   beginning to move

For you were the notched head of a snake,
   sensing forever warmth and form

For you were inexplicable death in the crib,
   the long house in betrayal.

And you were more terrible than this
   in a loud alley of visions,
     for you passed through unharmed, unchanging,

As the women screamed, unraveling silence,
   halving the door of the world,
     bringing forth monsters

As a child opened in parabolas of fire
   There at the borders
   of two lands burning

As the world split, wanting to swallow you back
    willing to give up everything
    to lose you in darkness.

    You passed through these unharmed, unchanging,
but now you see them
strung on our words of your own conceiving
as you pass from night to awareness of night
to know that hatred is the calm of philosophers,
that its price is forever,
that it draws you through meteors,
through winter's transfixion
through the blasted rose
through the shark's water
through the black compression of oceans
through rock—through magma
to yourself—to an abscess of nothing
that you will recognize as nothing,
that you will know is coming again and again
under the same rules.

If you enjoyed reading *Lord Soth*, be sure to read these other books in the DRAGONLANCE® Warriors Series:

The details of the early years of the greatest weapons-smith in the history of Krynn are revealed in *Theros Ironfeld*. Before he forged the fabled dragonlances, Theros was captured to work as a slave on a Minotaur ship, employed as a metalsmith for Gilthanas of the Qualinesti elves, and served as a soldier in many epic battles. After a draconian attack leaves him with only one arm, he is called to the Hall of the Gods, where he must make the biggest decision of his life. (ISBN 0-7869-0481-X)

Maquesta Kar-Thon details the exploits of a young woman who must capture a deadly sea monster for a minotaur lord in order to save her father's life. At eighteen, Maq is forced to become the captain of a ship and to battle pirates, Blood Sea imps and other evil creatures of the deep. Her quest must be successful. Her father's life depends on it. (ISBN 0-7869-0134-9)

In *Knights of the Crown* a spell thief named Sir Pirvan the Wayward begins an unlikely quest to become one of the Knights of Solamnia. His training starts as a squire of the Knights of the Crown, who have much to teach him about the virtue of loyalty. (ISBN 0-7869-0202-7)